Designed for love...

No one says no to fiery but talented home designer Neve Harper—which is how she convinces her elusive neighbor, Duke Kennicot, to help out with her latest renovation job. Not only is Duke a design aficionado, he's got the inside scoop on the cabin's owner. And since Neve's ulterior motive is a romance with the boss, Duke is her ideal wingman. Except from the moment they're alone in the remote Ozark mountain location, Neve discovers Duke is just as headstrong—and a whole lot sexier—than she ever realized. Duke has always made it clear she's not his type. Yet the simmering tension between them says otherwise....

Duke had been warned to steer clear of hot-tempered Neve, but his resolve is lessening with every heated exchange—and every smoldering touch. By the time Neve unearths a dangerous, age-old mystery buried on the property, Duke is ready to do just about anything to keep the brazen beauty safe....

Books by Roxanne Smith

Long Shot Romance
Men Like This
Relapse In Paradise
Running the Numbers

Bound By Design
To the Studs

Published by Kensington Publishing Corporation

To the Studs

Bound By Design

Roxanne Smith

LYRICAL PRESS
Kensington Publishing Corp.
www.kensingtonbooks.com

Lyrical Press books are published by
Kensington Publishing Corp. 119 West 40th Street New York, NY 10018

First Electronic Edition: February 2017
eISBN-13: 978-1-5161-0082-8
eISBN-10: 1-5161-0082-4

First Print Edition: February 2017
ISBN-13: 978-1-5161-0085-9
ISBN-10: 1-5161-0085-9

Printed in the United States of America

For Matt—my quiet forest, my favorite solid element—who may or may not notice a few striking similarities between his wife and Neve, and smile.

That's love, folks.

Author's Foreword

For this story, I delved deep into the realm of renovating, beyond what I imagined when I began the story with Neve daydreaming about granite countertops and matching tile backsplashes. I hope anyone familiar with the process of rebuilding appreciates the effort I put into making it as realistic as possible and forgives me where I failed at nailing it down. (Ha. Get it?)

Acknowledgements

Always, Dawn Dowdle, who helped me push this story when I was almost ready to give up on it. Marci Clark is an amazing editor, and I'm delighted I'm able to work with her for another series. Friends, family, support systems, and those who will definitely see something of me in Neve...thank you for being awesome and accepting of my "quirks."

Chapter 1

Neve Harper eyeballed the dismal kitchen with its cheap faux pine wall panels and misshapen laminate countertops, warping and cracked from poor material and poorer maintenance. "Oh, *lawd*, no. This'll never do. The space is too small for such a dark grain. And *paneling?* In the kitchen? Who the hell designed this place, Daniel Boone? I wouldn't open a can of sardines in this hole. Why aren't there windows? At least there's an overhead light fixture. Anyone else surprised it isn't a deer antler chandelier?"

The linoleum floor didn't help the overall appearance, either. If a pattern existed on the chipped, stained tiles, the design had long ago ceased being discernible. The matted threadbare rugs were such she wouldn't let Darcy the Pit sleep on them.

Cramped, gloomy, outdated, and uninviting. No wonder she'd been hired to redo the room.

The *one* room. She rolled her shoulders in a feeble attempt to keep annoyance from settling in and getting comfy. No room for unproductive emotions on the job. Some other designer had renovated the rest of the house already, but he'd done it by blowing his budget and earning himself a pink slip before completing the final—and priciest—room.

A dark, disgusting kitchen with a dark, disturbing budget.

Neve liked clients big on results, not the monetary weight it took to pull them off. *This is the last favor I'm ever doing for a friend of a friend.*

Like any other job, favor or not, her stellar reputation sat squarely on the line, and Neve had something to prove. She *always* had something to prove in this business, and someone to prove it to, even if only to remind everyone else why she was the *crème de la crème*, the best and brightest home remodeler and interior designer in Little Rock.

She tapped her chin with one artfully self-manicured finger and imagined the room a brighter, happier place—a shining beacon of culinary dreams. A place where cooking a simple meal offered an escape, an adventure, or whatever the hell one might need at the time.

She loved kitchens. Hated to cook, but loved kitchens.

"White." She barked the word. Her team of carpenters and tradesmen were either listening raptly or preparing to take the heat when she had to repeat herself. She hated to waste time more than anything else, and tonight she had a particular reason not to dawdle—drinks with Austin, her latest boy toy, at her favorite spot downtown. This half-job wasn't worth being late over.

"White *everything*," she called out amid men and women jumping into action. Whether taking notes or whipping tape measurers from their tool belts, they knew better than to stand idly once she started talking. "All the cabinetry has to go, budget be damned. I want some custom stuff in here. Ruby, draw up a few design options. Tony, let's get a skylight in the ceiling for added light. No way are we getting a normal window in here without giving up every inch of storage space, which is pretty damn meager to begin with. Quartz countertops. Don't concern yourselves with the backsplash until we've established a secondary color. Frosted glass cabinets." She sighed as she settled on the big sacrifice. "White appliances. Stainless steel jumped ship when we added the skylight, but let's not embarrass ourselves. I want quality. Ben, you're on flooring. Not white unless you can get a deal on porcelain tiles. Otherwise, something linoleum but on the higher end, please. I'll want options when I arrive with a color board in the morning."

Neve scanned the room again, this time calculating for freedom of movement. In tight quarters, the smallest change had the power to create the illusion of more space. The skylight would help, but there had to be something else. "The refrigerator is sucking up all the air in the room. Matt, I want to see what you can do about a recess for it. Maybe utilize the pantry closet. We'll expand the cabinets to ceiling height to make up for lost storage. Though, it's hardly worth noting. Ruby, are you listening?"

Without glancing at her young assistant, Neve imagined her startling like a mouse and turning an unhealthy shade of white and red that probably marked some kind of underlying health condition. Her infuriating lack of confidence was an illness all on its own.

"I want drawings first thing in the morning. I'll have color palettes. Be ready to discuss color scheme and décor at seven sharp."

Her gaze didn't leave the offending kitchen until she'd completed the instructions to her team and turned heel, her long, loosely curled chestnut-brown hair swaying out behind her from the force. She snatched her black leather biker jacket off the back of a dining chair and had her arms through the sleeves before she reached the door. She checked her watch. "Damn." No time to drop by the loft and freshen up before meeting Austin.

Ah, well. Didn't get any cleaner than the first day on the job. She headed design and planning while giving demo to her team. She sported no paint spatters or new bruises. Dark jeans hid any muck or grime she'd picked up during her initial inspection of the kitchen, and a cursory survey revealed her black T-shirt free of unsightly smudges.

She snorted as she climbed onto her bike, a royal blue Honda Rebel 250. Not that Austin would notice. He wouldn't care if she showed up in a garbage bag ball gown and clown shoes. She'd probably miss him more than she had the others by the time their fling came to its inevitable end. His laid-back style and cherubic features were such a nice foible to her frantic energy and sharpness.

"Neve?"

She paused in pulling the glittering black helmet over her head.

Tiny and timid, Ruby drew inward like a mouse hiding in a shadow when Neve glanced up at her. Her drab light brown pixie cut and big, frightened eyes made for an unflattering visage. Then again, the cap-sleeved prairie dress in a benign lavender didn't help.

The hesitance in Ruby's small, doubtful voice struck Neve's ever-exposed nerves like sandpaper on an open wound. Or, in the very least, an ages-old wound that ached like bad joints in cold weather. Neve had spent much of the beginning of her career in the backseat, handing over her best ideas to dismissive men who hardly gave her a second glance but didn't hesitate to stamp their names on her hard work and intellectual property. At some point, she'd had to learn to believe in herself. No one had come along and done it for her.

But what bothered Neve most wasn't Ruby's clothes or hair, or even the way she couldn't look Neve in the eye—it was Ruby's utter absence of one critical trait—*boldness*. A mandatory ingredient in the recipe of a successful designer. Bold attitude, bold ideas. Carving a space in an industry overflowing with wannabes took stones. It took gall. It took direct eye contact and a resolve to never back down, never show weakness.

Ruby's saving grace was her knack for creative space usage, which was the only reason Neve had agreed to take her on. She needed an assistant, someone useful to the team, not a kid to mentor.

Neve stuck her helmet under her arm and tried to curb her instinctive abrasiveness. The years she'd spent breaking through the mold and making a name for herself had left her with an attitude she couldn't quite seem to shake. Tolerance for weakness was just another way of *showing* weakness. And despite not wanting to be a mentor, she had hoped some of her confidence would rub off on Ruby during her internship. "Are you confused about my instructions?"

The girl practically withered. Shoulders slumped, eyes downcast.

Neve's jaw clenched. She inhaled deeply and refused to voice the sharp remonstration dying to fly off her tongue.

Ruby wrung her hands but finally formed a full sentence. "Yes, ma'am. I mean, no. No, I'm not confused. You were clear, totally clear. I just—"

"Spit it out. I have somewhere to be." If only Ruby utilized time as well as she did space.

"Tony wanted to know about lighting, that's all. Besides the skylight, I mean. Like, what kind of fixtures should I work into the design?"

Neve didn't count to ten. She'd stopped the practice years ago. It never accomplished anything except to waste ten precious seconds she'd never get back. She cocked her head to one side, licked her lips, and spoke with exaggerated slowness. "Your job is to give me templates. Options to choose from. Ideas to pick through, improve upon, or throw out."

The young woman squinted nervously at Neve. "Um, right. Yes?"

Points for making eye contact. "Then try that. Options, just like what you're doing with the cabinetry. C'mon, Ruby. This is beginner crap. You've done all this in design school, haven't you? I could've plucked some loser off the street and gotten as much as you've given me so far. I mean, why are you even here? Where's your passion, your drive? Your *oomph?*"

Ruby's mousy brown eyes, the exact shade of her hair, went wide and stayed there.

"Oh, *God*, no. Are you really…?"

Yes.

Yes, really.

Big, fat tears gathered at the corners of her eyes, and Ruby stared without making any move to wipe them away, so they plopped onto the apples of her cheeks in dollops.

Neve rested her chin on her free hand, formed into a fist for optimal chin-resting, and studied the fat drops rolling unchecked down Ruby's face.

They all cried at some point. Hell, Neve had cried. The first time, she'd been sent home for the day. The second time, she'd been thrown from the project altogether. That had been the last time she'd ever cried on a job site. And the things the men on the crew had shouted after her as she ran home bawling had stuck to her flesh like shrapnel. She'd learned to use it. She'd soaked it in, let it become her armor.

"Should I call your mom to come get you or something? I bet she keeps emergency milk and cookies in her purse."

Mean, but the dry joke served its purpose. Ruby came back to herself with a hurried wipe across her cheeks and a loud gulp. She sucked in air and made a breathy apology with gossamer words.

"It's fine, Ruby. But do me a favor. Don't whisper my name like you're afraid it'll summon the devil, then proceed to stammer over a simple question. You can't be weak and do this job." She stepped close enough to finger one of the girl's bell-cap lavender sleeves, frowning at the scalloped edge. "You can't dress like someone's Cabbage Patch plaything and rule the roost. It's a shame."

Ruby's eyes went big again, this time as round as melons. "Are you f-firing me?"

Neve patted her shoulder. The girl winced, and Neve stopped abruptly. "Sorry, uh…no, I'm not fuh-firing you."

Ruby's face went slack with relief.

"But once this job is done, we'll have to revisit the issue. I might settle on demoting you to Tony's assistant and getting myself a new one. I swear, if you cry again." Too late. Neve closed her eyes briefly, warding off her annoyance before her mouth got the better of her. "Go, Ruby. Just go. You have work to do. Cry all you want, but don't get the plans wet."

Ruby whirled away.

Neve had no clue if she continued with her blubbering or sucked it up. Didn't care so long as she could work at the same time. She pulled on her helmet, hooked the straps snug under her chin, and straddled the lightweight motorcycle. Damn if she didn't have better things to worry about than Ruby's jellied spine and her pointless light fixture concerns. The best-laid plans wouldn't matter when it came time to purchase the hardware, anyway. With the owner's lacking budget, they'd be lucky to get anything from an honest-to-goodness outlet instead of the local Jolly-Mart.

She shuddered. *Please not Jolly-Mart.*

Kitchens especially cried out for the good stuff. Granite countertops with inlaid flecks of golden yellow, glossy wood floors and a stylish, gleaming hood over an industrial-grade six-burner gas stove would turn that drab scene into a place of culinary wonder and enlightenment. Or just a warm, beautiful spot to sip hot tea and eat scones. Or, in Neve's case, cold beer and greasy takeout.

She settled into the leather seat of her motorcycle and ignored the wave of exhaustion that nearly compelled her to reach for the cell phone clipped to her belt and cancel her date. But weekends and average office hours weren't sacred to designers. She went weeks without seeing Austin when both their schedules filled up.

Talk about the perfect relationship. Zero demand, saucy nocturnal activity, and no expectations or compromises. As long as Austin didn't do anything stupid like the last guy she dated, who'd asked her to move in with him, she foresaw they had a long, mutually beneficial relationship ahead of them.

She shot away from the curb and arrowed her bike toward the exit of the cul-de-sac. She spared a glance in a rearview mirror and almost lost control of the handlebars.

Ruby stood on the pathway leading up to the house with her arms limp at her sides, gazing at Neve as she rode away like a possessed ragdoll. *That's goddamn creepy.* Between the white picket fence ensconcing the landscaped yard beyond her and Ruby's dated attire, the image in Neve's mirror could be 1950s suburbia. She revved the motorcycle's engine and rounded the corner, glad when Ruby dropped out of view. With any luck, Austin would be waiting when she arrived at Lucy's, her favorite bar downtown, with a drink in his hand and a lustful gleam in his baby blues.

Luck proved a giving lady.

Austin waited at a table for two adjacent to the big glass window overlooking the congested sidewalks of downtown Little Rock. The best spot in the house for people watching. Or people *judging*, Duke, her gay dog-sitting neighbor, liked to call it.

Yeah, she judged people, but only those who left the privacy of their homes in sweatpants or hair curlers and thereby truly deserved it.

Duke brought a small smile to her lips. He certainly didn't look gay. A lean manly man with a mean glare and thick black hair hanging pin-straight down his back, like some eighties metal guitarist. A long, grizzled beard hid what she decided must be a stately jaw to fit the rest of his broad, oh-so-manly face, and deep blue bedroom eyes that made promises his body refused to keep. At least for the women of the world.

She dreamed of converting him. Except when he tried to steal Darcy the Pit. Then she dreamed of throwing him off her fifth-floor balcony. After converting him.

Austin was a study in contrast. With tight golden-blond curls and big cornflower-blue eyes on a wide, serene face, he was as cherubic as Duke was wickedly handsome. His generous mouth set him apart from a dozen other too-pretty college boys she'd considered getting involved with. She immensely enjoyed those plush lips, particularly after teaching him how to use them to properly satisfy a woman.

A *real* woman, that is, not the flakes he went to college with.

His smile at her approach bespoke of pleasurable things. If he were a little older or a little more masterful in bed, it might be love. "Hello, gorgeous. Missing something?" He held up a dainty glass, a cosmopolitan by the look of it, with a cocky, inviting grin.

That mouth. Those lips. Neve came awake and reached for the glass. She chugged half before sitting. The liquor spread through her belly, adding to a warmth already there. "Three more of these, and I'll feel like I had a real drink. Make sure you get me a Jack and Coke next round, will ya?"

Austin leaned back in his usual relaxed demeanor, but his smile slipped a little. A brief flicker of something undiscernible crossed his face too quickly for Neve to peg. He sipped his drink, another fruity cocktail. "Bad day, sweetheart?"

She lifted her hand to signal their waiter, ignoring Austin's annoying habit of using generic pet names. "Terrible. My new assistant is incompetent, and my client is a cheap asshole with high-dollar expectations and no qualms about mixing designers. I'm finishing what some other jerk started."

Austin's eyebrows hitched up. "That some kind of no-no in your profession?"

"Depends on if the client likes my designs better, I guess. Ruby is my real problem. I don't get some people. If I'd been born a mouse, I'd dress like a fucking hawk, you know?" She flicked her gaze over the menu. "Still no crab cakes. I don't know about this place sometimes."

That odd, totally non-sexy stillness returned to Austin's expression. "You actually expect them to add a new menu item to please a single customer? C'mon, Neve."

His tone might have been flat, but Neve hadn't missed how it toed the line between joking and genuine exasperation.

She dropped the menu and glared at him. "Something on your mind?" God help her. If she had to listen to one more complaint about the poor lumbar support on his office chair at the university, she'd hurl her fork straight at those lush, pillowy lips.

Instead, he gave a tiny shake of his head and lifted a hand in a lazy apology. One corner of his mouth lifted in a listless semblance of a smile. "Nothing, nothing. Go on. You were saying you don't know about this place sometimes?"

She studied him.

He lounged comfortably and watched her with the affected innocence of a child. A little *too* innocent and definitely mocking.

Her lips curled cruelly. She didn't have to call him out. There were easier ways to wipe the smug look from his angelic face. "That's right. The menu is stale, the new chef is a Burger King castoff, and the waiters don't earn the ten percent I'm socially obligated to give them."

Naturally, their waiter chose that precise moment to approach the table.

Neve had to give the guy credit. With reddened cheeks and a tightly clenched jaw, he took their orders for another round of drinks and dinner salads with an aplomb Neve probably couldn't have mustered herself. No tip was worth her pride.

Apparently, their waiter felt differently. His stiff stride carried him away from their table.

Did she feel bad? A little. Austin had been her target. "He's definitely getting twenty percent," she grinned, tipping her glass toward their retreating waiter. "Did you see his face? I should notify Cover Girl. All these years they've been missing a lovely shade of blush in their selection. Maybelline has something close, but mottling is so hard to pin. It takes the exact amount of white splotches amid the angry red spots."

She waited for Austin's physical response—the straightened back and upward-angled chin—before lazily moving her attention his way. Neve liked Austin. She truly did. He wore his emotions like a fine suit, every exquisite detail on display. Sadness sloped his shoulders. Pride puffed out his chest. She read his body language like a roadmap to his feelings and she'd hit her mark. "Oh, I'm sorry. You were a waiter here, weren't you? Funny, the things we forget." She let her false sincerity fall away. "You have something to say, Austin. I suggest you say it and let's stop with the head games. You aren't dealing with some campus bimbo."

Austin's mouth stayed firmly shut, even as his soft blue gaze bore into her. "I said it's nothing."

Later that night, even as he pinned her arms over her head, breathed heavy grunts into her neck while thrusting into her, she recognized the familiar sensation of disconnect. Everyone liked to say men didn't get emotionally involved when it came to sex, but as usual, everyone was wrong.

* * * *

Duke waited until Angel Face shuffled into the elevator before rapping his knuckles across Neve's door. He avoided men around Neve at all costs. Being gay was harder than he'd thought it would be. Was Angel Face superhot? Should he make a smutty comment or smile coyly at his butt as he walked past?

I need gay lessons. Hell of a thing to come to terms with, especially after two years of pulling it off.

Pajama-clad and curled into a ball on her ultrachic sofa, a beige monstrosity set square in the center of the high-ceilinged room atop a thick white rug, Neve didn't pause in shoving yogurt-covered pretzels down her gullet to bother with a greeting. The scenery didn't differ—sofa, pajamas, snacks, bad television—but she seemed more subdued than usual.

He sat next to her and snatched the remote from the coffee table. "Just because you renovate and design for a living doesn't mean there aren't channels besides HGTV. Why can't I live next door to a chef? Or a chiropractor. Someone useful."

"I'm assuming it's because you were a real asshole in a previous life."

"Can we watch *Survivor*, maybe try a movie once in a while?" He swept a lock of his hair over his shoulder and grinned as Neve rolled her eyes.

She'd never hidden her envious love of his hair. "Do you do that on purpose? Play with your hair and wear tight black jeans and T-shirts to torture straight females?" She turned her attention to the flipping channels on the television. "Because I would."

"Really? If you were a hot lesbian, you'd deliberately entice straight men? That's brutal."

"That's me. Brutal." Normally, she made proclamations like that with a little more pride.

Duke chewed his lip and looked her over. She had her glossy, coffee-colored hair pulled into a rakish bun on the top of her head, wore her favorite plush robe over plaid pajamas, and one hand steadily ferried pretzels from the bag to her face.

Pretzel crumbs and all, he'd still get hard if he stared too long. Neve joked about converting him, but if she ever made an honest effort, he wouldn't hesitate to wrap her killer legs around his waist like a bow, wind a lock of her silken hair through his fist, and make good on every vulgar fantasy he'd concocted over the last two years.

Duke shifted to find a more comfortable position in his awkwardly tight jeans, jeans growing tighter with each vivid image popping into his cranium—Neve on her back with her hair fanned out like a dark halo, Neve's haughty mouth humbled by a moan of ecstasy, his palms on the inside of her thighs, spreading—

Jesus Christ, man. I need to get laid.

He landed on a hotrod channel before recalling he shouldn't. Or should he? He had a hard time balancing his act while trying not to be overly stereotypical. He clicked over to a shopping network and tried to appear interested in a china set the overly made-up host fawned over. "You all right, Neve?" He looked at her.

Her flat amber gaze met his in an almost mechanical way. Deliberate and threatening, her displeasure clear and coupled with challenge—a dare to prod further. Basically, with a single glance she told him to mind his beeswax.

Duke's balls instinctively crawled into his stomach. Glares like that were the reason he pretended he was gay. He thanked his lucky stars every day that Neve was so awful, the thing that both compelled him and made it easy for him to keep his distance. He had experience with alpha females, and while they were apparently his cup of tea, he was trying to wean himself from the habit.

They'd become something of friends, but only as a byproduct of being the sole occupants of the fifth floor in their midtown building. Years ago, the place had been offices of some industrial firm. A developer had bought it and split each floor into two mirroring loft apartments.

Duke liked the solitude in a city as busy as Little Rock, but it sucked having only one neighbor when he needed to borrow sugar. Especially if the neighbor was anything like Neve Harper, who had a tendency to speak her mind. It wouldn't be so bad if she had nicer thoughts. But sometimes, he just couldn't help himself. He had to poke, like she was an itch he had to scratch. He likened it to hanging out with a vicious dog—they smelled fear, so pretending you weren't scared was key—but the dog was a pretty one he kinda wanted to pet sometimes. "I'm not here for you. I came to see Darcy."

Upon hearing her name, Darcy the Pit hefted herself from the rug and padded over to nuzzle Duke's hand.

He grinned and stroked the pit bull's short, silky coat. Neve had so much style, even her rescued stray looked designer. Darcy the Pit had a coat the color of cream soda. Her eyes matched her fur, lined with the same delicate pink of her paws, belly, and nose.

Neve continued to pulverize pretzels. "Go home, Duke."

"Nah."

She curled protectively around her pretzels, like they were the only thing she could trust. "You came to torture me with your need for social interaction." She pushed a heavy sigh through puffed cheeks. "I think I'm nearing the end of my time with Angel Face."

Ah. Man trouble. "I'm sorry to hear that. He's…" Shit. "Scrummy?" *Oh, good one. Nice save.*

Neve stared at the television. "He's okay. It's just exhausting picking through a bunch of unskilled college boys to find one worth training. I'd hoped Austin would last longer, but his feelings are getting involved. What *kind* of feelings, who knows. Emotions aren't my thing. I just know they lead to bad things and are best avoided."

Not a broken heart then. He'd been worried there for a second. But this was *Neve*. If she had a heart, it was made of carbonized steel. At the same time, she definitely seemed more put out about Angel Face than the previous college studs she dated. "Sorry it didn't work out."

She rolled her eyes. "He's so passive-aggressive, it'll be weeks before he gets around to doing anything about it. I've got time."

Duke gave her ankle an encouraging pat. "Way to think positive, sport."

"Shut up and switch the channel back to HGTV before I get nasty." She struggled into an upright position at the same time her cell phone buzzed against the glass top of her coffee table. She set down the pretzels at last, dusted off her hands, and picked up her cell. Her eyebrows drew together quizzically at the identity of the caller.

Duke expected her usual tart greeting, but Neve answered in a mellow professional tone. "Neve Harper." A pause. "Hi, Mr. Dyer. No, of course it's not too late. What can I do for you?" Her legs unfurled. She sat up straighter as she listened, a storm gathering on her face.

Duke's curiosity beat out his urge to run for cover. "Your client?" he mouthed.

She zapped him with an annoyed glance that dissipated into an expression of mild shock, her gaze now locked on some point over Duke's head. Her mouth fell open. "How in the hell can you ask me to resign before seeing the finished results of the renovation?"

Duke cringed. One of *those* calls. Bummer.

Neve's free hand curled into a fist and her chin came up. "I haven't verbally assaulted anyone who didn't deserve it. And to be fair, Mr. Dyer, if you expected Ruby to get special treatment because she's your niece, you should've said so before hiring me. I would've turned down the job. Besides, I don't need your cheap project in my portfolio. Good luck hiring someone with half my talent. My team and I—"

The voice whirred through the phone, effectively cutting off Neve.

Her skin paled and her voice dropped an octave. "They agreed to finish the project under *Ruby's* management? This is a joke. Did Matt put you up to this? Because Ben wouldn't have the guts."

Somehow, Duke didn't think Mr. Dyer would call Neve at home for the sake of a laugh.

She nodded at Mr. Dyer's response. The messy bun atop her head wobbled. "I understand I demand a unique quality of employee, but do Ruby a favor, will you? Tell her she'd better grow a hefty pair of stones if she plans on making it in this business. There's worse than me out there."

Neve gained her feet and heaved in a breath after ending the call. The hand clutching her phone had turned white from her hard grasp. "Creepy little bitch. I've never been fired from a job in my life. I'm the cream of the crop, the best thing Little Rock has to offer. I'm Neve fucking Harper."

Duke sucked on his bottom lip. She was talking *at* him, not to him, which was good, because what the hell was he supposed to say? She wouldn't do anything too human like cry, but she might throw something or be more than willing to take out her frustration on the closest target, which happened to be him, if he opened his mouth and something stupid emerged.

Neither happened before her phone rattled again.

Already in her hand, she gave a little sigh at the caller. "Austin," she explained, regarding Duke.

"By all means," he urged, dipping his head in mock subservience. "I'm here for Darcy, remember?" To make his point, he reached for Darcy's pink belly. She rolled over with a lolling tongue to give him better access to her favorite spot.

"Her name is Darcy *the Pit*."

"It's a mouthful."

"You're gonna have a mouthful of teeth if you don't call her by her name."

His palms went up in surrender. "Okay, okay. You win." For now, anyway. Neve had been canned about three minutes ago. He could pick a better time to argue about her dog's longwinded name.

She gave him a withering stare and answered the phone. "Hey, Austin. I didn't expect to hear from you tonight."

Unlike the conversation with Mr. Dyer, Duke easily caught Austin's voice as it buzzed into Neve's ear but discerned about one word in every ten as he hurriedly mumbled over the line.

Neve resettled into her spot on the sofa, her feet propped onto the edge of the coffee table. A laugh from Austin creased her features into yet another look of concern. She flopped back and rubbed her forehead. "You want to have this conversation *now*?"

More buzzing from Angel Face. Duke didn't have to listen intently to make out words like *tact* and *asinine*.

Neve scoffed. "Even if he *is* their best waiter. Besides, I was speaking in generalizations. You want to know what I think of tact, Austin? I think it's a word people like you throw around because the truth is uncomfortable. Instead of facing it, you lie about how you really feel under the guise of *having tact*." Her shoulders sloped, her voice softened. "Look, Austin, this was inevitable. Happens every time with you young, idealistic guys. Sometimes they fall in love with me, sometimes they grow tired of waiting for me to become this nice person they suspect I keep buried beneath my bitchy exterior."

More indiscernible buzzing.

"No, hon. This *is* me." She shook her head like a disappointed parent. "Where did you expect this to go, anyway? Were we going to fall in love, get married? No. I'm a mature woman with an established career and reputation, and you're just over the legal drinking age. I just wanted to give you a different kind of education than you're getting at the university, that's all. If it helps, you were one of my best students," she added charmingly.

Neve pulled the cell phone away from her ear to quizzically study the screen. "That's weird."

Duke tugged on his long beard. Today it hung in a braid down to the collar of his T-shirt. "Oh? Getting hung up on is weird for you?"

"Who do you reckon has the guts?" She shrugged and chucked the phone back onto the coffee table.

It hit the glass with a resounding *smack* that made Duke wince. "May I ask now?"

Her gold-flecked eyes met his. They were surprisingly devoid of hostility. She was definitely more torn up about losing the job than losing the boy toy. "Ask what?"

He jostled her knee playfully, glad she wasn't poised to attack. "If you're all right. When I asked a minute ago, you mean-mugged me. Having eavesdropped on your last two calls, I have a reason now."

She rolled her eyes, but the ghost of a smile played across her wide mouth, host to thin but intriguing lips. "Save it, Duke. I bet I can come up with something I want more than your pity."

Chapter 2

"No, following me to work is not a *totally fab* idea. It's a terrible idea."

Neve grinned and hitched her bag higher on her shoulder. Duke hadn't done much to try to stop her besides complain the whole walk from their building to the bus station. "Be a sport. I've been stewing in my loft—sometimes in yours when you aren't home—for *days*. I drink tea with sad names like chamomile and watch even sadder television. Do you know what happens to fresh, delectable bread when it sits too long?"

"The maid eats it?"

"What? No."

He shrugged.

"It goes *stale*, Duke. I'm fresh, delectable bread in my prime and I'm going stale."

"Right." He led the way once the bus came to a stop at the corner, guiding her to the back where they sat opposite one another. He stared straight ahead like refusing eye contact would stop her from tagging along.

He had his long, gorgeous hair tied back into a demure, work-appropriate ponytail. Which was nice—he cleaned up good—but she itched to tug it free and run her hands through the satiny ebony strands.

She moved to the seat beside him, snuggling into his side for the sake of irritating him as much as possible. "Consider this payback for how often you crash my place to complain about my favorite shows and attempt to puppy-snatch Darcy the Pit."

He didn't look at her. "I never invited myself to one of your renovation sites, though. All may be fair in love and war, but the workplace is sacred."

She shouldered him playfully.

Look at me, begging for attention. Not having people to yell at is making me crazy.

"You work in a big, busy office. No one will notice me." Well, they might. She didn't have much cleavage to show off, but style counted for everything. The lacy edge of her lemon-yellow bra peeked over the low top of her black silk tunic. A hint, a tease, a shock of color to draw the eye. "If they do, tell them I'm an intern assigned to learn your job." She paused and tapped her chin. "What exactly is your job, by the way?"

Duke swiveled to face her.

Deep blue eyes like a starless night glared at her. If he ditched the beard, which he still wore in a thin braid reaching near to the open collar of his navy blue dress shirt, those eyes of his would dominate his face. How long would it take him to forgive her if she shaved him bald from head to chin while he slept?

"Two years." Disbelief colored the words. "We've been neighbors for two years, and you don't know what I do for a living?"

She waved him off. "Calm down, Pocahontas. You carry a briefcase. Your job is obviously boring and tedious." She eyed his chest, making sure to adopt the right amount of predatory interest. "At least you don't wear a tie. I'd draw the line at a tie. Because yuck."

He pressed his lips together in consideration. "This is probably how you got fired. And since when does Pocahontas have a beard?"

"She doesn't, but I didn't exactly study up on good nicknames before following you out the door this morning."

Neve gave her attention to the city scenery as they passed. The bus made for a nice change. Much slower than her Rebel, affording time to appreciate the lovely streets of midtown Little Rock as they meandered toward the city's center. Though, the constant stop-and-go as they unloaded passengers and picked up new ones was maddening.

"And you're wrong. I didn't get fired because of my penchant for awesome nicknames. I got canned because Mr. Dyer's precious niece can't hack it. She's taken my team and probably my design ideas, but her victory won't last long. She'll get eaten alive in this business. As for me, I'll try to squeak out a tear at her funeral."

"What are you going to do about your guys?" Duke swapped his put-upon veneer for genuine concern.

Damn him for being nice when she needed an excuse to be mean. And damn her traitorous, mutinous team. "I'm going to replace them. I might have a reputation for being a hard-ass, but I'm still the best in Little

Rock. Tomorrow I'll do something constructive like put ads in the paper. Today, humor me."

Duke rested against the hard plastic seat with his hands dangling limp between his long legs.

Long hair, long beard, long legs. So promising, yet so forbidden. Like all the best fruit.

"I'm a data analyst," he finally said. "I specialize in recognizing and analyzing market trends for the company. We manufacture bras."

"Get out." She shoved his shoulder. "Irony aside, I thought you wrestled bears. No, I'm serious. Look at those biceps." She gave one a good squeeze.

"If anyone asks, you're an analyst on loan from the university."

"Oh, I like role-playing. Tell me more. Do I have a haunting past that keeps me from being able to trust a man? Or a dastardly ex-husband who stalks me and watches me undress from the tree outside my loft?"

Duke stared straight ahead, poker face fixed in place. "There is no tree outside your loft."

"Semantics." She took the opportunity to study his profile and withheld a sigh of longing. Why were the good ones married, gay, or desperate? "You're right about Pocahontas. There's the hair thing, but you're so white, I feel I'm doing her spirit an injustice."

He closed his eyes briefly before turning to impale her with them. A *zing* went through her. What did it say about her that his ire turned her on?

"You can't act like this at the office. I'm an authority figure. I won't have you wipe out years of hard-earned respect with one stupid nickname."

"If you cut it to your shoulders, I can probably get away with Antonio Banderas."

His shoulders slumped. "Neve, please."

"Okay, okay. I can be reasonable. Perm it, and Slash is all you, baby."

Duke leaned forward and smothered his face in his hands. "God, deliver me."

"Not a Slash fan, huh? Fine. If you shave the beard and dye your hair blond, I'll call you Thor."

His expression when he lifted his head held every sign of true agitation. "You're being an asshole because you got fired and dumped in the space of three minutes last week, and that sucks for you. I'm sorry, but the bully train stops here." His gaze stayed steady on hers, a glint of steel where there was usually amusement. "I don't make a good victim."

Well, there goes my fun. She groaned and slumped in her seat. Her arms crossed defensively. "I'm not doing it on purpose. I don't *mean* to be mean, not always. Crap just spews out, kinda like my personality has the runs. Weird, right?"

Not totally true. On some level, she'd been seeking a target. And that was just like her. She used her crew and her interns for target-practice, because what else had she ever been? That was how the game was played and dues were paid.

Duke patted her thigh. "If anyone's personality has diarrhea, I'm not surprised it's yours. Try to make sure it doesn't come out again on my time. I'll let you tag along, but how about a little break in the 'tude, huh?"

"Fine, Gandhi, but you're mine until we get there."

His jaw clenched beneath a slow intake of breath. Neve expected another dire warning.

Instead, his face relaxed into a deadpan delivery. "I tried a perm once. Curls don't flatter my face shape."

A wide grin split her face. So much more fun when he played along. "How can you tell your face shape with it covered in so much hair? I've always wondered if it's weird for you to see yourself naked. I assume the hair on the upper half of your body overwhelms the lower half. Unless, of course, there's more hair on the lower half, in which case I'm at least ten percent less attracted to you than I was thirty seconds ago."

He let go a tiny sigh. "You're beyond tiresome."

"Hey, I'm not judging. Me, I'm a natural kind of girl. I let my bush grow like our maker intended, wild and untamed. Man needs a scythe to find his way down there, but the good ones don't mind."

"You didn't have to share that."

"Of course I did. We're *bonding*, Duke. See there? I even used your real name instead of one I made up for you."

Duke groaned and shut his eyes, once more leaning back. "Our stop is Dixon Street. Wake me when we arrive."

* * * *

"Wow. Snazzy digs."

Beautifully designed, the windowless, albeit spacious, office had been updated with tasteful Victorian flair. Understated crown molding, pale golden paint, recessed spot lighting, brushed-metal fixtures, and antique furniture completed the design with remarkable fluidity and cohesion.

Neve much preferred it to the ultramodern style that was all the rage. Sleek lines and understated finishes were fine, but the whole point was to put character and life into a space. Any contractor with thumbs could throw up a stark white wall and retro chandelier. A true artist brought out *soul*, though.

And Duke's office had soul.

She commandeered the cushy chair behind Duke's fine antiquated desk and spun in a circle. The chocolatey brown leather blended seamlessly with the décor, while offering both contrast and a definitive masculine element. Someone around here had serious style.

"Okay, Mr. Boss Man. Shit, sorry. No fun names. Will Mr. Kennicot or Mr. Duke do? Or plain old Duke? Oh, I got it. Duke of Bras." She didn't wait for an answer. She stopped spinning and squinted at him. "Do you want to know what Austin said to me last night? He said I need to find someone like me. What do you think he meant?"

Duke's cheeks puffed out in a tired exhale. She was wearing the guy out and they hadn't had coffee yet. He set his briefcase on the floor next to his desk. "Why are you doing this to me? Go find a counselor, a therapist, something. I can't help you."

She flattened her palms on the desk's surface. "You're a man, Duke. A gay man, yes, but a man nonetheless. You've got to have some insight for me. We're friends, neighbors. Hell, you know me as well as Austin ever did. Tell me what's wrong with me." She bit the inside of her cheek. "Not that I'm looking for a permanent relationship or anything. Merely curious, which is apparently what happens when I'm not allowed to be mean." She gave him a pointed look. "Being bitchy keeps me from thinking too hard about stuff. So, I blame you."

Yep, just curious. Not lonely, disappointed, or tired of the young college idiots she purposely courted because they posed no threat to her actual feelings. Nothing like that—that or creeping into her mid-thirties with an anvil around her neck that kept her from pursuing meaningful relationships because they never ended well. The same instinct that would make her run from a mountain lion made her turn heel every time she ran into an eligible man she actually liked. She couldn't stop. Ever since…well, since her last "meaningful" relationship. Instead, she trolled the clueless kids from the university, which were easy enough to come by. It was like fishing. Sit at a bar alone and wait. Why? Because those boys were looking for two things—a mom or a woman with some experience in bed. Neve could offer one of those things in spades. But God forbid a friendly architect offer to buy her a drink or take her out for dinner more than once. Suddenly, she just didn't have the time. Or an imaginary boyfriend popped up to prevent things from going further.

Gently, Duke gripped her elbow and forced her to vacate his chair. He took her place, opened a sleek white laptop, and proceeded to answer her question without meeting her expectant gaze. "Most people, myself included, appreciate when those around us take care with their words. Perhaps Austin meant to suggest you ought to look for a man as careless with his words as you are. Also, I'll point out it's not a good thing I know you better than the men you date."

She crossed her arms and nodded. "Pretty good for a guy who appreciates tact."

One shoulder lifted as he typed. "You asked."

She leaned against the desk and examined him. He studiously ignored her while tapping away. Poor Duke. He didn't deserve her hounding neediness, but she had one tiny, little problem. She didn't have any friends. And this thing with Austin got under her skin worse than she expected it would. Sure, the end had been nigh, but he'd dumped her less than an hour after peeling his sweaty, spent body from hers. A new record for the books.

And forget females. Women were impossibly sensitive and catty. With no siblings and aging parents she'd never been tight with, she only had Duke's tenuous friendship to call upon in her time of need.

I'm pathetic. My only friend is circumstantial and a gay data analyst to boot.

If he were straight...

She abandoned the idea. Say Duke *was* straight and they became involved. How long could a nice guy like him stand up to her hurricane-force personality? Like cheap linoleum, he'd be warped and chipped after a few months. Duke deserved someone nice and easygoing like himself.

While Neve needed a *real* tough guy, not one who merely looked the part with a grizzly beard, rock-star hair, and penchant for leather biker jackets. It wasn't like you had to be a club member to get one. Macy's sold those suckers year-round.

She gave up trying to learn anything from staring at Duke's hair and turned her back to him, to observe the rest of the offices. The place had glass walls, which struck her as completely pointless and counterintuitive considering the purpose of a wall was privacy. As far as a design element, they were a cheap answer to the question of sophisticated space management.

A glance to her left stopped her short. She came away from the desk to press her face against the glass wall and stare. "Who is *that?*"

In a corner office on the east side of the building, a handsome blond man sputtered with rage at...was that a *kid?* Blood-red face, finger pointing threateningly at the young boy, no older than fifteen. She had to give the kid credit. He stood his ground, hands balled into fists at his side while the blond guy purpled with rage.

"He's on fire," Neve breathed. "He's a maniac. He's yelling at a child."

He's perfect.

Duke joined her by her side and slid his hands into his slacks pockets. He cleaned up real nice, but she still preferred his dark, faded denim and black T-shirts. "My boss, Gavin Chambers. Head of Sales for the Little Rock division. That's his nephew, they're—"

"Really going at it. Man, he's pissed."

"Actually—"

She thrust her hands out and grasped Duke's arms, leaning into his confused gaze with determination. "Introduce me."

Black eyebrows snapped together. "What? No way."

Neve turned pleading. She hated to beg, but Duke would love it. Maybe enough to do what she wanted. "This is what Austin meant, don't you get it? He said to find someone like me—someone angry and unafraid to unleash his inner psychopath on poor fools like that gangly kid in there getting shredded apart by your boss. I bet we hit off. Go on." She released him and tried to push him toward the door. "Introduce me."

Duke wasn't the huge, muscled type. He had more of an athletic thing going on, like a super-toned cyclist or mountain climber. Solid as granite and completely immovable. And looking totally annoyed.

Time to switch tactics. She ran a slow, lingering finger across his chest. "You're clearly composed of spare grizzly bear parts, so I'll have to bludgeon you with reason."

He took her by the wrists and held her hands away from his body. His gaze slipped down to where her decorative bra peeked over the fabric of her tunic. Another tickle of warmth brushed her.

He let go of her wrists. "Hands off. You're making me look unprofessional. You want reason? I've got plenty for you. First, you're mistaken about Gavin. He's one of the nicest people I've ever met. He also happens to be shy with women. He'd need to know you for several weeks before it would cross his mind to ask you out."

"Fine." She planted her hands on her hips. "I'll ask him out. As for you, stop gawking at my breasts. I realize they're wonderfully perky, but it's uncouth. Shame on you." She chanced a peek back at Gavin. Still chewing out the kid. *Such endurance.*

Duke stepped past her, blocking the view. "It'll put him off if you ask him out, and yellow is a distracting color. Get a new bra. Or a shirt that fits. And anyway, you're missing the point. He's *nice.*"

She gave him a pitying smile and smoothed her hand over his shoulder, brushing away invisible lint. "Oh, Duke. I understand, sweetie, I do. What's more terrible than your boss dating your next-door neighbor? Imagine, coming by to visit Darcy the Pit and having to make small talk when he answers the door. Or worse, he bumps into to you at the mailboxes and wants to talk shop. Ew, and those awkward elevator rides. Five stories of heavy breathing and eyeballs with nowhere to go. I would hate it, too. But you can't stand in the way of fate, Duke. Love conquers all, even an unhelpful gay neighbor intent on making sure his lonely straight neighbor doesn't get any." She batted her eyelashes. "Love, that is."

He ogled her. "You're insane. You can't be in love with a total stranger."

"Why not?" She snapped her fingers as an idea came to her. "I've got it. Let's get professional with it, huh? Perhaps Gavin's office could do with a little updating. I do more than renovate, I'm a top-notch interior designer." At Duke's doubtful stare, she squared her shoulders. "All I'm asking is you get me in the door. I can take it from there."

To her great surprise, Duke seemed to consider. His beard moved in little jerky motions as he chewed his lip.

She resisted the urge to tug the little black braid down until she had his lips right where she wanted them, but he'd probably complain about appearing unprofessional again. "You're wearing your thinking face. I like it. Talk to me, baby."

His navy blue eyes searched her face for what seemed like an eternity. "You are remarkably stubborn. Perhaps I'll mention my designer pal in passing. If he seems interested, I'll bring you in tomorrow, but give me a day, will you? I have to work at some point."

"Nope." She shook her head. "No way. I'm not below compromise, however. Tell you what, I'll head to the coffeehouse we passed on the way this morning and get us something to replace the disgusting sludge your secretary brews, and you go talk up Boss." She scanned Gavin's office, but he and his guest had moved out of sight. A critical eye took in his office on a professional level. "We have to come up with something besides my trade. His office is impeccable."

Duke rocked back on his heels. One hand came out of its pocket to stroke his beard in a thoughtful gesture. "Maybe not."

She squinted at him. "Are you messing with me?"

"It's a long shot."

"You're no match for me, Duke. Don't make me *make you* tell me."

Both hands went up in surrender. "All right, all right. You asked for it. Gavin owns a cabin in the Ozarks and has this grand plan to turn it into a mountain retreat. The place is ancient, but the previous owner had plumbing installed about twelve years ago. He started to renovate, fell on hard times, and finally lost it to foreclosure a few years back. Gavin snatched the place off the market for next to nothing."

Neve whistled. "Remote cabin. A tough one. Smorgasbord of issues. Again, *remote*, which doesn't sound like much help in getting close to Gavin."

"You wouldn't work with the guy daily, obviously. Not unless you want to get a job here selling bras to outlet stores in the greater Arkansas area."

"Not particularly, no."

"But if you were renovating this cabin for him, you'd have to be in almost constant contact. He'd need to make several trips to the...remote... isolated...*private* cabin."

She blinked at him. "You want to wriggle your eyebrows suggestively, get it out of your system?"

He pressed on with his pitch. She recognized a sales pitch. But what was he peddling, exactly? "You'll have to take shopping trips together for light fixtures and hardware. By my estimation, you'd have six to eight weeks to convince him he's your soul mate."

She mirrored Duke, stroking her chin thoughtfully. He seemed mighty pleased with the proposition. It wasn't immediately obvious what he stood to gain if she accepted the job. Probably took a shine to the idea of sucking up to Darcy the Pit in her absence.

As for renovating a cabin, she'd never done anything so challenging. Her realm of expertise didn't extend beyond the interior. "Will there be a general contractor on site? What if I have structural issues?"

"An excellent question you'd better make sure to ask Gavin."

Neve nodded resolutely. Despite whatever Duke imagined he was getting out of it, Neve needed two things: a shot at Gavin and a job. Here was an opportunity to get both, or one if not the other. "Fine. I'll do it. Now, get in there. Time's a-wasting, Tonto. Save my new boyfriend from his impending stroke."

* * * *

Stupid yellow bra. Stupid Neve and her stupid perky tits and that goddamn stupid yellow bra. A few more minutes in the presence of her interesting fashion choices, and he'd have ruined everything.

Duke walked with his head down straight to Gavin's office.

"You need to grow up, you hear me?" The whites of Gavin's eyes had gone red from yelling.

His nephew, Nick, had come around a few times before to visit Gavin. He stared at the ground, a petulant set to his jaw.

"You have to make hard decisions in life. Time to be a man and live with the consequences." Gavin paused in his diatribe to lift inquiring brows at Duke's hesitant knock on the door.

He shuffled his feet. "I apologize, sir. A minute when you've got one would be appreciated."

An instant smile broke out over Gavin's face. The veins in his forehead receded and the mottled red of his cheeks faded as he inhaled and clasped his nephew's shoulder. "Sure thing, Duke." He gave the kid a good-natured jostle. "How'd I do, buddy?"

Nick brushed back a mop of unruly dark hair from his pimply forehead. "You did better than Dennis. I wish you could do the play with me instead. Thanks for helping me run lines, Uncle Gavin."

"Aw, it's nothing." Gavin shooed off the compliment with the wave of his right hand and hooked his left around Nick's thin shoulders. He addressed Duke. "This kid, I'm telling you. Broadway awaits."

"I don't doubt it, sir."

"I'd better go." Nick loosed himself from Gavin and hefted a fully loaded backpack onto his shoulders.

It surprised Duke when the gangly kid didn't topple over from the weight of it.

"The play's Friday. You're coming, right?"

"You kidding me? Wouldn't miss it, but I'd better get back to work myself. Tell your mom hello for me."

"Sure, Uncle Gavin." He waved good-bye, politely extending it to include Duke, and shuffled out the door and toward the elevators.

No one's destination remained a mystery for long in a place with glass walls. Probably the point. Hard to get away with slacking when the boss could watch you from behind his desk. Hard to get away with a number of things, actually, including a strange woman getting handsy in your office while the busybodies from accounting pretended not to stare from behind their monitors.

Damn you, Neve. Damn you and your stupid hands.

Normally, withstanding Neve came easier. But "normally" involved Neve in ugly pajamas at the end of a long day, short on patience, humor, and a threshold for human contact. Today, she was in rare form. Or in normal form, and he simply didn't know this side of her. He'd be in trouble if he ever did.

Gavin tucked his hands into his slacks pockets and watched his nephew go with an easy smile. "My sister's kid." He whistled appreciatively. "He's got chops. Did you see him? He landed the lead part, you know. Of course, drama has always run strong in the Chambers family."

From the faraway gleam in Gavin's eyes, Duke didn't doubt it. He let his boss's reverie go on another ten seconds before issuing a light, throat-clearing cough.

He wagged a finger at Duke and settled in behind his exquisite cherry desk. "Right. Have a seat, Duke. What did you need?"

Duke did as instructed and sat opposite, eyeing the brilliant, glossy surface of Gavin's clean work space. Clean desk, clean mouth, clean all over. That was Gavin. Also kind, thoughtful, helpful, and utterly unprepossessing.

Neve Harper's exact opposite.

He rubbed his hands together. Last chance to back out of his devious plan. Were it anyone else—quite literally anyone but Neve—he'd never have the stones to go through with it. He checked his conscience a final time.

Not a single quivering qualm.

Her delusions about Gavin provided him with the perfect escape route, one he'd been searching for. By the time she realized her error, which by his calculations ought to come right around the same time Gavin discovered Neve's brutal lack of social grace and basic human kindness, she'd have already signed the contract. She might hate Duke in the end, but she'd have to admire his cunning. She'd emasculate him, but with a sense of pride.

"I wanted to talk about the cabin, Mr. Chambers."

Gavin bolted upright, nearly coming out of his chair. "Excellent! Great news, Duke. I'm so glad you decided to take the job. I told you, didn't I? Wasting your talent downstairs designing booby compartments. Anyone can take your place here, but I want someone I trust working on my retreat. Only the best."

Duke swallowed. "I agree, sir, which is why I've gone to great lengths to find a suitable alternative." He held up a hand to ward off the interruption looming in Gavin's disappointed face. "Please, hear me out. Neve Harper is the best in Little Rock, perhaps even the best in Arkansas. As it happens, she's also my neighbor. The two of us got to talking a few days ago. I mentioned your cabin in passing, and you wouldn't believe it, but she lit of up like a darn Christmas tree, sir. Absolutely insisted on an introduction. She's in *incredibly* high demand, and I can't even promise she'd have the kind of time necessary for something like the full renovation you want, but..." He puffed out his cheeks. "Heck, if you can sign on someone like Neve Harper, I wouldn't sniff at the opportunity, sir."

Gavin didn't appear entirely convinced. He reclined in his cushy seat and smoothed his pale blue and pastel pink–checkered tie. One set of fingers drummed a neat staccato across the surface of his desk. "I've never heard of her."

Duke dug in his heels. He had to sell it. This had to work. If Neve couldn't get him out of this, no one could. He wasn't lying about her reputation.

He splayed a hand over his chest. "Sir, the project fascinates me. I'd love to do it, but on a personal level, a *professional* level even, I don't have..." He needed a word. Something artsy and temperamental. "Inspiration," he finished with a slight sad flourish. "So you see, I couldn't do the project justice. However, I can introduce you to Neve, and that's the next best thing. She has a real passion, sir. I'd love to bring her by tomorrow if your schedule allows it."

Gavin inhaled, his mouth a foreboding straight line. His light blue gaze traveled the room, avoiding Duke's carefully composed face. "You want me to meet this Ms....."

"Harper, sir. Neve Harper."

He nodded once. Another drum of his fingers over the desk. "Tomorrow?"

"Only if it's convenient for you. Ms. Harper is flexible."

Poor choice of words. Neve's lacy yellow bra leaped back into his mind. *Stupid, stupid, stupid.*

It'd be easier to continue his charade if he didn't have a hankering to sleep with the very woman he desperately wanted to avoid getting involved with. The guy who'd lived in the loft before Duke had regaled him with horror stories of their short affair, and Neve's dragon-lady transformation once it ended. He warned Duke against getting ensnared by her.

Duke hadn't taken the warning seriously until he met Neve. His first thoughts were overtly sexual. No way he wouldn't get involved. Years avoiding women, but with a glance at Neve, and he knew she'd be the one to unravel him. So, he'd wiped the drool from his chin and promptly introduced himself as her new *gay* neighbor, vanquishing any possibility she'd ever set her sights on him.

But, goddamn, it was torture.

"Convenient for me." Gavin's contemplative voice broke through the vision of Neve's enticing undergarment like an arrow through a cloud of smoke. "How about right now?"

"Well, sir, she—"

"Has impeccable timing if I do say so myself." Neve's mahogany hair whipped across Duke's shoulder as she blazed past him with an outstretched hand toward Gavin. "I'm Neve. So nice to meet you, Gavin. May I call you Gavin?"

Flustered by her frank introduction, Gavin blinked several times before taking the proffered hand. "Of course, Ms. Har—"

"Neve will do, thanks." She beamed at him and lowered herself into the chair beside Duke's, legs crossed, back straight, hands carefully poised in her lap after smoothing down an invisible fly-away hair. "I hear you've got a cabin you'd like to turn into a mountain chateau. How romantic."

Stunned into silence, Duke could only watch as the train wreck unfolded before his eyes.

Thankfully, Gavin hadn't caught the edge of sarcasm in Neve's remark.

She rambled on, taking control of the meeting as though she were on the other side of the desk. "I'll be straight with you, Gavin. I've never renovated a cabin before. But"—she held up a slender finger and turned solemn—"you won't find a more dedicated soul. My job is my life, my whole world, and I've never backed down from a challenge. You can check out my references if you'd like. In fact, I designed the lobby of a five-star hotel three blocks from here. Do you have plans for lunch? Their in-house restaurant is sublime, and you could see my handiwork for yourself firsthand. Within budget and beyond expectations, which happens to be my slogan. See."

Duke had no clue where in the hell she'd been keeping a stash of business cards. It didn't surprise him the placard was fire-engine red with fancy black script. More like something an escort would have than an interior designer, but totally Neve: bold and in-your-face.

He wanted to disappear. What part of *he's shy* hadn't she understood? Shy people didn't stand up well under bombardment. They needed gentle coaxing, subtle nudges.

To his utter amazement, Gavin's hesitant smile spread slowly as he took the card, eyebrows raised slightly at the intrepid design. "You do have a certain enthusiasm. The type to give a hundred percent."

She winked at him. Actually *winked*. "Plus interest."

Duke hardly believed his luck. He relaxed his tense shoulders. Neve had basically passed the job interview, and he'd be off the hook for good. He rose from his seat with a cheery wave. "I'll leave you two to sort out the details. Glad I could help." He'd done it. Escaped by the hair—

Gavin stopped him with a sudden raised palm. "Now hold on there, Duke. I haven't given up on you yet. No matter what, I still want you in on this."

Neve's head snapped in his direction. Her eyes were such a pale brown, they seemed tan sometimes, with big flecks of dark amber. Her gaze narrowed. She might've been a lion scrutinizing his lean-to-fat ratio. "In what capacity might I require a data analyst? To double-check my math?"

Gavin perked up, excitement lighting up his face.

Duke dropped his head. *Shit.* He had it figured out before Gavin opened his mouth.

"That's perfect! You two can work together. Duke, you turned down the job the first time because you wanted a partner. Well, now you've got one. I'm sure Ms. Harper won't mind." Expectant, he turned to her. "Would you?" Not exactly a question. Gavin wasn't giving her a choice, and they both knew it.

Her whole face seemed to harden and shrink in on itself like drying plaster. "Someone enlighten me. I'm obviously missing some critical piece of information that'll make this all come together."

For two years, Duke had miraculously managed to avoid Neve's infamous wrath. His streak ended today.

Gavin didn't miss a beat. "Duke's only filling in for an analyst on vacation. I thought you two were friends? He's actually head of our design team, but before he came here, he was a general contractor in Louisiana. Or was it Alabama?"

Duke closed his eyes and pinched the bridge of his nose. "Georgia, but that was a long time ago." He opened his eyes, almost pleading Gavin to drop it.

"Oh, come on, don't be modest. Vale House is timeless, Duke. The man responsible for Vale House is the man I want. No offense, Ms. Harper. I'm sure you're an excellent designer, but I won't settle. I'll hire you, but only if Duke's willing to sign on as well."

Duke didn't think she was listening. She glared at him, once narrowed eyes gone wide with shock. "*You* did Vale House? *The* Vale House, famous Savannah plantation?" She blinked several times. "Your office. You designed it, didn't you?"

Vale House, his supposed masterpiece. Yeah, he'd renovated and restored one of the oldest still-standing plantation homes in the South and earned renown in his field for perfectly replicating the spirit of pre-Civil War life in a house that had been nothing but shambles when he started. He'd given five years to the plantation and lost more than time because of it. He clamped his mouth shut against an ugly remark and batted away unpleasant memories. "I'm not interested."

Coldly confident, Neve came to her feet so all three of them were standing.

This was the woman Duke was used to dealing with. Where had she been all morning? The peek-a-boo bra was suddenly less enticing, her eyes less entrancing. His damnation and his saving grace—the part of her that made him want her and drove him away at the same time. "The hell you aren't," she declared. Simple but definitive. "You're taking the job, Duke, because without you, I lose it."

Gavin regarded him with concern. "Tell you what. I'll hire Neve here as head honcho. She can bring on whoever she likes for general contracting if the cabin needs it. I mean, the place has four walls and a roof, and that's pretty much all I can tell you about its condition. All you have to do is consult." He shook his head and grew quiet. "Your talent is wasted here, Duke. You're meant for greater things than designing bras. Come on. What do you say?"

Damn nice people. Duke wanted to be cold and hard like Neve, but even the bitterness coating the back of his throat couldn't stop him from saying yes to Gavin. Because Gavin was nice, and he wanted a nice cabin out in the woods, and why couldn't Duke sit around in the woods for a couple months and do something nice for his boss? Why the hell not? He dared a glance at Neve.

That's why not. Dragon lady smoldered behind her unwavering glare.

Duke regretted ever mentioning the cabin. "Fine. Under the condition I'm there only as a consultant, and I don't answer to Neve."

From pleading to delighted, Gavin's beaming smile took up his whole face. He came around the desk to grasp Duke's hand with both of his. "Thank you, Duke. Thank you so much. It's all I ever wanted."

As Duke shuffled out of the office behind Neve several minutes and one signed contract later, a headache began to blossom from the back of his skull. What in the hell had he done? His plan had backfired bigtime. Not only had he committed to a job his soul cried out against, he'd jimmied himself into a hell of a pickle with Neve, whom he'd be stuck with for weeks out in the middle of nowhere at some remote cabin, hundreds of miles from normal, kind human beings.

As soon as they were a few yards down the hall, she whirled on him. Pursed lips made her high cheekbones prominent. Small breasts, angular features, thin lips on a wide mouth—nothing at all attractive about her, least of all the stinging wrath she was seconds away from unleashing on him in a place full of see-through walls. He'd be the talk of the break room for months after this. He braced for impact.

She closed in, but her voice was shockingly quiet when she spoke. Her glittering eyes made up for it. "You want to know why I'm so direct, Duke? Why I don't believe in bullshit like tact? It's because I can't stand a goddamn liar. This is far from over, booby boy." She stalked away from him.

Her hair flew out behind her as if trying to escape. Her hips cut like razors in her long, angry stride, her ass swaying from side to side with purpose. Nope, nothing attractive at all.

Chapter 3

Duke had never been to war. He imagined waiting for Neve to storm his loft felt a lot like waiting for a decorated general to launch a well-planned assault. He tugged his beard, unbraided and left to run wild. He ought to shave it, but he liked how it hid his face like armor. He'd feel naked and exposed without his raiment of hair. By the time Neve's booming knock sounded on the door, he'd almost prepared himself.

She stood on the other side of the threshold in her pajamas, which didn't surprise him. Unlike him, Neve didn't need protective gear. Not when her personality was such a weapon. She'd twisted her long hair into a bun on the top of her head and had on gray sweatpants with a hole in one knee and a white T-shirt so small it strained over her tiny breasts. Braless, she hadn't left a damn thing to the imagination. Size, shape, and even the slightly darker shade of her nipples all on fine display.

Dear God, give him back the racy yellow bra.

Would she be so comfortable showing off her assets were he straight? Probably. Neve never lacked for confidence. Her golden eyes no longer snapped and buzzed like a flickering flame, but they bored through him with an intensity that made him look away.

She pushed past him and headed for the refrigerator. "Make some of your gay tea, but hurry up. Let's get this over with."

He rolled his eyes but started for the kitchen anyway. He snatched up the olive green kettle. "Chamomile is not gay tea."

"Quit being so sensitive. All tea is gay tea."

He'd agree if he weren't pretending to be offended. He filled the kettle at the faucet and switched on the gas burner. He folded his arms, rested against the counter, and watched Neve bury her head in his fridge.

She pulled a takeout container from the shelves. His dinner. She sniffed the box. "Onions?"

"Nope." Possibly the only thing they had in common. Besides their jobs, information he'd deliberately withheld.

She snatched a fork from the drying rack and deposited herself on the sofa. "This is going to be fun," she mumbled around a mouthful of sweet and sour pork. "We're going to learn a lot about each other tonight."

Duke tugged his hair into a ragged ponytail at the nape of his neck. "Man, you're ballsy. I don't owe you an explanation."

She forked another huge bite into her mouth. "Like hell. You intentionally kept your job a secret. We're in the same damn profession, and you've hidden it for two years. This morning you outright lied about what you do. Now, normally, I'd agree with you. I don't give a shit how you earn your living, Duke, but this seems oddly personal. You're going to explain this covert bullshit to me, or I'm going to make the next six to eight weeks pure hell. Your choice." She didn't bother to look him in the eye as she delivered the threat.

He took it to heart. Duke pulled the kettle from the burner when the whistling began. "You'll do that anyway. It's part of your charm."

"You make jokes, but you've never seen me at my worst. You've never done anything to—" She stopped.

Duke glanced up from pouring hot water over tea bags.

Neve poked at her rice.

"To what?" he pushed. "Piss off the queen?"

No answer, but she at least managed to meet his gaze. She didn't shrink under his questioning look. That wouldn't be Neve-like.

He shook his head. Who cared, right? Apparently, he did. He came around the island and set two steaming mugs on the coffee table. He sat next to Neve and angled toward her. "Don't stop now. You said we're going to get to know each other. Nothing wrong with you going first."

She blinked and dropped the fork as though her appetite fled before the answer. "You've never done anything to let me down."

Wow. Why did that answer shock him? Perhaps he never considered she had reasons for being such a bitch. Then again, there was something to be said for impossible standards. And that he'd let her down implied she relied on him. For what, exactly? Neve had a steady string of boyfriends. Every few months some new idiot strolled out of the elevator looking like he'd won the lottery.

Intrigued, he plopped against the cushions. His sofa wasn't svelte and stylish like Neve's but a hand-me-down with a network of holes and patches he'd used to cover other holes. There was history and a few stains, but he liked stuff with a past.

"I design bras. I didn't tell you about my old job because it isn't relevant. We don't talk about that sort of stuff. When would I have brought it up? The thought never crossed my mind to randomly mention we once had something in common." More like having stuff in common with Neve had toed the line of "getting involved."

Her gaze was still hard. She didn't attack, though. "How did you go from renovating plantations in Georgia to designing bras in Arkansas?"

"Renovating didn't come until later. After attending an art institute, I met a contractor at a bar. Random act of the universe. I started helping him on job sites, giving input here and there. I liked it enough I dropped out of the institute and went to work for him full-time. Eventually, when I felt I'd surpassed my mentor, I branched out on my own. End of story."

Her impeccably shaped eyebrows went up. Women had this thing about their eyebrows where they never seemed to get them right. Too thin and weird-shaped or bushy like a squirrel's tail. But Neve's were nice. "Vale House? Bras?"

He groaned, impatient with rehashing history. "You know the rest. An old geezer with even older money hired me to restore Vale House. I did the job, then I quit the profession. Went back to art design, moved to Little Rock, took a nine-to-five at a bra company making easy money. Trust me, bras are nothing compared to houses. They're easier, for starters, and tend to come with better benefits."

Neve flashed a smile. She might be made of brick, but at least he could get a laugh out of her occasionally. She finished his leftovers and moved to throw away the container and rinse her fork.

Duke waited, eyeing her as she moved comfortably through his home.

"I understand tact." She rested her hip against the island, her arms folded, and regarded him with her best poker face. "For instance, I'd never dream of telling my sweet granny she's got pickle breath when there hasn't been a pickle within ten miles of her house in a decade. I wouldn't call out a kid for having underdeveloped motor skills. Those circumstances require a diplomatic approach. I might offer Granny a Tic Tac, but I'm not cruel."

"Neve, c'mon, you don't owe me an explanation." Leave it to Neve to forget women were supposed to be emotional creatures. She was going to get him with logic.

"The general populace is different. I admit it. I've got some crazy high standards and even higher expectations, but there's no excuse for lying to spare someone's feelings. You're not doing favors when you hide the truth from people. In the end, lying does more damage than good." She glanced away briefly. "Trust me. You can say I'm harsh with my deliverance, but I won't ever lie to you, Duke. I despise lying, lies, and liars. Unless you're a small child or my sweet granny, don't expect any different when we're working together. If an idea sucks, I'm going to tell you it sucks. And I'll expect the same from you."

He squinted at her. Her philosophy struck him as surprisingly unrealistic for such a grounded woman. "Everyone lies. It's human nature."

"It's cowardice, but I won't argue about it being our nature. Yeah, we all lie. We lie because we're afraid—afraid to cause hurt or anger, afraid to be the messenger who gets shot, afraid to share, afraid to hate, afraid to love."

Afraid to relate. Duke smoothed a hand over his beard. "There're other reasons to lie."

She ignored him. "What were you afraid of when you didn't tell me what you did for a living? Afraid we'd have something to talk about? I don't get it."

"Not a damn thing." It was like having someone read his mind. No wonder people didn't like Neve. She picked open their brains and threw the contents in their faces. "Sorry. I don't go around spewing random information about my past. It's not like you and I sit down and have heartfelt discussions like we're best buds or something. Why *would* I tell you?"

Her mouth clamped shut, her lips pressing together until the skin around them turned white. He waited for an outraged outburst, an ugly insult.

Instead, Neve made a visible effort to relax her shoulders and take in a quiet breath. "I'd like to start on the cabin this weekend. If you'll arrange for a rental car, I need to spend the next few days finding a general contractor in the area. There's a town called Red Hill nearby, and I'm sure they have a local guy."

"You're going to hire locally instead of getting a team together here in Little Rock?"

She gave him a flat smile. "I support small business. See? I'm not a complete asshole."

"I never said—"

She pushed away from the counter, ducking her head and waving her arm. "Forget it." She opened the door to let herself out. Her bun had lost its shape, falling into a limp ponytail.

God, he couldn't wait for this to get started so it could end. "Great. It's gonna be loads of fun. I can't wait."

She took a step, gripped the edge of the door and stopped, her head down. "Don't lie to me again, Duke. I hate liars."

The door slammed shut. He threw his head back and yelled after her, "I am not a liar!"

* * * *

"You take liar to a new level of scum."

Duke shrugged one shoulder and gazed around. "It's not that bad."

I'm going to kill him. I'm going to strangle him with his own hair. Frustration and awe at the condition of the cabin made it difficult to push words through Neve's throat and past her gritted teeth. She opened her arms wide in exaggerated appraisal of the main room, which also happened to be the *only* room. "Are you blind? Gavin needs a wrecking ball and a construction crew, not a designer."

Wall to wall logs formed the floors and ceiling, which arched high in an A-frame style. No insulation. No electricity. Minimal plumbing. Neve wanted to cry. She'd wasted hours on the trip out here.

Duke stood firm in the center of the room, black strands of hair falling pin-straight around his shoulders. Definitely long enough to wrap around his neck a few times. "The contract is signed, Neve. The location trailers will arrive soon, along with Vince Taggart and his team. They'll spearhead the tough spots while we focus on design."

Her temper flared. "Which 'tough spots' would you be referring to? The questionable foundation, the rotted steps out front, the half-completed plumbing installation, the blocked fireplace, the lack of lighting, or the complete and total absence of a bathroom?" She crossed her arms, cocked her head, and waited for an answer to make sense of what she'd been hired to do with the empty composite of dusty wood.

"It's no biggie." He smoothed down his beard. His other hand rested on his cocked hip. "Vince's crew is bringing along a Porta-Potty."

She inhaled. "Do you want to die? Because we're in the middle of nowhere, and I can probably hide the body pretty easily."

Duke put a consoling hand on her shoulder and ducked his head as if to share a secret. "Isn't this why you hired Vince and his team? Sure, there are some structural issues. I expected as much. This place has been abandoned for years. The way I see it, we have more time to design a new floor plan. The timeframe shouldn't change. We told Gavin between six to eight weeks. It'll be closer to eight than six, but still well within range. Although, there's one other thing I haven't mentioned yet."

She'd hired Vince Taggart because he came locally recommended. No telling if he had the chops for the full extent of the job, though. Neve had expected the hole in the floor where part of the old logs had rotted through and for the fireplace to need a good scrubbing and chimneysweep. But this…

"I'm a designer. I can remodel and rearrange what's already there, but I didn't sign up for this."

"If we work together, we can do it." Sincerity swamped Duke's steady blue gaze.

Neve shoved his hand from her shoulder, causing him to lose his balance. He recovered with only a slight unhinging of his jaw.

Funny, he'd gone out of his way to distance himself from her the last two years, keeping secret the one thing they would've had in common. He was only out here because she'd forced his hand. It wasn't a team effort. It was a hostage situation. "Only, we aren't working together, are we? This is my gig. From what I understand, you're here to mumble bullshit and call it consulting, so save your pathetic pep talk. I'm going to search for cell reception, call Gavin, and give him my professional opinion of this dump. You stay here and chant or something." With care, she avoided the hole in the floor and survived the dangerous descent down the precarious front steps.

The cabin sat elevated off the ground by the thick stump of an oak tree at each corner, and likely one centrally located beneath the cabin. At the time it was constructed, the space beneath would've been used as a larder for packing goods in snow through the long winter of the Ozarks.

Generally, Neve found people unfamiliar with the Arkansas mountain range seemed surprised at the snowfall. Because, of course, Arkansas was considered part of the South, with a capital S. And everyone knows the South is muggy and hot, with lots of old grannies sitting on their big porches eating apple pie and inviting strangers in for their famous sweet tea. Mountains were still mountains, and snow blanketed the range every winter.

Winter was a long way off, though. Summer commanded the acres and acres of untouched Ozark forest that stretched out from the high hilltop where the cabin perched. Walls of green reached for the sky, but by the time they finished the cabin, provided they avoided major snafus and kept to the schedule, the hills would be poised to explode into the vibrant colors of fall—golden yellow, bright orange, scarlet, and crimson. An autumn rainbow would blanket the scenery until the leaves all turned the same tired shade of brown and fell to their slow deaths in the soil below.

Well, that was dire.

Neve blamed the gloomy turn of her thoughts on Duke. She'd failed to get anywhere near Gavin in the process of taking on the project, and now she didn't even have a project to keep her occupied. She'd spend the next three weeks sitting on her thumbs waiting for Vince's team to do the necessary major lifting before anything on her side of the drafting table could be put into action.

"Neve, wait." Duke's impatient plea ended with a grunt.

She turned around in time to witness his boot catch a warped plank and send him flying. Instinct pushed her to try to catch his fall, but she failed to reach him in time, which was fortunate, as she narrowly missed being crushed beneath his weight and the momentum of his three-foot drop to the ground.

He landed with a thud and groaned. He rolled over, one hand clutching his side. "*Ouuuch.*"

Neve leaned over his prone form. "Did you need something?"

"An ambulance." Breath rasped through lips screwed up in a grimace of pain. How she noticed through the thick web of his beard was a mystery. "I think I cracked a rib."

It was a quarter-mile trek back to where they'd parked the rental car at the end of the steep, winding gravel path. The final leg to reach the cabin coursed through forest too dense and rugged for anything besides a four-wheeler to traverse. Gavin would have to let them clear a path in order to move supplies. Hiking the distance wasn't an option for a team hauling lumber and machinery.

"Wait here. I'll hike to where I can get reception." She patted his shoulder and straightened, holding her cell phone aloft. Definitely no bars out here.

Duke groaned again. "Wait here. Ah ha. You're hilarious. Wait, maybe it's not—" He yelped and grimaced as his fingers gingerly tested his side. "Damn. Okay, yeah. It's cracked. Go, hurry."

"Lucky for you, I'm headed that way."

Lucky for him, she missed his mumbled reply. She headed for the marked and well-beaten path back to the gravel road and kept her phone held high in case a bar or two sprang into action. She kept a steady eye on the signal icon, paying small mind to her surroundings.

Snap. Neve paused and scanned the thick swells of green foliage on either side of the wide trail. She swallowed and brought the phone to her chest. It'd make a better weapon if it had reception, but it'd have to do against…what sort of predators roamed the Ozarks? Bobcats? Coyotes? If a mountain lion or black bear shot through the trees, she'd be worse off than Duke, despite his vulnerable position. They wouldn't even be hungry anymore once they were done with her, and he'd never know she unwillingly and begrudgingly saved his life.

Another crack sounded through the undergrowth to her right.

Neve swung toward the noise and braced for an encounter, fists up, one clutching her cell phone like a dagger. She'd laugh at her silliness if goose bumps weren't playing the fiddle over her skin.

"I ain't going to hurt you." Hands up, the stranger emerged from behind the screen of the tree line and engaged her with a disarming smile. Tall with tight faded jeans, a cowboy hat, and a two-pound belt buckle.

Neve released the breath held hostage. She'd take Yosemite Sam over a black bear any day. Easier to aim a well-timed kick to a man's groin than outrun something with four legs. She lowered her makeshift weapon, refusing to feel mortified. "You make a habit of sneaking up on people in the woods? Next time I might have something more dangerous than a cell phone aimed at you."

The man's smile widened beneath a neatly trimmed mustache. He had a friendly enough countenance. Non-threatening hazel eyes watched her with mild amusement from beneath the curled brim of his hat. Those sideburns, though. They inched dangerously toward mutton-chop territory. He slid his thumbs into the belt loops on either side of his zealous buckle. "Timothy Hux." His head dipped forward in the customary cowboy howdy-doo. "My ranch is a few miles southeast of here. I noticed the car come up the road early this morning. Figured that Little Rock boy done gave up and sold the place. Thought I'd walk over and introduce myself to the new neighbors."

Walk through dense woods with a perfectly clear path yards away? "Gavin Chambers hasn't sold the cabin. I'm Neve Harper. He hired me to fix the place."

The rancher's smile faded somewhat. "I suppose that figures." He stuck out his hand. "Sorry to have startled you. You need anything, give me a holler. I'm over the hill there. If you head back down the mountain, the sign for Lady Killer Ranch is on your right. It's easy to miss on the way up, what with how the road twists and turns."

Duke and his injury sprang to mind. "Actually, I could use your help. My friend—colleague—fell off the rotted front steps at the cabin. He fell on his side and can't move from the pain in his ribs. He suspects he cracked one. What's the quickest way to get an emergency responder up here, Yosemite?"

Amusement glinted behind his steady gaze, belying the straight line of his mouth. He pulled a walkie-talkie from behind his back where it must've been clipped to his belt. Pretty handy in a place where cell phones were about as useful as a third butt-cheek. A *bleep* sounded when he pressed a red button on the side. "Miles, Tim here. Come in."

Loud static crackled in the air and startled a few nearby birds into flight. Their takeoff rustled the leaves overhead.

"This's Miles. What's up?"

"Send Owen to Beels Cabin, would ya? We got a fella needs first aid. He better bring Laurel 'round, too."

A moment of silence, then more static. "Sure thing, Tim. I'll send them your way."

"Copy that." Yosemite clipped the talkie back onto his belt and grinned politely at Neve. "All right, city girl. We ought to head back before your friend gets nervous. Or a bear sniffs him out while he's helpless." He turned toward the cabin.

Neve groaned. Traveling away from cell phone service went against the point of having left Duke alone in the first place. She'd have to get in touch with Gavin after helping Duke. By then, Vince would have arrived with their location trailers, and at least Duke would have somewhere to rest. Not like he had any plans to do any real work, anyway.

She stepped in beside the rancher. "Beels Cabin, huh?"

"Says the town registry. I suppose Mr. Chambers can call it what he likes."

"I've named it Gavin's Cabin. Couldn't resist. By the way, I like your ranch's name. Lady Killer." She slid her gaze his way, a brow arched in query. "Is that indicative of the owner?"

Timothy's mustache twitched as his lips curved upward. "Well, now. I can't go giving away my secrets to the first pretty lady I run into out in the woods. Some stuff you ought to find out for yourself, I reckon."

Neve returned his smile. He had a certain languid quality she admired in a man. Nice eyes when they twinkled, like they did now, lit with mirth. *I'm here to worm my way into Gavin's confidence, not make nice with friendly ranchers.* Good point. Besides, she ate men like Timothy Hux for breakfast. "I don't believe for a second I'm the first pretty lady," she teased, despite her internal warnings. "But I'm sure I've got my answer."

He chuckled and issued a low whistle. "No offense, but you've got trouble written all over you."

Neve bestowed her best devil-may-care smile on her new friend and winked for good measure. "In permanent marker." *Okay, really, stop.* "What else can you tell me about the cabin? If your ranch is a family gig, you should have generations of stories about the area."

He touched the rim of his hat, an affirmative gesture. "My great-great-granddaddy homesteaded this land. Back then, your friend's cabin didn't exist, and the property stretched from the hilltop on down to where the gravel road branches off from the highway. Now, legend says his boy— that'd be my great-granddaddy Ben—fell in love with one woman after he done got married to another." He thoughtfully rubbed his chin. "A big deal at the time, 'course. As if an affair weren't outrage enough, Florrie was, uh…the politically correct term is African American, but they were called worse things in Ben's time. He made himself a pariah when he built the cabin for Florrie, right on his land, not a mile from the ranch proper, where he lived with his wife and boys. He even deeded her the land, too."

"The cabin hasn't been bought back by the ranch in all this time?"

Timothy shrugged one shoulder. "I don't see no more point than my daddy did. Can't farm this rocky slope. The land itself ain't much to bother with, and you seen yourself the shape the cabin's in. Seems like a lot of money to pay for more work to do."

"Whatever happened to Florrie and Ben? I'm having a hard time imagining it culminates into a happily-ever-after for anyone involved. Except maybe Florrie." Single landowner? Relationship of love? Given the other options at the time for unmarried black women, it sounded to Neve like an ideal set-up.

"Oh, definitely not Florrie. My great-granny, Lulu Hux, lost her mind over the whole thing. A few years after Florrie took up residence, Granny Lulu killed herself in a jealous rage, but not before taking Ben's beloved Florrie down with her. Murdered her right inside the cabin. Then shot herself in the head with Ben's pistol." Another shrug. "So the story goes, anyhow."

Neve's stomach flip-flopped. "Lady Killer Ranch doesn't sound as charming as it did a minute ago."

Timothy's soft laugh said it didn't bother him much. "Locals sort of renamed the ranch after the murder-suicide went public. Ben wasn't no hero, that's for sure. A couple generations later, the story lingers about their ghosts. Granny Lulu can't move on for guilt, and Florrie can't move on for want of vengeance. I reckon both spirits are still around and running circles 'round each other. Not sure how that works, but ghosts weren't never a care of mine."

"Wow." Neve nodded. "I've jumped right into a *Scooby-Doo* plot. I'll be sure to let you know if I run into any ghosts, one probably chasing the other with a fry pan or something."

"Heck, you better fetch me if you run into Granny Lulu. She'd be mad as spit if I didn't stop by to say hello."

Duke hadn't shifted his curled position on the ground at the foot of the offending steps. His head twitched as they drew near. "Neve? Is that you?"

"Yep, and I brought back-up."

"Back-up?" His incredulous tone made her want to kick him. Maybe not directly in his injured rib but close enough to send uncomfortable reverberations through it. "We're twenty miles from the nearest town."

Twenty-six, actually, but who was counting each and every tedious mile in between Red Hill, the closest point loosely termed civilization, and Gavin's cabin? Not her.

She bent over Duke again. His beard had picked up some dirt and a blade of grass. "Ungrateful whelp."

"From Red Hill, maybe, but not from the nearest ranch." Timothy stepped around Duke to enter his field of vision. "Cracked rib, eh? Two of my best cowhands are on their way. They'll get you taped up good, and you'll be making firewood of them rotten steps in no time."

Neve tapped her chin. Not a bad idea.

Duke stretched his neck to angle his face toward Neve and peered up through one open eye. "Did he say cowhands?"

"Whispering won't stop him from hearing you."

Timothy smiled and worked his hands into the front pockets of his impossibly tight jeans. They'd put any pair of leggings Neve owned to shame. "What works on a cow ought to work on a man. Bones are bones."

Duke let his head loll to the side like he'd given up on life. His sleek hair had come loose from the tieback and fanned around his shoulders. "Only you, Neve. Only you."

Twigs snapped from the direction of the trailhead as a couple in their mid- to late-forties hurried toward them. A pear-shaped woman with a head of dark corkscrew curls and the same style jeans as Timothy, complete with a seemingly identical buckle, led the way, followed by a man in similar dress. Dappled sunlight reflected off his bald head. The hair appeared to have scrambled from his head to become eyebrows, which were black and bushy like a skunk's tail. He had a blue duffel bag in his left hand.

"The cavalry has arrived," Timothy announced. "This here is Owen Pritchard and his wife, Laurel."

A lot of dipping heads. Owen hitched his chin at Duke. "This your man, here?"

No, it's other guy lying on the ground in a fetal position. Neve checked her sarcastic response. "He tripped coming down the steps and thinks he has a cracked rib," she explained as Owen handed Laurel the duffel bag and dropped to a crouch to examine Duke.

Duke coughed and winced.

Laurel joined in on the touching and poking and pressing. "Might be cracked," she finally declared, gaining her feet, while Owen continued to study the injury. "Not broken, luckily, but check in with a doctor when you get back to the city. When y'all headed out?" She aimed the question at Neve.

"We aren't headed anywhere. We'll be spending the next eight weeks working on the cabin and living in a tin can at the end of the gravel road, up where we parked our car. I'm Neve Harper." She offered her hand, and Laurel took it. "This is Duke. He's only around to consult. Nonessential personnel."

Owen's lips pressed together and his eyes squinted in concern. "Well, Red Hill has a decent physician. Make the trip to town and follow-up with an x-ray to be sure. Soon as you can, hear? We'll tape it to help with the pain, but only for a few hours. It'll heal better without a wrap on it."

Duke nodded miserably.

Laurel hunched down again beside Owen and they worked together. He pulled a roll of adhesive tape from the duffel, at least three times the width of the stuff you'd pick up at a pharmacy. Veterinarian supply.

Timothy must've read her mind. "There's a large animal vet on the other side of Red Hill, but we're so far out we've had to learn a lot ourselves. Laurel and Owen ain't schooled proper, but they handle minor injuries at the ranch. Your friend should be fine."

Duke croaked something.

Unable to catch it, Neve knelt at his side and leaned in close. "What's that?"

"You told him we're friends?" He took in a ragged breath. "I thought you hated liars."

Chapter 4

"Neve, tell me the truth."

She growled and bared her canines the way Darcy the Pit did when she ran into a strange dog she didn't like. Hopefully, Duke would take the hint. "For the last time, Laurel and Owen didn't give you horse tranquilizers. Besides, they both decided it's a muscle thing. No injury to the bone, and you'll be fine by the end of the week."

Reclined into a half-laying, half-sitting position after sleeping through most of yesterday afternoon and on through the next morning, Duke gingerly lifted his arm, not without a slight grimace, and ran his fingers over the dusky purple bruise roughly the size of his palm. "But there's no pain. I slept straight through the night. How's that possible?"

"Obviously anything is possible if my name can be mistaken for Ned, and you and I are given a single location trailer to share for the next eight weeks." She made no attempt to soften the bitter hem of the remark.

Irritated hardly did her mood justice.

How Duke managed to wake up from a thirteen-hour nap and look like something out of a dirty lady's magazine didn't help smooth her temper, either. The sleek black strands of his hair draped over his shoulder, coming to rest their tips across his nipple. She wanted to run her thumb over the tiny hard bud if only to see the look on his face.

Such a waste of beautiful male. A loss to females the world over, but the fact didn't dissipate her agitation with their set-up. "Like I said last night before you conked out, get used to the sofa. I'm not giving up the bed. And if you think Darcy the Pit loves you, try getting into the bedroom while I'm asleep."

His eyebrows rose in lieu of a hands-up surrender. The injury to his ribs limited his usual gesture-happy communication. "Hey, I'm not taking the heat for the trailer mistake. It's not a big deal, anyway. The next eight weeks are going to fly by, and the sofa bed is perfectly fine with me. I'm not complaining, am I?"

Well, I am. She'd spent thirteen years living alone—longer if she took into account her lack of siblings. Ever since moving out of her parents' house and into her first apartment at nineteen. No dorm life for her. She'd have ended up in prison for murder long before completing her degree in interior design. For the first time in her grown life, she had to share personal space with another human being on a semi-permanent basis. "Eight weeks may not seem like a long time, but I'm sure it feels long when the bathroom is coed."

"I'm gay, remember? I'm supposed to be meticulous and well-groomed."

"Supposed to be?" Her arms were already crossed. She added a challenging lift of one eyebrow.

He rolled his eyes, still puffy from long hours of sleep, and waggled his fingers at her dismissively. "Complain all you want. Me, I'm glad I'm not sharing with Vince or any of his guys."

Neve ignored him as he closed his eyes and appeared to attempt going back to sleep. She'd work better without him, anyway. She sat on the crooked bench seat of the dinette table and sketched an approximate representation of the cabin. Simplest floor plan ever—a square. Also a problem. Gavin probably expected some kind of private sleeping and bathing area. "We're going to have to install walls," she murmured. "At least two for a bathroom, if we're doing a studio-apartment style with the bed open to the rest of the space."

Did Gavin want an exposed sleeping area? Would he entertain at the cabin, use it for a lover's retreat, or only visit alone?

She tapped the eraser end of her stubby pencil on the thick page. "I need to get with Gavin for a few details before I can draw a floor plan. Some stuff is obvious—there's no insulation or essential bathroom fixtures. But I need information. Speaking of, didn't you have something to tell me?"

One of Duke's eyes opened, a cobalt slit against his pale skin and dark hair. Did she imagine the hint of trepidation behind his gaze? "What are you talking about?"

She furnished him with a flat stare. "Did you bump your head when you fell? You said, mere moments before your tragic fall, there was some 'other thing' you'd yet to mention."

A mask of relief stole over his face. So, she hadn't imagined his apprehension. Curious.

"Right, right. Uh, well, Gavin had some last-minute requirements he neglected to get included in the paperwork. It's a small complication. Nothing we can't cleverly work around, I'm sure."

Neve's head flopped forward, chin to chest like a limp doll. "You mean *another* complication. Because there's already a list." She straightened and ticked each item off on her fingers. "A single location trailer to share, meaning only one of us is likely to return to Little Rock alive or in possession of all their limbs. You're injured and, despite it not being as serious as we first assumed, still means at least a week of bed rest, so we're already down a team member. Then there are the structural concerns and the cat-fighting ghosts and—"

"Neve!"

She blinked. His eyes were squeezed shut, lines gathered in the outside corners like pleats. She pushed buttons. It was her thing. And normally, people let her. Sometimes, they whined, pouted, flinched, or ran the other away…but they didn't shout. She cocked her head to the side and waited.

His face took on a pleading expression, an impressive feat with eyes shut. "You're giving me a headache. Yes, there are problems with the cabin, and less than ideal living circumstances. Yes, this is going to suck, but it will suck a lot more if we're both being assholes, which is what will happen if you don't get off my ass."

"I thought you liked things on your ass."

"I'm serious." His eyes popped open. "Vince brought a whole team with him. Maybe one of them would like the honor of being your whipping boy, but I'm not interested in the position."

She had to give him credit. He blended seamlessly between malleable and showing off brass ones that almost made her proud. One day, she'd find out exactly how far she could get away with pushing Duke Kennicot. But not today. So, she let her snarky thoughts on what positions he *did* like skitter through her brain without passing her lips.

He smoothed his hand over his face, a show of weariness, and ended with a tug on his beard. "I can leave tomorrow. Head back to Little Rock and give you the job and the trailer. Everybody wins."

"Like hell." Gavin's deal had been set stone. No Duke, no project. If he left, she'd be sent back to town right behind him. "You and I are going to strike a deal."

He craned his neck to observe her with obvious suspicion. He searched her face and narrowed his dark blue gaze. "Stipulations?"

Neve stroked her chin and took a moment to consider. What, precisely, did she need to accomplish here?

Gavin ranked first in her lineup of priorities. The college boys and their easy brush-offs were no coincidence or mere habit she'd formed out of desire for hot, young bodies. Better an ending she expected than to let herself truly care for someone who'd leave her anyway.

And men always left. Real men. Grown, reliable, responsible, dependable men—the ones who paid their mortgage on time and brought home flowers for no reason. *Those* men always left. At first, they loved Neve's candid approach to life. They adored her unwavering dedication to honesty and truthfulness. They liked knowing where they stood, how she felt, what she did and didn't like in bed—things a lot of women kept tied down. But eventually, they grew weary of confronting the truth, because the truth wasn't always a pretty thing. They wanted to hear how special they were, how tough and strong, how *big*; the best she'd ever had, the cleverest, the bravest, the sexiest.

They wanted to conquer her, bend her until she fit the shape of their egos. And when she refused to budge or soften, they moved on to more yielding women. Maybe that was why she attracted them in the first place. She was a challenge they thought they could overcome, a game they wanted to win. They hadn't appreciated her, just the way she provoked their testosterone to new heights. So, when they went, she let them.

The trick, she decided, had to be finding a man with flaws, who'd have to accept hers in return.

Gavin had anger issues. Maybe instead of leaving her, he'd simply blow his stack. She had a defense against anger, but it was hard to argue with a man's back.

Neve's long gaze met Duke's and, for an instant, she wished it were him. He took some of her crap, a sample here and there, but not all of it. He even managed to incite her guilt a few times, which wasn't easy, because most people deserved what she dished out. In another life, a man like Duke would be the one she chased. He'd be the one she wouldn't let get away.

"Here's the deal," she finally said, snapping out of her daydream. "You help me get close to Gavin, in an obviously figurative way, given we're a hundred miles from Little Rock, and I'll keep the dogs locked up tight. You know me, Duke. I can be playfully mean or a real bitch, but there's not much gray area in between. Like a dial with only two settings."

He harrumphed. "You were perfectly nice to Yosemite yesterday."

She wagged a finger and smiled coyly. "Not nice. I was *flirting*, which may also be a degree of my personality. Mean, very mean, and sexually aggressive. However, I don't mind admitting it's a lot of work to be a bitch, and I don't have that kind of time for you. Seducing Gavin and renovating his cabin—a double entendre I intend to abuse at every opportunity—are my priorities. You help me, I'll be my version of nice."

A sly grin hitched up one corner of his mouth. "So, you'll flirt with me?"

She cocked her head to one side in a show of pity and frowned. "I wouldn't waste my precious ammo on a cause that degree of lost, sweetheart. Besides, I'll need it to schmooze Yosemite. He and his cowhands came in awfully handy yesterday, and that's the sort of friendship a discerning woman fosters. No, flirting is out of the question. My intent is more along the lines of softening the blows. Take it or leave it, because it's all I can offer."

"Sold." The blatant relief on his face was nearly enough to hurt feelings she didn't know she had.

She gave him a flat smile. "Good. Now, my little puppet, tell me about Gavin's special requirement."

"Okay, but then you have to tell me about these cat-fighting ghosts. Also, if you yell at me, the deal is off."

"The deal is off if you keep stalling. Shut up and tell me."

"You realize I can't do both of those things."

She inhaled deeply. "Why do you want me to kill you? I swear, you're begging for it."

He released a defeated sigh. "Gavin wants everything we add to the cabin constructed from reclaimed wood, with the obvious exception of any glass or tile surfaces. Any walls we put up, cabinetry we build, or flooring we add. Basically, outside of staining or sealing the planks already in use, there's little we can alter."

Neve summoned every last ounce of patience she had to keep herself from flinging the sketchpad across the trailer. "That's fan-fucking-tastic. Would he also like a hollow log for a toilet?" She narrowed her gaze at Duke accusingly. "Now I understand your refusal to sign on for this. It's twice the job I was led to believe."

He raised his index finger like a shield. "Hold on a minute. It's true, Gavin enlightened me some time ago about his desire to use reclaimed wood, but I had no notion as to the state of the cabin. I expected to have more to work with, same as you."

Reclaimed wood, huh? Slowly, the corners of her mouth turned up until she blasted Duke with her full smile. "You wouldn't believe it, but a certain rancher invited me to come a-callin' should I need anything. I bet his ranch is chock-full of old barns and decrepit storage sheds he'd let us dismantle for the right price—a price far cheaper than what a lumberyard would ask. This reclaimed wood fad is all the rage right now, and the law of economics means the price rises with demand."

Duke regarded her with a tilt to his head and a queer light in his eyes. "A fine place to start with Gavin might be that smile right there." He cleared his throat and glanced away. "We need to work on your potty-mouth, though. Gavin's a clean dude, inside and out."

She gave Duke her most savage smile. "Don't worry your pretty head. I can teach him to appreciate a little grit."

* * * *

The leafy canopy of white oaks, loblolly pines, and towering catalpas kept the summer sun at bay as the morning marched toward midday.

Neve clutched her sketchbook to her chest, pencil tucked behind one ear, and meandered down the overgrown path toward the cabin. Duke might have an excuse to spend the day lying around, but she had a crew to put to work. Vince Taggart and his team had already abandoned their trailer for the worksite, and Neve chafed at being late.

Beels Cabin. She liked her name better, but the story intrigued her. Timothy Hux struck her as the friendly sort, a real howdy-neighbor kind of guy—a screaming red flag in her book. She hadn't missed the slightly calculating gleam in his studious hazel eyes. She knew men well enough to recognize it hadn't been the appreciative observation of a man attracted to a good-looking woman. He'd analyzed more than her snug-fitting Levi's.

Neve determined to get a read on the mysterious rancher's motives for poking around the cabin. Maybe if she behaved and treated everyone, especially Duke, with the utmost civility instead of the usual fun nicknames she liked to bestow, Providence would bless her with a visit from the friendly Mr. Hux and spare her the hike to Lady Killer Ranch with a self-awarded dinner invitation.

Though, in fairness, a few miles' hike through pristine Ozark wilderness hardly seemed like any kind of punishment. And Darcy the Pit, happily snoozing at Duke's side back at the trailer, would love nothing more.

Behind her and off to the left, twigs snapped and bushes rustled.

Neve stilled. An image of Yosemite popped into her head. Was this going to turn into a thing, this sneaking up on her from the cover of the forest?

Darcy the Pit's squirming light brown body shot from the busy undergrowth of the tree line, tongue lolling from her wide, smiling mouth, and her whip-like tail wagging in furious joy. She head-butted Neve's shins and licked her hands like she didn't know which she wanted to do more. Lick or head-butt? Head-butt or lick?

Affection unfurled in Neve's chest like a flower coming to bloom in a foreign landscape. Sometimes she believed she was as heartless as people said she was. But she had one in there, thumping away, and Darcy the Pit proved it for her time and time again, even when she doubted herself. No one with a heart could withstand Darcy the Pit's blinding, infectious joy.

If only men loved the way pit bulls did. Neve rubbed the short fur on Darcy the Pit's barreled chest. "Mommy's sweet girl, yes, you are! Yes, you are."

Darcy the Pit soaked it in, and in a pure burst of unbridled canine jubilation, rocketed down the path toward the cabin. Probably questing for prime fetch material. She'd return with a branch twice the width of her head and whine when Neve refused to toss it for her.

"Be reasonable," she called after her. Couldn't hurt to try. Maybe one day the lively pit bull would heed her warnings.

The cabin came into view after another five minutes' hike. Such a gorgeous backdrop for a ramshackle pile of dusty old logs well past their prime. Neve pushed away the fear of failure and focused on the task at hand.

No crewman. So, where had Vince and his team disappeared to? She hadn't checked the vehicles. Possibly they'd gone to town for supplies. If Vince was half as good as his reputation, he'd have already made a cursory inspection of the cabin, much as she and Duke had done, and compiled a list of necessities to get started.

She stopped next to the steps Duke had launched himself from yesterday morning. They were splintered, a gaping maw of pointed, jagged teeth. She didn't need the ominous symbolism to keep her from attempting to enter the cabin. No, siree. She'd let Vince stabilize the place first.

She squatted next to one of the oak pillars acting as foundation pieces for a closer gander at the rigged job. From a top-notch city-slicker point of view, it scared the hell out of her. But way out here and eighty years ago, the four pedestals of the toughest wood around would've been an ingenious solution to the issue of a firm foundation on loose soil.

Maybe I need to get a little rustic. Something to consider. No sense approaching a cabin like she might a high-rise condominium in downtown Little Rock. Forget steel and poured concrete; use the resources at hand.

Her gaze traveled from the oak pedestals to the splintering steps and back again. She rose from her crouched position with a cocky grin to do Casanova proud. "Well, hot damn. Why am I always alone when these magical bursts of genius strike?" She whipped the pencil from behind her ear and drew a rough outline of what she had in mind. A simple fix. Hopefully, Vince would agree. If not, she'd help him see the light—by shoving it down his throat if need be. With a smile, of course.

Darcy the Pit whined, rushed to Neve's feet, sniffed furiously, and disappeared around the rear of the cabin. Another whine compelled Neve to follow.

Around the back of the cabin, Neve's lip turned up at the distance between the building and where the grass flourished into bushes and eventually thick clusters of trees. "Not much of a backyard, huh, girl?"

Darcy the Pit's attention focused elsewhere, specifically on the hole she'd begun digging next to the northwestern oak stump elevating the cabin.

Neve shouted, forgetting in an instant her own rule of using the dog's full name in her haste to issue the command. "Darcy, no!" Neve rushed toward her, shooing her from the shallow pit. "You'll bring this house of sticks down on your head. Quit. Shoo." She shoved the dog away and hunkered to block her access to the hole. "Go on, I mean it, shoo! Don't you know anything about loadbearing tree stumps, dummy?" Neve started to scoop dirt back into the dip until her fingers brushed something hard. A rock, probably.

Darcy the Pit whined again, shuffled her paws, and glared intently at where Neve had her hands in the dirt.

Maybe not. Neve huffed, rolled her eyes, and started to dig, carefully, muttering under her breath. "I can't believe I'm digging a hole *for* my dog. If this isn't love, I don't know what is. It's not healthy, this relationship of ours. Don't think for a minute Duke would do this for you, because he wouldn't. You remember that the next time you go showering him with your sloppy dog kisses. Despite his gnarled beard, he's kind of foppish. I'm a little fuzzy on what foppish means, but it's not flattering." Her nail scraped against a hard surface. "Okay, girl. I found something."

She kept going until she removed enough rich brown soil to see the grains of wood on the item buried. Perhaps a box or plank of wood long forgotten. Neve continued digging around where her fingers found the edge, and she scooped enough to reveal the rectangular wooden shape, no more than seven inches long and five across. Definitely a small box. "My, my. You've got one hell of a sniffer, mutt."

Darcy the Pit pushed her huge head past Neve's arm to stick her snout in the hole and snort.

Several minutes and two chipped nails later, Neve had it. She pulled the small wooden box, no more than three inches in depth, from the moist earth and brushed away clumps of clinging soil. She weighed the strange thing in her palm—hefty for such a small container. Could be solid, but the way the weight seemed to shift made her doubtful.

It had been buried with the intent to keep it hidden and unopened, judging by the strange metal contraption serving as a locking mechanism.

A cluster of oddly shaped metal protrusions were affixed to the spot where the lid met the container. She turned it in her hands. It almost looked like the small treasure chest of a particularly devious pirate. Small holes in between the metal spires of the lock might serve as a keyhole, but what kind of key would fit such an odd latch?

A funky one. Or a nonexistent one. The hardware comprising the hinge had to be internal. No breaking in that way. Her battering-ram instincts rallied her to take an axe in hand or light the thing on fire, but something—something precious, if the hellacious lock meant anything—resided within, and she didn't want to make the discovery at the cost of destroying it.

She sat back, winced at an acorn jabbing into her right butt cheek, and considered what she had.

Timothy Hux had some serious history in these hills. He might know something about where the chest came from, or why someone would go through the trouble of burying it beneath the cabin.

He said his great-grandfather built the place for Florrie soon after marrying his great-granny Lulu. If Ben Hux married in his mid-twenties, which for the sake of the era Neve would assume was likely, the cabin might be seventy years old or more.

If only she'd picked up better vibes from Yosemite. Given the peculiar and violent history surrounding his family and Gavin's cabin, Neve decided against involving the rancher. Best to keep family out of it. Besides, given possession laws, the chest and whatever it contained belonged to Gavin. She'd show her unique find to Duke, and together they'd figure out how to reveal its secrets.

Neve held the treasure out to Darcy the Pit. "It's your prize, after all."

Head tilted, she sniffed, took a lap around Neve, sniffed again, and padded away, curiosity appeased.

"That's my girl," Neve praised, making the dog's tail go from zero to sixty. "Sniff 'em and leave 'em." She stood, stretched her stiff knees, and brushed the dirt from her jeans. She whistled for Darcy the Pit and rounded the side of the cabin. The items in her hands almost flew from her grasp when she collided into something large and solid.

Vince Taggart made an *oomph* as she rammed into his chest. They both stumbled back from the unexpected impact.

Agitation and guilt jolted through Neve. "Damn it, Vince. Don't you know better than to sneak up on people?" She fumbled with the box in her hand, balancing it against the sketchpad tucked beneath her arm.

"What you got there?" A stubby finger aimed at the box. His other hand came up to adjust the filthy baseball cap perched on a head of thick, steely-gray hair. Inquisitive green eyes narrowed.

"Nothing. Just my box of...stuff. Like, rocks and stuff I collect for, uh...design ideas. Inspiration from nature sort of crap."

"Why's it covered in dirt? You're also covered in dirt."

Curious old fart. She cradled the mysterious box protectively against her chest with the same arm she used to pin her sketchpad to her side. The other arm she snaked around Vince's shoulders as she led him toward the front of the cabin and away from the disturbed patch of dirt behind her. "Nature is dirty, Vince, and sometimes one must dig for inspiration. Literally. Now, I'm glad you popped up because we have some things to discuss." She dropped her conspiratorial air and reclaimed her arm as they approached the broken, splintered steps leading up to the open front door.

Vince adjusted his hat again, pushing it up only to tug it back down to exactly the same spot. "Oh, you ain't lying. Where to start is the real question. The inspection is complete, and the list is a mile long."

Neve pointed at the busted stairs. "I say we start right here. See how the cabin sits on those oak stumps? We're going to borrow and use a similar approach with the new steps."

The older man rolled his shoulders and spit, something he probably imagined she'd find undignified and offensive. "I believe building stairs falls under my expertise."

"Certainly," she agreed. Then she spit, too. The wad landed inches from Vince's. "But telling you how to make them look falls under mine." No reason to harp on. She cocked her chin toward the cabin. "I love a good loophole, don't you? Gavin wants all-natural, so we'll give it to him. This new staircase of his is going to be a real statement piece in more ways than one." She smiled thinly and pointed at a pile of busted floor slats Vince's team had removed from the cabin's interior during their inspection. "Those loose pieces, where'd they come from?"

Vince shrugged. "Stacked in a corner of the cabin. Leftovers from construction, maybe? The place has been vacant for decades."

"The last owner tried to spruce the place up a bit before falling into debt and selling it. I noticed the slats during my walkthrough with Duke, and they're not the same makeup as the cabin. Newer stuff. I'm betting from when the plumbing was updated. Either way, great news for us. Those slats will form the bones for our new stairs. We're going to use a series of logs laid over the top horizontally to form the actual steps. In front, though, we'll insert small logs vertically. They'll look—"

"Like they're supporting the steps. Almost like organ pipes in three rising rows." He chewed in the inside of his cheeks as his shrewd eyes lit up. "Huh," he grunted. "Neat idea."

She didn't bother to be offended by the wonder coloring his voice. Eyes squinted in study, fingers rubbing the gray gristle of his unshaved chin… professionally, she had Vince Taggart's attention. His respect would follow.

"Get a few of your men on it. I want it constructed as a single structure we'll dig and set with a concrete base. What's your take on the foundation? For authenticity's sake, I'm in favor of keeping the pedestals."

"I agree, once we add a little fortification. They're sturdy, natural, and already here." He smacked his lips in a satisfied manner and leaned back on his heels, thumbs hooked into his belt loops. "The stairs are the easy part. The place is primed for plumbing, but the job isn't complete. A plumber can tell us more, but it's going to be a larger project than I'd anticipated."

Neve shook her head. "One thing at a time, pal. My first concern is ensuring the cabin is structurally sound. Check the roof for leaks, patch the hole in the floor so we can move safely inside, and get with Duke about any permits we need to apply for. He's handling the administrative duties. If we're set by the end of the week, we'll move inside and start punching out new windows and building walls."

"Huh." Vince's grunt held less awe and more grudge than the last one. "Reclaimed wood. I say getting your hands on a good supply ought to come before planning any walls. Just in case."

She whistled for Darcy the Pit and smiled wryly at the old geezer. She liked him. "I'll keep your advice in mind. You know, Vince, I think we're going to be best friends by the time this is over. I can smell it."

He lifted a brow. "That ain't our budding friendship you got a whiff of." He nodded past her.

She turned to catch Darcy the Pit sniffing her latest deposit of warm, steaming fertilizer a few feet away. Neve shrugged. "I didn't say it was a pleasant smell."

Vince resettled his baseball cap again and chuckled, walking off toward the group of men setting up workbenches and spotlights in the small clearing beyond the cabin.

Neve's lips curved, despite the scent of fresh dog poo permeating the air. *One down.*

* * * *

Duke smoothed down the rough, wiry hairs of his beard and winced at the tug on his tender ribs. He'd be taking it easy for the rest of the week, whether he liked it or not, no matter how badly he'd rather do other things.

Get a start on the stupid cabin, for one. Finish the job, wipe his hands of the whole mess, and go home. Back to designing bras and applying himself to nothing more intellectually straining than trying to win over his neighbor's dog.

He'd settled back into more a comfortable position at the same time his cell phone went off, the familiar jingle blasting into the stale quiet of the trailer. Duke bit back a groan and reached for it. Gavin's name glowed on the screen. Duke dropped his head, closed his eyes, and injected a note of cheer into his forced greeting. "Hey, Boss."

"Hey!" One day, Duke would work up the nerve to ask Gavin just what the hell he was so happy about all the time. "I wanted to give you guys a few days to settle in before checking on you. How was the drive up?"

Duke recalled the long, quiet ride through the middle of nowhere. "Great. It's beautiful this time of year. Summer's in full swing."

"The cabin's a gem, isn't she?"

As in raw, uncut, and unpolished. "She sure is."

"Well, how's everything else? Have the trailers arrived with Vince and his team? Are they nice? The trailers, that is. I'm sure Vince is great if Neve chose him, but I wouldn't mind your personal opinion, of course."

"Everything's great. I promise. The trailers are great." Lying already. Duke checked the sigh gathered in his chest. Gavin would feel terrible about the mix-up and there was little he could do about it now. As the budget sat, Duke would rather not have a second one rented, especially if Neve's plan for wood didn't pan out, and they had to find a lumberyard. Besides, he and Neve were both adaptable. They'd make do.

The sofa bed was against the wall of the small trailer, near the dining table and kitchenette. Beyond, a small open area operated as an office space and, at the far end, a small private bedroom behind a thin particleboard wall. Neve's domain. Or the dragon's lair, depending on her mood and his frame of mind.

"I'm glad to hear it," Gavin broke into his wondering thoughts. "So, what can you tell me so far?"

"Uh…" It'd be easier to answer Gavin's questions if Duke hadn't been confined to his bed for the last day and a half. Winging it, he injected a busy tone into his voice. "Vince and Neve made their initial inspection. A few issues, nothing major. A hole in the floor we need to patch, and the front stairs are…" *Are a heaping pile of busted splinters, caved under the weight of my sheer manliness.* "Rickety. We're working on that, as well as contacting lumberyards for reclaimed wood." He swallowed and recalled Neve's deal. Somehow, he had to get them talking. "Actually, uh, I think

Neve has some questions for you concerning the layout. I'm consulting, but she's in the thick of it. Probably best you talk to her. I'll conference dial her, and she can give you the details—"

"Oh, no, no. Not necessary, Duke. I've no need for the nitty-gritty. Have her make a list of her concerns and call me tomorrow. I'm sure Neve has more important folks to deal with."

"More important than the client?"

"Sure. Plumbers and painters, right? You're my go-between. Besides, you said she's in the thick of it. I hate to turn you into a secretary as well as a consultant, but it's for the best if she stays focused on the job while you handle communications."

Neve was going to *love* this. She'd given him one job: get her close to Gavin.

Boss was kinking up the works, and it didn't even make sense. Why avoid the person directly responsible for his precious cabin? "Are you sure? She'll need direct input from you at some point, sir. Especially when she gets into picking out fixtures and furnishings. You don't want a middleman muddying up the creative process between client and designer. She'll do her best work if she gets the vision straight from you."

"Nonsense. I trust you implicitly, Duke."

Something hefty rode on the words, but Duke had no time to sift through and wonder at what it meant. A headache blossomed in his left temple. "Whatever you say. You're the boss."

Gavin gave a contented sigh. "I have to thank you again, Duke. I truly, truly appreciate what you're doing for me. I'll be driving up to see the place at some point near the end, and I'd like to take you out for lunch while I'm there. Just the two of us, my treat. Oh, also one last thing. Tell Neve I've hired her an assistant. I don't want you stuck with all the errand running and busy work."

"Thanks." *I think.* Duke ended the call and reclaimed a more comfortable position on the sofa bed.

He tried to imagine Neve's face when Gavin showed up to take *him* out for an executive lunch while she stayed behind, knee-deep in wood varnish and pipe laying, to say nothing of the assistant she had no hand in hiring. *Poor idiot, whoever you are.* He tried to resist a grin and failed.

It promptly fled when Neve opened the front door in her brisk manner, only a sharp knock preceding her entry. "Everyone decent?"

"Like I'd walk around otherwise in our communal living space."

"Never hurts to hope." She came inside with a wide smile. She looked far too happy.

Duke's hackles rose. Then he noticed she had one hand behind her back. He struggled into a sitting position, wincing at every pull on the muscles over and around his ribs. "I don't like it when you're gleeful. You frighten me. What do you have there?"

Her shoulders sloped and she rolled her eyes. She dropped down next to him and angled her body to conceal whatever surprise she had. "Even injured and bedridden, you're a pecker. Have a little faith. I called a truce, remember?"

Yeah, he remembered. It'd last until he told her about Gavin's intention to communicate solely through him. He offered her a weak smile and brushed his hair back from his face. "Old habits. What is it?"

The smile still fixed in place, Neve brought her hand forward. In it, a small wooden box. A really *old* wooden box.

Duke sat up farther, ignoring the sharp tinge from his ribs, and gingerly took it from her. "What the hell?" Seamless. No hinge connecting the lid to the body, and the strangest metal contraption he'd ever seen serving as some kind of medieval locking mechanism, like a metal starburst with multiple holes. Even with a key, unlocking the box would be a bitch. "You found this?"

She nodded, a hint of pride in her smile. "Darcy the Pit sniffed it out, I dug. Someone buried this thing behind the cabin, next to one of the foundation pillars. Strange, huh? Something important must be inside. No one goes through all that trouble to make a box with no hinge and an elaborate lock to hide their saltwater taffy stash."

Duke turned the box over and ran his fingers across the uneven grain of the wood. "I agree. Have you shown this to anyone?"

"Vince caught me with it. I told him it was mine."

"Good. Neve, this is old. I mean, *really* old. And like you said, someone went through no small trouble to hide what's in here. We should probably keep it to ourselves for a while. At least until we figure out how it opens." He turned his attention to Neve's critical study of the box in his hands. "Including—"

"Yeah, yeah, yeah." She waved him off, her eyes never leaving the chest. "My new rancher buddy. He's going to prove useful, I guarantee it. However, knowing you can use someone is hardly the same as trusting them, and I didn't get this far in my career by being a bad judge of character. There's something…calculating, maybe?" She shrugged. "I don't know, exactly. Something about Hux is odd. You can relax. This is our little secret. Now, what do you think's inside?"

Her glee was intriguing. Lately, every time Duke turned around, he was noticing some new, not-terrible side to Neve. Her smile was big, her eyes bright and shiny. Like a kid finding a penny in a parking lot.

With effort, he regarded the box once more. It might've been polished smooth twenty or thirty years ago, but time, humidity, and dirt had all left their mark. Not large by any measure. Neve had held it comfortably in one slender hand. Big enough, however, to keep a decent secret. "Coins, maybe? Lost maps, notes between clandestine lovers." He lifted the shoulder on the uninjured side of his body. "The cabin's plumbing schematics. I don't think we should try to force the lock."

Neve cocked her head to one side. "Yeah, I thought of that. Could destroy what's inside."

"The key is a lost cause. There's no telling if it still exists or where it might be."

"Would it help if we had the key? Look at that thing. It's meant to be opened by someone who knows how to open it."

He nodded. Made sense. "Like if you're meant to open the box, you'd know how."

"Right. Except, I'm not a stickler for the rules." She reached for the chest. In her hands, it seemed a little larger. "I bet anyone who knew how is long dead. It's at least half a century old, don't you think? What should we do?"

Why'd it surprise him she asked his opinion? He didn't really care for the warm, tingly way this new side of her made him feel. He scratched his chin through his mired beard hair. "Out here, the world is older. Time moves slower. Small towns like Red Hill cling to their pilgrim days, the age of homesteading and establishment. They revere the past. Who but Southerners reenact a war they lost hundreds of years later? I think we start with nearby museums."

Neve's face lit up and she pointed a finger at him, pistol-style. "Nice. You're absolutely right. Little hole-in-the-wall museums are everywhere out here. One of them is bound to have something similar on display, especially if it was the work of a local craftsman. What about locksmiths?"

"Another good idea," Duke agreed.

She nodded. "So long as it didn't come from a traveling Chinese immigrant salesman, there's hope."

"There's always the Internet. I can do a search."

She bent over and patted him on the head like he was Darcy the Pit. "It'll be the most useful thing you've done since we arrived."

"I figured out the front steps were broken, didn't I?"

She gave him a begrudging smile. "I do love a hands-on partner."

He waited and considered. He hated to spoil her rare good mood, but he'd didn't want to deal with the aftermath of coming clean when she was feeling otherwise. "While you're in such high spirits, I have some unfortunate tidings from Gavin."

Neve left the sofa bed and set the mystery box on the picnic-table-style dinette table. Then she slid onto one of the long benches. "I can't have a good day, can I? Everything has to be tempered with a dose of crap." She threw up her hands in an impatient gesture. "Well, go on. What now?"

Duke sucked in air. "Gavin intends to communicate exclusively through me and he hired you an assistant."

Nothing. No response. Not an eye roll or locked jaw.

A great bubble of tense silence filled the space between them until Duke wanted to rise and bolt. How did one person create such immense tension without a single utterance? His eyes couldn't quite meet hers. He imagined her great amber eyeballs drilling into him. He waited for the ball to drop. For a curse or a shout, but the awful silence continued.

Another moment passed.

Finally, when he could stand it no longer, he risked a peek at Neve.

Her hands were folded demurely on the tabletop, and she watched him with a slight curve to her lips. "You should see your face. I can probably get Laurel and Owen over here with some more of their horse tranquilizers if you're feeling tense." Knowing amusement glinted from her honey-colored eyes.

Slowly, the pressure bled away. Goddamn her. "You shouldn't toy with a man's emotions. You're telling me you're not pissed?"

"Oh, I'm pissed. But you don't know me as well as you think. Right now, I'm on a job. My motives for taking the job notwithstanding, work is something I don't take lightly. Nor do I put personal business above the contract I signed. My outbursts are reserved for dumb apprentices and men a'scared of a woman telling them what to do. I've already had one such battle this morning. Gavin's hiccup doesn't mean much by comparison, and the fix is relatively simple. Next time he calls, you're unavailable. You're stuck in a tree, digging a hole to poop in the woods, something. Anything. Eventually, he'll be forced to get in touch with me. We establish a rapport. A new routine takes place. Problem solved. As for the assistant he hired, a bad one won't last five minutes and a marginally adept one will be much appreciated. Not that I've got my hopes up or anything."

Only Neve could come up with such a response. He wanted to roll his eyes, but she had a real way with words he couldn't help but appreciate sometimes. "Sorry."

She leaned forward to prop her elbows on the table. "Don't apologize. I'm giving you a hard time. Sure, I'm prone to rage but I also made a deal with you I intend to keep. Until you fail, utterly and spectacularly, I'll honor my end of the bargain. I'm being *nice*, Duke."

Huh. Nice. How about that. He prodded his ribs. "I'll be ready to work tomorrow."

Neve stood, yawned, and stretched, with her arms reaching for the ceiling. "No, you won't. I want one hundred percent out of you. This week, your duties are administrative. We need permits and details from Gavin concerning the layout of the cabin. I have a list of questions. Next week, you can join us in the manual labor. Ugh." She dropped her arms and reached under her tight gray T-shirt. "I shouldn't have worn my new bra out here. No time to break it in." Beneath the fabric, her hand tugged at a front clasp and pried the lemon yellow strapless bra free. Without it, the smooth edges of her nipples fought to escape the confines of the body-hugging fabric.

Duke's mouth went dry. *Stupid yellow bra.*

Neve ran a hand over one of the cups, then approached him and held it out. "You're a bra guy. What's wrong with this thing? There's not supposed to be a wire, but I'd swear there's a damned wire in here somewhere." She glanced up when he didn't respond.

He stopped staring at her nipples to meet her gaze.

Her brow snapped together, and she leaned down to look directly in his eyes. Her small breasts hovered inches away, and she placed a hand on each of his knees to steady herself. "You okay, Duke? You're sweating." She straightened and put a hand over his forehead.

For a split second, he imagined she kept moving forward, her hands sliding all the way up his thighs, her lithe body climbing over his, straddling him, firm nipples pressed into his chest.

He swallowed. "It's...I'm hot. It's hot. I should go outside. For air."

Air and space between her body and his. He'd be pissed if, after everything, a bra was his undoing.

She dropped her hand from his forehead and shrugged, her attention again focused on the bra. "Well, do something with this thing, will you? If you can't, I'm going braless. It's killing me."

Duke stood on shaky legs and made for the door. No one would get a damn thing done if Neve sashayed around with her pointy little nipples staring at everyone for the next eight weeks. He snatched it from her on his way out the door. "I'll fix it."

Chapter 5

Neve cupped her mouth and shouted. "Duke, wait up!"

He paused midstride, turned, and blew out his cheeks impatiently.

Besides his manic, pent-up energy from a bedridden two weeks, he struck a rather dashing figure this morning in a pair of fitted dark denim jeans, heavy work boots, and a black T-shirt curving comfortably around his form, the way an oft-worn piece of clothing tended to.

In his left hand, a clipboard with notes written in Duke's nifty, precise handwriting. He still leaned slightly, favoring the injured side of his body.

Neve decided he deserved it, even as she pitied him.

Last week he'd attempted to climb a ladder to help Vince on the cabin's roof, only to misstep and aggravate the injured ribs in a mad scramble to stay on the ladder rather than fall and break his back.

Pity or no, his impatient expression when she caught up to him struck a nerve. She stopped a yard away and lifted her chin. "You have something more important to do than talk to the person in charge, Mr. Kenni*cock*?"

His deep blue eyes widened slightly, enough to wipe away the bored, half-lidded expression he wore. "No, of course not. I'm ready to work, that's all. I'd apologize if it weren't for the totally fab nickname. We're even in my book."

Neve pursed her lips and took the last stride to stand next to him. A soft breeze blew through the trees and made the tips of his loose hair dance around his toned arms. Usually, she relished the part of the job where she put people in their place, but it seemed a shame since they'd been getting along lately. Still, if pulling rank was how to get his respect, so be it. "Don't forget which one of us took this job in earnest, Duke. You're a consultant, here to offer your opinion when I ask for it and act as a go-between for me and my client. You're not running things, you're not making any decisions, and you're not to treat me like anything less than King Shit."

He bowed deep, bending at the waist. "Your Majesty."

"If you're not in too much of a hurry, do you think you'd like to be brought up to speed?"

"I was on my way to see for myself."

"I don't have time for the tour, even if you don't have anything better to do."

The line of his mouth went flat. He was listening now, reminded of whom he was dealing with.

Mission accomplished, albeit joylessly. "First of all, what do you think of installing a back door? The cabin's in desperate need of natural light. Instead of ripping through the wall for pointless windows, I want to make one giant one to walk through. French doors, predominately glass, north-facing, along the same wall as the kitchen cabinets and countertops."

Duke stroked his long beard, tugging on it when he reached the ends. His considering gaze roamed the trees surrounding them. "Yeah, okay. The lighting is a legitimate issue. It'll also make the cabin seem larger."

Neve shook her head. "Just like a man to think the back door makes it look bigger." She slapped his shoulder. "I'm glad you agree, princess, because it's already done. Vince punched out the space for the French doors last week, and also a small window near the front door." She ignored his shock. "The roof is repaired and sealed, the foundation fortified and secure, and the front steps I instructed Vince to build are being dug and set as we speak. Flooring is patched. With your helpful input from Gavin, I drew up blueprints for the walls I want constructed to create a private corner space for the bathroom, leaving the bedroom open to the rest of the cabin as per his request. I have to say, I admire the choice."

"Uh, Neve?" A worried brow rose as Duke squinted at her. "Don't we need material to build walls?"

"As well as cabinetry and countertops, for which our master carpenter, one Finn Welk, who arrived yesterday, has already begun to draft plans," she informed him in one lofty statement. "I'm taking care of it today. What I really wanted to discuss with you, though, is the trip we're taking tomorrow. There's a flea market and a mom-and-pop hardware store I want to check out. We're driving one of Vince's trucks and hauling a storage trailer. I figure buying local will add to the special vibe Gavin's aiming for, and until I know what I can dig up around here, I can't very well place an order for furnishings, plumbing parts, or cabinet hardware." She snapped her fingers as she recalled another item and dug around in her pocket, coming up with a crumpled note.

Duke tentatively took the proffered ball of paper. Why was he always waiting for her to snap? Unless he'd done something stupid, she had no reason to lash out.

He briefly scanned her writing. "Red Hill Historic Museum."

"It's the only one in town. The Red Hill Historical Society runs it. Even if there's nothing in the museum, it might be worth tracking down and interviewing a few older members."

Duke nodded his approval and pushed the note into his front pocket. "It's a date." His eyebrows snapped together. "I mean, it's not a date. Not a *date* date."

She studied him. Interesting. Pink-tinged cheeks, shifty eyeballs, fidgety hands. Symptoms she recognized, but they didn't belong on a confidently gay man. In fact, the last time she'd observed the signs of a crush, they'd been painfully obvious on a client's young teenaged son who liked watching Neve a little too closely while she worked grout into newly laid tiles.

But Duke?

Was it possible for a gay guy to develop an attraction to a woman? Did he have some latent bisexual tendencies he'd neglected to share? Wouldn't be the only secret he'd kept from her. She had no clue how that kind of thing worked and didn't want to risk calling him out. If she scared the badger, he might dive back into his hole, never to be seen again. She smiled, however, thoroughly amused, and vowed to give him hell when the job was over. The ride back to Little Rock would be sweet, delicious torture.

"God, I hate when you smile." He appeared truly distressed. "Anything in particular you'd like me to do today?"

She smiled wider. "Yeah, come with me to Lady Killer Ranch. It's time for some recon. Maybe Yosemite's a real anal-retentive farmer, rancher, whatever, and there are no old buildings he'll let us dismantle. If that's the case, we need a lumberyard on speed dial yesterday."

Reluctantly, Duke bobbed his head in agreement and gave another yank to his poor over-yanked beard. Why did he torture the poor thing so? "You're right. Without material, we're at a dead halt. We're just inside national forest boundaries. Closest lumberyard with reclaimed wood is fifty miles east."

Neve's heart fell into her gut, and the first wave of doubt drenched her. "Transportation would gobble up a huge slab of the budget."

Duke squeezed her shoulder encouragingly. "Let's head over there now. If it doesn't pan out, we're heading to town tomorrow anyway, right? Adding getting an estimate from the lumberyard to our to-do list."

Worry gnawed at her insides at the same time she offered Duke a muted nod. She might've set herself up for failure. Vince and his team counted on her to come through with material, and Gavin expected her to stay within budget and timeline. She'd blow both if Timothy Hux couldn't be charmed by a sassy city girl.

A pocket of doubt in the back of her mind kept coming back to the calculation on the rancher's lean face. If she'd missed the mark on this one, it would come at the expense of her job and, worse, her reputation.

She swallowed and smiled halfheartedly at Duke. "We're off to see the rancher, the magical rancher of Ozark."

"He doesn't have to be magical. Just malleable."

* * * *

Peachy, as Georgians like himself were wont to say. They were off to visit the friendly rancher and his merry band of cowhands. Duke did his best to keep his disdain for Hux from showing. Neve might attribute his interest to a schoolyard crush or some other ridiculous and embarrassing theory, so he kept his opinion to himself, as well the frown tugging at his lips.

It wasn't that he didn't appreciate the care they'd given his injured ribs or the pain-dulling drugs they'd given him. He did. But it chafed his professional ego to rely on something as tenuous as a friendly neighbor to come through on such a vital necessity. Were he in charge of the cabin renovation, he'd have contacted the lumberyard last week, budget be damned. Neve's solution, while creative and potentially a boon, was a risk.

Besides, something about the old rancher struck Duke as smarmy. He intended to nail down exactly what he disliked about Tim during their hopefully short visit.

Though the ranch entrance was only a mile or so from the cabin, the bumpy, unpaved mountain road made for slow travel. Nearly twenty minutes of tedious crawling passed before they came across a gated drive almost entirely hidden in the dense growth of the surrounding forest. A small battered sign read LKR, the ranch's brand.

Oddly, it pointed in the wrong direction. The road dead-ended up at the cabin's parking area. Coming from town, the sign would be all but invisible, explaining how they missed it on the way up to Gavin's property the first day. Only coming back would a passing eye catch the faded post.

Why didn't they fix it? Ten minutes with a shovel would do the job.

"Do you suppose it's hidden intentionally?" Neve's ponderous voice mirrored his musings.

"It seems so, doesn't it? Backward sign, overgrown entrance."

Her mouth quirked up, and Duke gave himself over to a short study of her profile. Lips too thin by half, a painful sharpness to her cheekbones, huge eyes that reminded him of flowing lava.

They turned on him like they sensed his thoughts. "There's something going on here. First, Hux practically snuck up on us through the woods the day we arrived. If you hadn't gone crashing through the steps, forcing me to make the trek back up the hill to the car, he might've slipped right through the trees without ever announcing his presence." A considering glance swept Duke's face. "Maybe that's the thing niggling in the back of my mind. Hux wasn't on the path, but slinking through the woods. Not a friendly neighbor on his way with a friendly handshake, but a spy."

Despite how it reminded him of a bad television plot, Duke shivered. Nothing like creepy supposition to get his mind off Neve's unattractive yet weirdly entrancing physical features. "Maybe he thought we were some teenagers out for a joy ride or something. Empty cabin out in the woods? Sounds like the kind of place to attract kids looking for somewhere to drink a few or smoke a little."

"Maybe."

He navigated the turn into the ranch at a single-digit speed. Pockmarked and pitted, the road seemed nearly impassable. He'd have to turn around if it didn't improve. Unwisely, they'd taken the rental car rather than one of Vince's trucks. However, once they rounded the corner, the lane smoothed out so perfectly the road might've been paved.

"Ha!" Neve practically bounced in her seat. "C'mon, that's intentional. Has to be. It looks like an abandoned road no sensible person would drive down, but as soon as it's out of sight of the main drag, it's perfect. Smooth as my ass the day I was born." She shook her head, arms crossing. "He's hiding something. Maybe the ranch. Who knows, but nothing else explains how the clues are adding up."

"But from who? And why? We should ask him."

She turned on him wide-eyed, the picture of horrified. "Do you want to get chopped into tiny pieces and fed to his livestock? You don't admit to a psychopath you're onto him, crazy. Don't you watch movies? True crime dramas? It's a poker game. It's all about bluffing and reading the other guy before he reads you."

"You know, he might just be lazy." Made sense, in a weird way, but also far-fetched and silly in the light of day. "Or really busy," he added for good measure.

"No. Not Yosemite. I told you, there's something about him, something weirdly calculating. A man like that doesn't do anything without a reason."

The trees thinned out as the land opened up. They were traveling into a kind of valley. A wire fence sprung up and lined the road on either side. It spread wider as the land broadened, enough for two vehicles to easily pass one another. Cows began to appear in small clusters between the trees, growing more concentrated the farther into the valley they went. A few had large curved horns. Big horns.

Pricey cattle, Duke noted. Apparently, Lady Killer Ranch did well. Hux wasn't hiding from debtors.

Eventually the road curved to run alongside a creek shallow enough to walk across. Another mile down the road, the forest receded to nearly nothing, and a great expanse of meadow swelled and dipped.

The main ranch house became visible at the far end of the wide meadow, its back up against where the tree line began again.

"Beautiful," Neve breathed. Her head pivoted back and forth. At first, Duke assumed she was talking about the view. Then she pointed north. "There. That building looks old and out of use."

It certainly did. Large, barnlike doors hung open and loose on old hinges, likely rusted and coming loose from the wood structure. An open square window on the second level showed nothing but blackness from within.

For whatever reason, apprehension settled in Duke's stomach. He invited it to stay. Something told him Timothy Hux might very well offer to let them dismantle an old barn, but at what cost? Probably one Neve would willingly pay.

She rolled down her window and peered across the field. "Well, what do you think? It definitely looks abandoned, right?"

Duke leaned forward over the steering wheel for a glimpse. "It appears to be a storage shed of some kind, probably for hay."

"It doesn't seem like he's using it."

"Well, I'm no farmer, but maybe it's not hay season."

"I'm no farmer, either."

The disappointment weighing heavy in the sentiment almost made him laugh. Like she'd have done things differently and learned about hay farming just so this one moment in her life would make sense.

"You're a bit of an overachiever."

"There's nothing wrong with expecting to succeed."

The creek continued to flow alongside the dirt road, growing wider and deeper, until they crept closer to the ranch house. There, it gurgled off to the right, arching back in a half-circle and disappearing behind the house. Tim Hux probably fished right off his back porch.

A small pang of envy hit Duke square in the chest. He'd grown up in the wild woods of southern Georgia, fishing and hunting with his dad and brothers. Somewhere along the way, he'd turned into a city boy and traded fresh game and canvas tents for protein powder shakes and a midtown loft. He smiled, imagining an early retirement back to his roots.

"We're facing a potential disaster, and you're over there grinning like an idiot." Neve's disgust only made him smile wider. She pointed at the front of the house as he drew up the car and parked. "There's Tim. Someone's with him. Might be his brother, Miles, the one he radioed to send Laurel and Owen that day." She opened her car door and gave a cheery wave to the two men.

Duke swallowed his disappointment at having anything more important to do than enjoy the scenery. He exited the rental and followed Neve up three wide, creaky steps and onto a rickety wrap-around porch stretching roughly eight feet out from the house.

Tim and his presumed brother crowded around Neve, all big smiles and tight jeans.

Either they were trying to flatter her or truly found her attractive. The latter he couldn't wholly fathom, despite his own weird attraction to her. Even standing there, she was too lanky. Arms too muscular, long, loose curls too thick, hawk eyes too challenging…hips too swingy, shoulders too square. He thought of her braless. Tits too small, nipples too aggressively pointy…

Duke cleared his throat and stopped short of their intimate circle. "Nice to meet you proper, Mr. Hux," he inserted, offering his hand to the rancher.

The rancher turned to him, and his sharp hazel gaze swept over Duke.

His first real good look at Tim, who he'd only briefly seen from his back through vision clouded in pain. He had an instant understanding of Neve's assessment. Definitely something caught his attention in the man's canny stare. As quickly as Duke noticed it, it dissipated.

A wide, friendly grin spread beneath Tim's generous mustache. "Well, look at you, up and at 'em. Nothing broken after all, eh?"

Duke stretched sideways, the muscles going taut. "Some stiffness. We're heading into town tomorrow. I'll have it looked at while we're there, but I sure do appreciate the help. I'd ask you to pass along my thanks to Laurel and Owen." If the shrewd rancher liked the shroud of friendly neighbor, Duke would wear it as well. Like Neve said, read the other guy before he reads you. He didn't want Tim to pick up on his disquiet.

Tim clapped him on the shoulder. "Well, what're neighbors for? Duke, this here is Miles, ranch foreman and my little brother. You and Ms. Harper have a knack for timing, I tell you. We were headed out to pasture when

Miles saw the car coming on up the road. Another five minutes, we'd have missed you."

Indeed, two white and brown spotted horses, paint horses if Duke had to guess, were saddled and tied to a post at the far end of the long wrap-around porch.

Miles didn't smile as wide or have a grip as sure when he shook Duke's hand. He hardly made eye contact.

The shy one, Duke decided. Miles didn't have Tim's height or impressive sideburns, but they did share the same green-brown eyes and pale brown shade of hair. An obvious enough resemblance.

Miles stepped back and put his hands in his pockets. "Nice to meet y'all." He nodded toward Neve then peered at his older brother. "I'll head out. You see to our guests. Owen can ride with me." He made his exit with an accepting bob of Tim's head.

The rancher's steady gaze returned to Neve, running appreciatively over her as though she were the prettiest thing this side of Little Rock. "Guess that just leaves us, don't it?"

"Kind of." Duke crossed his arms. He clamped his jaw shut to keep from saying something less pleasant than stating the obvious.

Neve ignored him and matched Tim's smile with one that oozed charm and a hint of tease.

Why had he come along to personally witness this awkward ogle-fest? And why the hell didn't Neve ever pretend to be charming for *his* sake?

Oh, right. Because why schmooze a gay guy?

As if she'd just noticed he still stood there, she glanced at him and started. "Oh, let's not forget our third wheel." She winked then and stuck out her tongue the moment Tim turned his back.

Before he knew it, he was smiling with her. *Damn it, she's good. The snake* and *the charmer.*

Tim guided them toward a cluster of six picturesque rocking chairs at the far end of the porch, facing west, naturally, for optimal sunset-watching. Two groups of three, they were angled to slightly face each other in a sort of half-circle to foster companionable conversation.

Quaint.

"Y'all have a seat. Make yourselves comfortable. I'll get Laurel to bring out some of her famous iced tea. Hope you like sweet. Only flavor it comes in."

Neve didn't hesitate, bounding toward the middle rocking chair in the first cluster of three with a childlike grin. "Lovely. Sweet tea would be fantastic. I'm parched."

With a tip of his wide-brimmed hat, Tim disappeared behind a screen door. A loud clatter followed as it slammed back against the frame. It bounced off from the force and slapped against the frame a second time.

Duke rushed to Neve's side and whispered fiercely, "What are you doing? I didn't come to watch you play smoochy face with the handsome cattle rancher."

Her mouth formed an upside down U, and she tossed an errant lock of hair behind her shoulder. "You think he's handsome? He's a little on the thin side. I personally like some definition on a man."

He squeaked as her hand reached out and splayed over his thigh as he crouched next to her rocker.

"For example, a girl wants thighs she can depend on, you know? Thighs that can support her when she crawls onto his lap, not snap like twigs under her weight." Her gaze drifted away, and a shoulder lifted in a slight shrug. "Unless she's on the bottom, in which case he's boring, and who cares what kind of thighs he has."

Duke cleared his throat of sudden dryness and his mind of sudden, unwelcome visions for the second time in the last few minutes. He escaped Neve's slender roaming hand by taking the rocker next to hers. "What kind of game are we playing here?"

"The kind I almost always win. Different jobs require different tools. Vince Taggart needs me to spit a loogie bigger than his before he can respect me."

Duke squinted at her. "You actually did that? Hocked a loogie to impress Vince?"

"Of course I did."

He looked out over the meadow and nodded to himself. "Of course you did."

"Hocking an impressive wad of lung butter is but one of my varied and highly useful tools. Our rancher is playing along, but I'm not getting anything out of him using my wiles. And he won't be won over with toughness, either. Working on a ranch, he knows all about tough women. Laurel would kick my ass in any physical arena. So, what tool do I use on a man with no obvious susceptibility?"

Shocking. Neve had a penchant for manipulation. He turned his mind to the question. "Logic, I guess. My dad appreciated a logical argument. Some people prefer to barter." He shrugged. "Hell, who knows."

Tim rejoined them, pushing through the screen door and allowing it to slam back against its frame once again, a tray of three tall glasses balanced perfectly in one hand with no apparent effort. He handed them each a glass, ice cubes tinkling musically, keeping one for himself. He lowered into the chair on the other side of Neve and set the tray to rest on the planks at his feet.

Duke sipped his tea and would be hard-pressed to deny it came damn close to the tea his granny used to make. Thick as syrup and sweet enough to curl his toes. The day seemed hotter here in the open valley without the dense cover of the trees to block the summer sun. He appreciated the cool glass in his hand. He sipped again and tried to pay attention to Tim as he babbled on about the ranch.

"My great-granddaddy Ben built most everything you see. Wasn't but a tiny little cabin 'fore then, much like the one you're fixing now. He inherited the ranch and the land and made it thrive. Places tend to do that when there's love going into the care. And Ben Hux loved his land."

Neve's hand swept toward the storage building they'd noticed on their drive in. "So, Ben built these, then?"

"Yep. He added onto the original house, built the cowhand quarters, the hayloft, and a second barn. When he was a boy, he owned everything for miles and miles around. No need for fences. Then he began selling off patches of land here and there. Fences went up to mark new property lines."

Duke did the math. It took money to build, even when materials were cultivated on-site from your backyard. Didn't make sense so put so much effort into expanding the main hold only to sell off the bread and butter of the ranch in pieces. "Why sell the land?"

He half-expected Tim to ignore him, but he glanced beyond Neve to give Duke an unhappy glare. He didn't appear to appreciate the question. "Ben gambled. Hell, he met Florrie at the tables. Lucky times meant expansion. When the luck dried up, so did acres and acres of Hux Ranch."

Neve guzzled tea and smacked her lips. "Your great-grandpa sounds like a real jerk. Gambling, cheating on his wife, selling off his inheritance. Poor Lulu."

Duke recalled the ghost story she'd passed along about Florrie Beels and her unfortunate end at Lulu's hands, and Lulu's end at her own. He didn't empathize with how she chose to die but couldn't deny it probably sucked to have been married to Benjamin Hux.

"So," Neve continued conversationally, "about these old buildings. I noticed the hay barn on our way up. Seems a little haphazard. Like maybe you don't use it much these days."

Tim grunted and peered at her. Definitely not a stupid man. "I've been wondering when we'd get to the point of your visit. You damn sure ain't here for Laurel's tea."

"No, but it's good enough to warrant a future visit with less business and more pleasure." Neve all but purred the response.

Duke stared ahead to stop his eyes from rolling back in their sockets. She wiped her brow. "Boy, it's hot down here. There's always a breeze farther up the mountain, but down in the valley it's not enough to disperse this killer heat." She set her glass on the porch railing and angled herself to face the rancher more directly. Her hands folded neatly together in her lap, and one leg crossed the other. A business stance.

Duke reclined farther in his rocker and waited for the master to spring her trap. He wasn't disappointed.

She began with a polite throat clearing, he guessed more for show than any need. "I have a passion for what I do, Mr. Hux. My job is to make things beautiful and give them soul. It's more than slapping paint on a wall or throwing down a set of matching rugs. Someone else might look at this place and see a weathered log cabin in need of a fresh layer of paint and some stainless steel to bring it up to date."

"But not you?" In Tim's tone, Duke caught the edge of sarcasm. Couldn't blame him. Neve laid it on kind of thick.

"I see something we're losing. History disappearing before our eyes. Every change, every added layer, every replacement wipes away something of the past. You can't get it back after that. Like this porch. It's old, creaky. I could do a rebuild, with uniformed wood slats dyed to perfection. It'd be fresh, shiny, and brand-spanking-new." She sighed. "But it'd lose its soul in the process."

"Right. Porch soul."

Neve didn't hesitate but sat up straighter and spoke firmer. "That's right. From the living tree the wood came from, to the callused hands of your ancestors who toiled with a fraction of the tools we take for granted today. The same hands that have tilled this land for generations. You think they'd have succeeded where so many failed if they were as cynical as you, Mr. Hux?"

Duke surprised himself by realizing he'd come forward in his rocker and hung onto each passionate word. Another tool in Neve's arsenal, or an honest display of heartfelt emotion?

More surprising, Tim sat back and blinked like she'd doused him with cold water. Then his brows snapped together in annoyance. "Why don't you get to asking what you came here to ask?"

Every drop of flirtatiousness fell from her words. "I'll pay you to let me dismantle an old building on your property and use the wood for my renovation project. Beels Cabin is a piece of history. It deserves to be cleaned up, certainly, but more so, that cabin deserves to be preserved. Gavin won't be the last owner. I don't want to ruin or change it by bringing in some gleaming factory-polished wood to add walls." She reclaimed her tea and relaxed into the rocker, almost nonchalantly, as if their whole project didn't hinge on Tim's response. "I'll pay well, Tim. It's worth that much to me."

"All this just to get your hands on some old wood?" He couldn't quite mask his incredulity.

A spark of intuition hit Duke square in the chest as he recognized how Neve had manipulated the rancher. She'd made him feel threatened with her talk of renovating his porch. To find out she only wanted the old, dilapidated hay storage building must've been a huge relief.

"Not any old wood," she corrected him. "Old wood with *history*. History, I'd point out, directly related to the cabin. Think of it. The walls inside the cabin will have come from the very ranch that borne it."

A tense silence followed.

Duke idly stroked his beard, chin to tip, and considered how disappointed Gavin would be when they blew half the budget on lumber and transport. He dared a chance peek at Tim, struck dumb to find him grinning like a fool at Neve.

"Tell you what. I'll let you have the old hayloft. Won't cost you a dime." Duke blinked. "It won't?"

Ever the shrewd one, Neve cocked her head. "What *will* it cost me?"

The rancher's smile dazzled. Who knew he had it in him. "Dinner with me here at the ranch. At a time of your choosing, of course. I understand deadlines."

Thankfully, Duke had stopped himself from laughing out loud. He'd have only looked like an ass when Neve extended her hand.

"You've got yourself a deal, Yosemite."

Chapter 6

"A date, though? Really? With smarmy Yosemite?"

Neve ignored Duke's indignant protests, just as she'd done last night when he'd hounded her all the way back to the cabin. She also turned a deaf ear on Darcy the Pit's unhappy whines as the two of them formed a train behind her. In her world, if the grass still clung to its morning dew and her first cup of coffee hadn't been fully inhaled, it was too early for anything—including an argument with her project "consultant" or an explanation to her lazy dog as to why she couldn't go back to sleep.

Darcy, sweetie, I need you to give one last good sniff around the backside of the cabin before...well, it's a secret. One I can't let Duke in on.

Since yesterday had yielded them a source for the reclaimed wood, Vince needed to get a team over to Lady Killer Ranch as soon as possible to start dismantling the old hayloft. Barn. Whatever. She'd never heard of a rancher who slept past daybreak. Tim would likely be up and waiting for her people to show.

How they'd transport the supply remained a mystery. Getting the wood up the mountain along the main drag from the ranch, easy. A few pickups and a couple hours. Getting it down the footpath to the cabin presented another issue they'd have to tackle with tactical precision. She'd ask Duke, but her gut said Vince would be the guy to come up with a workable solution.

Rather than concerning himself with *real* problems, Duke seemed inexplicably hung up on one of the solutions. "I'm serious, Neve. You said yourself he's hiding something. What if he—"

If she had red police lights attached to her head, they'd have started flashing. She stopped on a dime and whirled to face Duke.

He came to a sudden, fumbling stop as he tried to avoid crashing into her and narrowly succeeded.

She jabbed him in the chest. Sometimes people didn't understand boundaries. She excelled at pointing them out. "You jealous or something?"

He blinked rapidly and stepped back. His Adam's apple bobbed in a great swallow, and his eyes went wide. "What? No. God, no."

She jabbed at him a second time. "Then get off my ass. I did what I had to do and I'd welcome an explanation as to how it's your problem. Except, you can't provide one because we both know this has nothing to do with you, *consultant*. This is my project, my name on the contract next to Gavin's. You had your chance to be the shot-caller. Yesterday, I came through on a crucial supply. Period. Now, I've been led to believe you're some kind of genius in your field but have yet to witness a shred of evidence to support the theory besides your decades-old claim to Vale House. Which, while impressive, doesn't do shit for me here and now."

His face reddened. His deep blue eyes grew hooded. "I was injured for two weeks. It's not my fault I haven't been involved."

His mumbled excuse did little to douse the flames of her temper. Quite the opposite. "Nor is it mine. You want to be on my ass about something, why not ask how in the hell we're supposed to get over a ton of wood slats down this goddamn trail without bulldozing trees. Or ask me who we're to trust to keep the progress on track while we're in town shopping and enjoying amateur sleuth hour at the museum." She brought up her clipboard for a quick glance and scribbled his name next to one of her task bullets. "You're supposed to be skilled. Now try being useful. I charge you with figuring out how Vince and his boys are going to get the lumber from the road to the cabin. They can't use the storage trailer we're taking to town. You have one hour to find a solution and tell Vince before I leave for Red Hill, with or without you."

Duke's abashed expression of big, round blue eyes and unhinged jaw did something to her anger; it waned almost as quickly as it had come on. She had powerful urge to soften the rebuke. That didn't sit well with her. She couldn't afford to play favorites or get soft on the job.

Darcy the Pit settled against her leg with a low whine.

Neve closed her eyes briefly and bit her lip against the annoyance that flared in her chest. If he were anyone else, she'd skin him alive. "I've told you before, the job comes first. Succeeding beyond expectations, not merely meeting them, is what I do. No matter what. I've been running things for three weeks without anyone questioning me, which is how this works. I answer to one person, and it isn't you," she explained quietly and meaningfully, hoping he understood it wasn't personal. Her spiel was the closest thing to an apology she could give.

She left him there, studying something infinitely interesting on one of his boots. She didn't have time for whatever Duke had stuck in his craw. Neither did he, and now he knew it.

In truth, she had reasons for her bad mood that had nothing to do with the cabin, an issue in itself. Personal matters shouldn't come between her and her focus, but the whole point of taking on the job seemed to be fading into the background.

Gavin Chambers.

He still insisted on receiving reports and giving directives through Duke. It hardly mattered; she'd been too busy the last three weeks to have bothered with him anyway. With his injury, Duke had nothing better to do than act as secretary. And now, in a completely backward turn of events, she owed the shady rancher down the road a date and was no closer to her original goal of getting to know Gavin. Most frustrating, perhaps, her current trajectory wasn't likely to change soon.

Neve stopped midstride in front of the cabin.

A tiny blond head bobbed around two of Vince's men working on a sawhorse. They used the wood slats they'd found abandoned inside the cabin to create handrails for the new set of front stairs, now dug and set and looking fabulous and woodsy.

A satisfied breath escaped Neve even as she approached the girl and steeled herself for some kind of problem.

The girl turned at the sound of Neve's approach.

Not a child, after all. Just a freakishly small woman. Under five feet tall if not an even four. Short hair in a pixie cut, much like Ruby's style, but unlike Ruby, this girl dyed hers a shade of bright, buttery blond, which Neve admitted did the haircut some justice. She had wide eyes, set somewhat far apart, devoid of makeup, and they looked at Neve with something like wonder.

Neve crossed her arms and cocked her head at the young woman. "Which local village did you wander in from, and do your parents know where you are?"

The sprite stuck out her hand. Her smile seemed to stretch the full width of her face. "Ha, you're funny! I like funny. *Hate* stuffy." She rolled her eyes to the sky and presented Neve with an exaggerated frown. "Stuffy people suck."

The animated girl would be almost amusing under any other circumstance but not on Neve's job site. "No, really. Who are you?"

Her hand stayed stuck out like a stubborn cowlick. "Oh, of course! I'm sorry. I'm so scatterbrained sometimes. Not with work stuff, though, I *swear*. Super-focused on work stuff. I've looked forward to meeting you. You're my hero. You redid my best friend's dad's house three years ago, and it was *amazing*. I changed my major that year. I'm excited right now, but I'll mellow out." Her eyes went to her proffered hand and back to Neve, almost pleadingly. "Kay Bing, your new assistant. I arrived last night and slept in my car because I didn't want to wake anyone. Though, Gavin assured me he'll get another trailer up here. I parked behind your trailer. You probably didn't notice my car."

"It escaped me." Neve reluctantly took the girl's hand and tested for a firm grip.

Kay didn't hesitate to give her a reassuring squeeze.

At least that boded well, but the Babble McBabbling thing had to cease. "Before this goes any further, Ms. Bing, tell me the truth. Do your parents know where you are? Also, when does said 'mellowing' occur, because the sooner the better. I have a short fuse and zero patience."

Kay snickered into her palm. "So funny!" Then she straightened her shoulders and put her arms at her sides like a soldier at attention. "The mellowing starts the minute the job does, ma'am. I'm tireless and possess a personal desire to succeed, as well as a professional one." More quietly, she added, "Gavin warned me I might not get a second chance to prove myself if I make any mistakes. So I won't make any." She smiled again and relaxed her posture. "Where do I begin?"

Neve took a deep, fortifying breath. Kay Bing would be a total disaster or the best thing to happen to Neve's career in many years. She prayed for the latter and scratched a few notes on her pad. "Okay, kid. Can I call you kid?" She wrapped an arm around Kay's shoulders and guided her toward the cabin.

"You can call me Bob if it strikes your fancy, Ms. Harper."

"Neve will do. Lucky for me, you showed up at the perfect time. Lucky for you, I'm handing you the means to prove yourself right off the bat. I'm going off-site today. Normally, I'd take along my assistant and leave Mr. Kennicot to spearhead. However"—*we have a little date with a museum*—"as consultant, he prefers to accompany me on this buying trip. While I'm away, you're my eyes, ears, and voice." She dropped her arm and reluctantly handed Kay the clipboard harboring her master list, among several others, to which she'd made a few new connotations.

Kay scoured it with hungry eyes.

Neve continued, "There are no excuses to fall behind, and I expect the items with your initials next to them completed by day's end. If it's not done, you're not done. Your job overall is to keep up the momentum—which I will graciously spur before I leave—prevent snags and iron out wrinkles. As you see on the list there, I've assigned the cabin's cabinetry design to you. They happen to be one of my weak spots. Finn Welk is our master carpenter, and you'll turn your designs over to him after I've approved. Vince Taggart is our general contractor. See him about blueprints for the cabin so you know your specs. You have limited space to work with, especially since I shortened a wall to make space for a set of French doors. Be creative but smart when designing the corners. No blocked utensil drawers or wasted space. The main location trailer is where my office is located. Feel free to make use of it. First thing tomorrow, I want a rough draft, and make sure Finn is in the loop and on standby. Your plans are useless if he's busy with another project."

Kay exhaled, though Neve didn't recall her taking in a single breath, and gazed up at Neve, the unmistakable gleam of awe shining. "Abso-*freaking*-lutely! Dream come true! Oh, man, I can't wait. I'm so on top of this."

Holy hell. She'd given Tinker Bell too much fairy dust. "Mellow. Remember? I have to go now." She turned heel to seek out Vince.

"Right, mellow. Got it. I'm just going to shadow you until you leave."

"Um…yeah, okay. Don't get underfoot." Why not? She'd catch up quicker on their progress if she trailed along. And for whatever strange, unaccountable reason, Neve liked Kay.

Inside the cabin, men scrambled with tape measures and laser levelers to ensure accuracy. Vince stood in the gaping hole where the French doors would be installed and frowned.

She'd yet to instruct him on what to do for the back steps. She intended to remedy that today while she had Duke well away from the cabin. She called to Vince, waving for his attention, and bobbed her head toward the exit.

He nodded and jumped down to the ground outside.

Kay hot on her heels, Neve followed and brushed off her hands. It was significantly quieter outside the cabin, despite their proximity to it.

"How are we looking, Vince?"

Nothing seemed to put the man at ease like delivering a progress report.

He shuffled his booted feet and spit. Then he angled a slightly embarrassed glance at Kay, but she smiled benignly. Not her first job, then. Excellent. "Exactly how we ought to. Three of my men are already at the ranch disassembling the old hayloft. There are flatbed trailers to haul the wood down the road, but I can't seem to come up with an easy way to get the lumber down to the cabin."

"Duke will have a solution within the hour," Neve assured him.

Doubtful, he shifted his greasy, dirty hat. "Well, that's good, I suppose."

"I'm going into town today, so hit me, Vince. Give me everything you got." He blew out a puff of air and straightened his shoulders. "We're measuring for the new walls now. Personally, I'd recommend we begin constructing built-in furnishings like cabinetry and such. We don't want to be waiting for that stuff once the insulation and secondary walls go up. We'll want them pre-made, pre-sanded, and varnished and waiting in the wings for a quick install. We've got both the plumber and the electrician coming in a few days, early next week. That'd be Andrew Bale and Jake Lansky. I know Lansky. Worked with him a few times. He's going to push the idea of solar panels, and I think with how the cabin sits in an opening it might be worth it, but he'll need to install a secondary power source—maybe a small generator—for winter. Finally, I'd like to know how you want the back steps done. Same as the front, or you got something else up your sleeve?"

Neve cast a surreptitious glance at Darcy the Pit while she sniffed around the oak pedestal. The same place she'd sniffed out the strange box. Her heart fell when the dog crouched and peed. If there was anything else buried, Darcy would've given some sign of interest.

Well, at least now she could move ahead with her secret construction plans. "Actually, Vince, I do have something in mind. First, allow me to introduce Kay Bing, my new assistant, courtesy of our ever-thoughtful sovereign. She's me while I'm gone today, and don't let anyone treat her otherwise. She's also responsible for those cabinets you want so bad, so make sure you give her whatever she needs—specs, blueprints, one of your guys to help her, you name it. The first thing I want when the lumber arrives from the ranch is an accurate inventory taken. Nothing goes to waste. There won't be a pile of slats hidden beyond the tree line when the cabin is complete. Whether to make shelves or patio furniture, everything gets used. Hell, we've got a master carpenter on site. Let's use him. Those cabinets won't keep him busy forever." She lowered her voice, put one hand on Vince's shoulder, the other on Kay's, and brought them in close for a huddle. "One final item. A secret."

"Oh, a secret! I love secrets." Kay grinned like a lunatic and squeezed her hands into little fists.

Neve ignored her for the sake of time. Duke might be coming down the path that very minute. "This isn't in your plans, Vince, but I trust you can do the math. You're going to build me a deck. A large one, at least five feet deep. Duke is not to know about it. I don't need his approval but I also don't have time to argue with him over it."

Vince once again readjusted his dirty ball cap. He leaned slightly away, like he wasn't sure about Neve's discreet plans, but a gleam in his shrewd gaze gave away his approval. "Can I ask why we're putting on a back deck instead of a front deck?"

"You can ask, but there's no point in sharing until it's confirmed we have enough of the reclaimed slats from Lady Killer Ranch to pull it off. Which you ought to know by this evening after you've taken the inventory, right?"

A small smile full of respect snuck across Vince's face. "Yes, ma'am."

She nodded and gave the small backyard another quick appraisal, blessing the lack of trees. Come fall, the deck should remain mostly free of fallen leaves, making maintenance less of a chore. It would also provide a nice sunny spot amid the shade.

She grinned back and patted them each on the shoulder. "I'm out of here. Good luck, you two. As in, don't let me down." She turned to walk around the cabin back toward the trailer up the hill.

"Hey!" Kay's panicked voice called after her with no small amount of nervousness.

Neve liked that. Nerves were good. They'd make the girl think, make her use her head, and keep her from becoming overly confident.

"What're you going to do?"

Neve turned around but kept walking, moving backward and hoping she didn't stumble over a wayward tree root. She held out her arms and made a cursory inspection of herself, from ripped jeans and dirty work boots to the faded T-shirt a size too big. "You think I'm going into town looking like *this*?"

* * * *

"I can't believe you're going into town looking like that."

Neve shook her head. The stylish gay male stereotype had failed Duke spectacularly.

A tic in the side of his jaw sprang to life. "I told you, I spilled orange juice down my shirt front. I had this on underneath and more pressing concerns than grabbing another shirt from my bag."

Despite the monumental task she'd charged him with, he hadn't done a damn thing besides anxiously tug on his beard until Vince's guys returned from their first trip to the ranch on four-wheelers hitched with flatbeds. Tim Hux, inexplicably shady and unnervingly thoughtful, had foreseen their transportation dilemma and provided the solution out of the kindness of his little ranching heart.

She hadn't given Duke an answer he liked this morning, but at least he was smart enough to keep his grudge against Yosemite to himself. Gift horses and all that.

"You had no pressing concerns. Yosemite did your job for you." She shouldn't needle him. She really shouldn't. But then how else to entertain herself during the thirty miles of sprawling, winding, indecisive mountain road at the crawling pace of forty miles an hour?

Tedious in average circumstances, towing the storage trailer behind them meant exercising more caution than usual. As nice as the scenery was, it didn't quite entertain her like Duke struggling to figure out his fashion faux pas.

He refused to look at her.

She didn't mind. He wore his long hair braided down his back and his beard braided down his chin. A pair of stylish aviator shades made for a ridiculously sexy profile she could hardly stop staring at.

"Why don't you quit acting like a jerk and explain what's wrong with a plain white tank top?"

Neve groaned. "It's not a tank top, Duke. It's a wife-beater." She tugged on one of the straps. She enjoyed the improved view of his toned shoulders but not enough to excuse the shirt. "There are two subcultures who can get away with wearing plain white wife-beaters in public. The first are pot-bellied men in trailer parks who do, in fact, beat their wives. Think spitting tobacco and mustard stains, red suspenders optional."

Duke's nose scrunched up. "Your visuals go for broke."

"The second group are saggy-pants gangsters. Complicated finger configurations, gaudy gold chains, a concealed weapon or two. Noting the pattern yet?"

"I told you, it's an undershirt. What if I told you only supermodels, porn stars, and super-hot chicks should wear five-inch stilettos?"

Neve shrugged and wriggled her toes in the purple peep-toe heels. "I guess I'd ask what the hell you know about any of those things. But seriously, I'm not going anywhere with you like that. You're too old and not enough of a douchebag to pull it off, nor do you fit the acceptable criteria."

He sighed, the helpless sigh of a man too tired and worn down to even manage exasperation. The sigh of a man who knows he's lost. She adored it.

"Fine, Neve. To appease the fashion gods you worship, I'll buy a shirt to wear over it. Happy?"

"Oh, I'm never happy. But at least I won't be embarrassed."

Red Hill did its moniker justice. Or would in the fall, at any rate. Red oaks smothered the city. Clustered tightly together in the dip of the valley, even the mountains rising up and bursting into their own cacophony of autumn color would be no competition against the oaks in the height of their season—a bright starburst of marvelous vermilion.

The city planner deserved a raise.

Duke pulled up to a local shop selling everything from frozen yogurt in ten different flavors to brightly colored T-shirts. He unbuckled his seat belt. "I'm buying a shirt. No, I won't get you frozen yogurt, but I will ask where the flea market is while I'm inside."

She huffed. "Fine. I only eat real ice cream, anyway. And yes, I have a vague idea of the highway where they hold it, but specific directions would be lovely. Almost as lovely as the choices you have." She hitched her chin toward the front window of the small shop.

A display of three T-shirts strung like paper cutouts in lime green, pale orange, and a tie-dye. Duke grunted. "I've always told myself I need more color in my life."

Alone in the vehicle, Neve stretched in the roomy cab of the pickup. She loved her little Honda Rebel, but there was something to be said for a truck that growled like a bear every time Duke pressed the gas pedal.

She flipped down the visor and inspected her reflection. She hadn't done much to improve herself besides a bit of blush to wake up the rest of her face. Renovations always did a number on her complexion. Days spent in high-gear—every item addressed, no task forgotten—and nights consumed with poring over blueprints and design palettes weren't exactly noted beauty regiments. Few understood the immense amount of work that went into harmonizing a space. The greatest, most expensive rug in the world was nothing but a pricey disaster if the color or pattern clashed with the wallpaper. Every element—furniture style and placement, hardware finish, wall décor, even the kitchen utensils—required a certain conformity to blend into a cohesive body of comfort and style.

A familiar chirp interrupted her thoughts. She'd heard the noise somewhere before...

She glanced down at the cup holders between the seats and spied the culprit. Duke had left his cell phone behind. She grinned and picked it up. Who didn't love a good secretary?

An out-of-state area code. Family, perhaps. She pressed the green button and did her best emulation of Duke's secretary at his office, the one who made horrendous coffee and had given Neve dark looks from beneath her false eyelashes. "Mr. Kennicot's line. How may I assist you?"

Total silence met her greeting. Well, not *total* silence, as breath rasped over the line.

Eyebrows hitched, Neve cooed, "*Hello.*"

"I'm sorry," a woman replied. She didn't sound sorry. More like annoyed. "Since when does Duke have a secretary answer his private number?"

Neve made her reply extra sweet. "Since now."

A laden, unhappy sigh made clear the woman's displeasure. "I'll call him when he can be bothered to answer himself."

Before Neve could issue another sarcastic response, the call dropped. She burned with intense curiosity, at least until Duke exited the shop sporting a Hawaiian button-up shirt. Neve forgot the call completely and covered her mouth with her hand. *What the...*

He climbed inside and started the engine without a word. His guileless smile spoke volumes, however, and he had the nerve to wink as he pulled away from the curb. "You were right. This is much better. It says, 'I'm on vacation.' Pure irony, since I'm not. Not even a working vacation, or I'd be having more fun."

Neve fingered a wide sleeve. Loud, but still better than the weird man tank. "You like this better than the tie-dye?" Seriously, not a *lick* of fashion sense.

At least half his mouth managed a self-deprecating smile. "The T-shirts in the window are child sizes. This is what fit. More importantly, I have directions to the flea market." He checked the rearview mirror before merging into a turn lane. His cell phone buzzed, and with no small amount of irony, he handed it to Neve, his eyes firm on the road. "I'm driving. You want to get that for me?"

Praying it wasn't the same rude lady with the 912 area code, Neve took the phone and smiled at Gavin's name on the screen. *Finally.* "Hi, Gavin! Neve here."

"Oh...oh, hey, Neve. How are you? I thought I dialed Duke."

Did she imagine the deflated tone of his voice, the edge of disappointment? Not likely, since he seemed to make little effort to hide it.

She adopted a more formal attitude. Maybe she'd been too familiar. "I'm well, sir, thank you. Duke is driving at the moment. I'm more than able to provide you with a progress report on the cabin."

"Actually, I wished to discuss a private matter with Duke."

"Ah." The wind fled from her sails.

The way Gavin had injected a longing note in Duke's name...

A spark went off inside her brain like flint striking steel. Here she was, the person in charge of Gavin's precious cabin, and yet he didn't want anything to do with her. She considered the facts. Why exactly was Duke, a specialist in pre–Civil War era revivals, working on such a project if not but for Gavin's adamant insistence he do so?

Enlightenment blossomed, and the whole world seemed to open up for Neve, silent but magnificent, like fireworks in the vacuum of space. She'd taken this job for the sake of getting close to Gavin.

And Gavin had hired Duke with a similar agenda.

She wanted to deny the obvious, as far-fetched as it seemed, but the notion had the undeniable reek of truth about it. Neve flopped her head against the headrest and put a cork in the massive groan threatening to tear from her body. What a waste of her time, her energy, her extended olive branch to Duke—all for nothing. No soul mate waited at the end of this long, difficult renovation. Just another item on her résumé. Well, great. Just fucking great.

In it for nothing, but in too deep to walk away. She cared. This mattered. She wanted Gavin's stupid cabin to come through the process new and wonderful and to be everything Gavin wanted, despite how she longed to shred his body into tiny pieces and thread him into the drapes. She'd been so sure after witnessing that temper of his.

Women were constantly complaining how men were such assholes. Well, here Neve was actively searching with nary a one in sight. She didn't want a sweetheart or a nice guy she'd annihilate in a matter of weeks. But had she been in the market for one, she'd be swarmed by jerks on all side, naturally, because life was the biggest jackass of them all.

And poor, clueless Duke. His boss was in love with him, and he had no idea. Did she illuminate the circumstances?

She had rough hands for such a delicate matter and no actual proof, only a hell of a hunch. Hell, maybe Duke reciprocated the feelings. They were grown men. They could work it out on their own terms.

That decided, she put on her work face and let Gavin off the hook. "We're in town on a shopping trip today, but if you call tomorrow, I'm certain Duke will be available."

Gavin thanked her without bothering to shadow his deflation. He didn't ask a single question about the cabin or what purchases Neve intended to make.

Proof, if I needed it. She ended the call and shook her head in disbelief as she gazed out the windshield. "Life never ceases to amaze me. It's a steady stream of curveballs and left hooks."

Duke made quick work of a surprised glance in her direction. "Pretty deep for a ten-second conversation. What did he want, the answers to the universe?"

"Just a private word with you." She puffed out her cheeks in a forceful exhale. No sense dwelling. She had more important things to focus on. "The flea market is supposed to be a multi-county affair. People come from all over the place to trade here, so we should have plenty to go through. This far off the beaten path, we're bound to come across a few hidden gems. Personally, I'd never come out this far to shop for a client in Little Rock. Not cost-effective."

Duke clucked his tongue. "I've crossed state lines to get my hands on a period piece at auction that was basically antique firewood, then proceeded to put a shameful amount of material and man-hours into restoring it. That's the whole point, in my opinion."

"Renovation isn't restoration. I bring the old into the present, and you take things back to their past. No wonder we can't get along. Do we have anything in common?"

"Not a single thing, by my calculations."

She eyeballed his hideous shirt. "I concur." She also concurred with Gavin's attraction. Damn Duke, damn him and his perfect profile.

By all things righteous and holy, his grizzled beard ought to deter from his appearance, not compliment the pure essence of *maleness* he exuded. Duke didn't play by the rules. He wasn't too pretty or flamboyant, nor foppish and effeminate. Even his long hair evoked images of Jared Leto... or maybe Fabio, if only she knew what the rest of his face looked like beneath his curtain of beard hair.

Damn him, damn him, damn him.

At least the flea market didn't disappoint. To save time, Neve had Duke drop her off with the trailer and sent him to the local museum to ask about the lockbox, then on to the hardware store to order the porcelain bathroom tiles and pick out complimentary plumbing fixtures, which included the commode and a pedestal sink. Also, a single deep sink for the kitchen. They'd make more of the day by splitting up, and surely she could trust the man with a few off-the-shelf buys.

Besides, she wanted a chance to pout without Duke noticing. Her spirits were low, and he'd notice. She didn't have any heart to put into mouthing off some sarcastic explanation.

The flea market was no Macy's. For every treasure, there were ten thousand pieces of junk. Everything from ripped ottomans to broken radios, splintered canes, piles of stained clothing, threadbare comforters, poorly made quilts, cheap plastic dishes, and cracked mirrors. People would sell nearly anything at a flea market, but only with willing buyers. Some of the goods said more about the would-be purchaser than the seller.

A lifetime of experience had taught Neve the ultimate lesson when it came to bulk bargain shopping—good stuff didn't bob to the top of the trash pile any more than diamonds floated to the surface of the earth. They had to be mined. Sometimes she had to break a sweat and get her hands dirty to find real treasures lurking in the depths, a task she relished. She uncovered what no one else had the gumption to dig for.

From an old woman, who turned out to be an old man, Neve purchased a small open-faced bookcase with two tiny drawers crafted from local cedar with the original knobs. It needed a good scrubbing and a polish and stain but was sturdy and at least thirty years old. Perfect sitting area addition. She imagined it placed below the window they'd created next to the front door or placed at an angle in the corner near the fireplace with a decorative lamp on top.

At the next stall, she picked out a reasonable amount of tarnished silverware and serving utensils, already relishing assigning the task of polishing to Duke.

At a furniture vendor of above average quality, she examined each and every table and set of chairs for both character and flaws before settling on a handcrafted dining set. The round tabletop balanced on an intricately carved pedestal. The four accompanying chairs were small but perfect for the limited space she'd designated for an eating area.

She didn't recognize the grain, but the few scars and gouges in the otherwise smooth surface made her giddy. This furniture had seen some shit in its day, probably served families for generations in these hills and hillocks, and more than likely outlived its maker by a few decades.

In the next several hours, Neve picked up two matching nightstands in dire need of a new coat of stain; a tall, narrow dresser over which she'd hang the gold-framed mirror she'd found buried under a pile of rabbit furs; thick canvas curtains dyed forest green with red dots running down the hem; and a set of amber-colored glass dishes.

At the last stall, a hardballing young man sold her a set of dusty crystal chandeliers for half their worth. She guessed the seller assumed they were glass. Had he bothered himself with the task of cleaning them, he might've noticed the light refractions were like no glass he'd ever seen. But perhaps not.

Any other client, Neve might've turned away from the idea, saved the image of twin crystal chandeliers hanging in the center of an antique cabin in the middle of the forest for someone else. It wasn't the sort of thing a client thought to ask for, but Gavin struck her as the type to appreciate the touch of decadence and whimsy amid the understated charm of the woodsy cabin.

She texted Duke. It was downright pleasant to have the use of her cell phone back. *Small curtain rod for front window while you're at the hardware store, plz. Not white. Done here. Ready 4 lunch.* He returned her message with *k*, which she despised.

Awhile later, they met in the dirt-packed parking lot, Neve trailed by a trio of beefy men she'd hired to load her purchases into the storage trailer.

Duke stood back with his hands on hips and watched them stack her haul. "You make friends everywhere you go, don't you?"

"Draw 'em like flies." She paid the men, smiled pitying at the one who asked for her phone number, and climbed inside the truck. The air-conditioning was at full blast, and she stuck her face in front of the closest vent. "Full trailer, empty stomach. What can we do about that?"

"Eat." Something in Duke's voice suggested his day hadn't been as advantageous as hers.

The Red Hill Delicatessen boasted the "Best Hoagies in Town!" painted boldly in red across their front window. Probably the only hoagies in town, Neve judged by what she'd seen so far. "Town" seemed to consist of a single main street, nearly all small local business, and a few scattered residential areas beyond that.

Duke's frown over his sweet tea preceded his bad news. "No luck with the chest." He disregarded the straw and took three manly gulps, his Adam's apple jouncing like a fishing bobber. "Nothing like it in the museum. I took a chance and asked around. No one knows anything. One of the men I talked to was ninety if a day, John Bilson, and he was at a complete loss. He's not even convinced it's a lock."

"It's definitely a lock."

Duke shrugged. "I think so, too. He made me an appointment with Cherish Rancourt, head of the Red Hill Historical Society. He says if anyone knows about the lockbox, it'll be her, but she's out of town. I won't get a chance to meet her for another four weeks."

"Peachy. So, if she's got anything to tell us, we won't find out until we're nearly done with the cabin."

Duke's spirits seemed to improve with the arrival of their lunch—roast beef and cheddar on whole wheat. "By then, we'll be down to the fine details I've got nothing to do with—pure interior design. I'll have plenty of time to widen the search grid if we have to. By the by, I've got your curtain rod, the commode, a pedestal sink for the bathroom, and a drop-in singe sink for the kitchen. Porcelain, of course, but off-white. And I ordered the porcelain tiles for the bathroom. I went with a glazed amber color. I think it'll compliment the wood grain. I chose fixtures within the same spectrum but slightly off for contrast."

Neve nodded her approval, impressed. Then she wanted to smack herself. She'd seen his office. Duke had talent, even if he wasn't applying it to the project at hand. "A gold star for you, Duke. Well done."

He nodded but didn't speak. It'd be impossible with the huge wad of sandwich he'd muscled between his jaws with superhuman force.

Neve didn't bother to hide her disgust. He even ate like a straight man. "If you choke, I'm having your sandwich order engraved on your headstone."

He gave her a thumbs-up.

Chapter 7

Four weeks left. Duke could hardly fathom how the first four had passed so quickly. *It's halfway over. Another four weeks, possibly three, if it all stays on track, and I'm free and clear of this mess.*

The last week had seen Neve subdued, her head down, concentrated on the project. She kept her end of the bargain. The razor edge of her tongue never dulled completely, but she tempered her remarks with a smile or a wink, despite how Duke failed over and over again to convince Gavin to take his concerns to Neve. He'd have nothing to do with her, and Duke had to wonder why in the hell he'd bothered hiring her.

Easy. So I'd take the job. But why? Why did it matter so damn much?

He didn't have answers. What he did have, finally, was something useful to do.

Neve's hands were full with double-checking her assistant's plans for the cabinetry and the measurements for major plumbing installations. If the calculations were off by so much as an inch, they'd have to scramble to rearrange the components. If she altered the toilet or shower placement, it had better be now while master plumber Andrew Bale and his team were there inspecting the pump house the last owner constructed over an underground spring.

The man was about as impressive as any other plumber, master or otherwise, which was to say unremarkable with the exception of his expressionless face. He had the sort of stern look that never seemed to change, whether he was happy or displeased.

Duke gathered little from his passive appearance, except that he was a man of few words. Short, succinct words. Like Neve when she was in full-on production mode. He worked like hell, too, taking no more than a few hours to track down Duke and give him his report.

Andrew's thick eyebrows came together like long-lost caterpillars. He kicked a pile of dirt his team had churned up during their inspection. "The last owner dug themselves a pump house, but that's about it," he lamented. "My team will have to dig and lay pipe. While they do that, I'll get to work on installing interior hookups. You show me where you want stuff to go, and I'll get to marking. Tiny cabin like this, we'll have it done by week's end."

Neve chose that opportune moment to introduce herself. "Neve Harper." She stuck out a hand, confident he'd take it, which he did. Hardly a squeeze had time to pass between them before she dropped her hand and guided them toward the cabin. "This way. The bathroom is interesting. The cabin had no interior walls, so we've constructed a couple. The new construction won't have insulation installed, but the outer walls will. You'll need to take both insulation and the secondary wall into account. That, or I considered the possibility of having the pipes come from underneath, but I'll bow to your authority. Hell, you can run the pipes overhead if you want, but it's not what I prefer."

"More costly," Andrew agreed.

Duke settled into the background and watched Neve take command of the situation. Andrew Bale seemed like the kind of guy people might find intimidating but, at his lack of a smile, Neve's grew bigger. "Oh, goody. I get to do all the talking."

She liked Andrew, Duke mused. No fuss, no muss, all work, no strong personality getting in the way of the job. Just there to get the work done. And how could Duke guess at such a thing? Because, all else aside, Neve was fascinating to watch in her element. He'd spent weeks seeing the way she handled Vince and his crew, her efficient use of the assistant Gavin provided. She kept everyone busy but didn't rush them. No idle hands, but no accidents, either. It was a steady, grinding pace that put every crew member on the site into a pattern of busting ass and resting well, because they knew they'd be pushed just as hard the next day. Vince had a good team, and that helped. But Duke suspected no one wanted to be outdone by the boss lady. So, everyone tried to put in the same verve and energy that she did each day. It took a special kind of leader to propel any group to such a high level of production.

"We've got all the appliances on standby for measurements," Neve was saying as she led the way, two steps ahead of them. "Toilet, pedestal sink, but not the shower stall. Not yet. Don't be delicate with the floor. We're putting down tile long after you and your crew have moved on. One of the more tedious things in a renovation, laying tile. What about you, huh?" She cast a teasing glance over her shoulder at Andrew. "Besides the obvious, what's the worst thing about laying poo pipes? Is it laying poo pipes?"

Red spread through the man's face until Duke could almost feel his embarrassment. She didn't know when to quit.

Lo and behold, Andrew grinned. He almost looked confused about it. "I enjoy laying pipes."

"Right." She grinned wider, a playful, facetious smile. "They're clean the first time around. Probably *fixing* poo pipes is the worst."

Neve talked all the way, so by the time they entered the cabin and reached the newly constructed room they'd intended to turn into a bathroom, Andrew had nearly every bit of information he needed to get started right away. She didn't hesitate in her stream of information, but Duke noticed, with the exception of a few jokes sprinkled in for fun's sake, every word had purpose. "Four-by-four. Tiny. Here"—she pointed to the original wall on her left past the open entry—"I've marked where I want the sink and commode. Move what you need to within the space I've designated. If anything has to be rearranged for any reason, inform me."

Clear, decisive direction. She didn't wait for Andrew to grant her authority; she took it and left no room for argument or doubt it belonged to her. She pointed to the adjacent wall. "There's a blank space about two feet across here. I want a towel rack there if at all possible. The room will be sparse but functional."

Andrew grunted his approval. "Pretty grand for a simple cabin, you ask me. Smart arrangement. It'll seem a little roomier."

Neve took the compliment in stride and held her hands out toward the east-facing wall to her right. "The shower is going to share this new wall here with the kitchen sink on the other side. Ought to make for less piping and therefore cost less dollars." Her sly gaze slid to Andrew.

He nodded once. "Right you are. It'd cost a good deal more to hook up both sides of the cabin."

Neve grinned. "Not my first plumbing rodeo."

"Oh, I believe it." Andrew examined the small space a final time. "That's all of it? Sink, commode, bath, kitchen sink? Everything appears marked and measured, but I'll do my own calculations."

She pressed her lips together in a line, tapped them with her forefinger and gave Duke a pointed look.

Oh, God, did I forget something? Damn, where did that list she gave me disappear to? Before he had a chance to start patting his pockets for the assignments Neve had doled out for the week, she made a strange request.

"Duke, I think I hear the electrician calling your name. Scram."

"What? But—"

Her amber gaze hardened, like watching sugar crystalize. "I need a moment with our plumber here. Would you mind?"

Ah, sweet dismissal. He shrugged, though it chafed. He'd done Vale House, damn it. He wasn't some newbie. But Neve ran the show. She'd proven it, too, taking Andrew's respect before he'd even had the chance to offer it. Still, Duke walked away from Neve with something like dread. She was already conferring in murmurs with the old plumber. Definitely up to something.

In an uncanny happenstance, Duke ran into Jake Lansky and his two crew members on the path coming from the road. After a short exchange, where the word *dude* was used with a total lack of irony, Duke accepted the instantaneous dislike Jake encouraged with little to no guilt.

In his thirties and probably a woman's idea of good-looking, Jake had the rakish devil-may-care thing going on. Jeans too tight and shirt too expensive for the kind of work he'd come to do. The heavy work boots he wore appeared brand new. He regarded Duke with the careless attention of a bored teenager, an attitude bound to rub Neve the wrong way.

Duke would love nothing more than to put the young man in his place, but he had no true authority. Little more than Gavin's mouthpiece out here, only Neve had to take notice of anything he offered. Besides, Neve had proven she could handle herself, and personally, he couldn't wait to watch her put a verbal whooping on Jake Lansky.

He beckoned him and his crew to follow and guided them back toward the cabin.

Neve stood outside, with her arms crossed, dappled shade casting a pattern across her skin and her baggy white V-neck T-shirt. It was worse than the tight gray one she favored, the way the fabric draped and shifted over her small breasts and showed an expanse of pale creamy skin at her neck. She simply stood there, the center of the world, without even trying.

*A speckled Neve in her natural habitat...*Wisely, Duke kept the joke to himself and introduced Jake.

"So, uh, where do I throw up the panels?"

Duke winced at Jake's artless greeting and the tone of indifference.

Neve cocked her head to examine him. "Neve Harper," she introduced herself formally. "I don't recall we've come to a decision on the solar panels. I'd like to discuss a secondary energy source."

The young man didn't seem to hear. One of his crew had been carrying a ladder, which he placed against the side of the cabin for access to the roof. "Oh, you definitely want solar panels. They're like free power." When he did bother to glance at Neve, his gaze swept over her from head to toe with one eyebrow hitched in undisguised appreciation.

Duke had the sudden urge to take the young man by his giblets and deliver a lesson in respect. Instead, he grinned and waited. This was going to be so good.

Neve's response was immediate. "How old are you, Jake?"

He grinned and ran a hand through his glossy black locks. "Old enough."

Neve didn't explode, although Duke hadn't dismissed it as a possibility. Instead, she let her gaze move up and down Jake, sizing him up, much as he'd done to her seconds ago. "Old enough to own a car? A house?"

He must've mistaken Neve's scrutiny for returned interest, because her questions seemed to put him off. The young man shuffled his feet, suddenly uncomfortable and glancing at his crew as if for support. "Yeah, I got bills. What's your point?"

"The point is you can't pay them if I fire you. If you have a car payment to make each month, a mortgage, or a family counting on you to feed them, my advice would be to keep them firmly in mind every time you open your mouth to speak to me or to anyone else here. You'll give respect before you get it. Or turn around, head back the way you came, and quit wasting my fucking time, okay, cool guy?"

Impatient, demanding, belittling, and absolutely right.

Duke welled up with pride. Not that Neve wouldn't punch him if he said so, but he admired her paunch. At the same time, was this why she had such a hard time in her personal life? What worked in the field to command respect and admiration didn't necessarily jive in the more delicate arenas of society.

She needs someone who respects her.

And like that, Duke understood.

Not a man here had the balls to stand up to Neve or speak a word against her. They valued her expertise, respected her grit, admired her leadership—but they didn't want to go home to it. They wanted malleable things, women waiting with a hot meal and a back rub. Neve would never be the quintessential little woman. But she wasn't the problem—the douchebags she chose to date were. If someone in her field knew her, worked besides her, saw her as both the natural leader she was *and* a woman, someone— *Like me. Shit.*

He hadn't expected the train of thought to take him there, but yeah, he supposed he'd seen a few sides others hadn't. Her love for Darcy the Pit, her determination, even her ability to compromise and stay focused on the task at hand, despite her disappointment with Gavin.

Like a chastised child, Jake swallowed and nodded.

Neve cut off any response Jake might've conjured with an effective dive into the matter at hand. "Now that we're speaking as one professional to another, let me try again. I'm not concerned about a heat source. The fireplace is in working condition." She sniffed. "I won't get into what it took to make *that* happen, but it's worth mentioning worse things than bats can take up residence in an old chimney."

Duke frowned at the memory of the massive spider nest.

"Anyway, if all we have are solar panels, turning the lights on is going to be a real bitch come winter. Give me an inexpensive and effective secondary power source."

Jake bobbed his head in a complete accordance. "Uh, well, we're pretty far out. I'm not sure about the local energy company, but generators are pretty reliable."

Duke took a chance on drawing attention to himself. "Actually, there's a ranch down the road. I don't recall power lines, but how realistic is it Tim runs the place on full-time generators?"

Jake turned into a professional before their very eyes. He cleared his throat, his confidence obviously shaken by Neve's pointed rebuke, but Duke had to give the kid credit for bouncing back. "Probably not a gasoline-powered generator. They're loud and pricey. Propane is a much better option, but there's still the cost of refilling the tank." He shrugged apologetically. "And a propane company probably won't come out this far. It's something you'd have to do yourself."

Neve chewed her lip and stroked her chin. Duke idly wondered if she'd picked up the habit from him. "Propane it is, then. The cost should be low, considering the size of the cabin and the solar panels working most of the time. The cabin will have large appliances. I'm talking refrigerator and—" She paused abruptly, peered at Duke. "Other things. Next week, we're putting in the spray-foam insulation, and Duke here will be building the log profile boarding to serve as a secondary wall. I understand each wall has to have an outlet, but I wouldn't mind a few extras scattered around. Please get with Kay—she's my assistant—and Finn, the resident carpenter, for schematics of the kitchen cabinetry. Specifically, I want an outlet behind the fridge, and at least two others for countertop appliances. I've also marked where I want my overhead fixtures. They're odd, but I've got my reasons. I'll meet you inside in five. Feel free to inspect the roof for the panels."

Jake looked Neve in the eyes and seemed to consider her for the first time. He gave her a half-cocked grin that made Duke want to punch him. "You're thorough."

She answered with a sly grin. "You have no idea."

Duke felt his lip curl. *Jesus, is she flirting with this kid?* Maybe, maybe not. But while Jake might take the comment as coy, he'd find out Neve meant it pretty damn literally if so much as a single wire was out of place.

She turned to Duke, hitched her chin toward the tree line, and continued in the same commanding tone once they had some semblance of privacy. "My tiles arrive at the hardware store early tomorrow morning. I want you to take Kay with you."

Duke scratched his head. He liked Kay. Cute, if a little intense. "Uh, sure. Is it my weekend?"

Neve surprised him by smiling. "We'd never produce a child that goddamn perky. But seriously, there's this thing happening between Kay and Finn. Normally, I don't give a shit, but we're pushing here. I mean, plumbing lines and the wiring of the cabin have to be complete by the end of the week. If we don't get the insulation and boarding done at the end of week five, we'll officially fall behind schedule for the first time. Their flirting is adorable, but I need Finn to finish the custom cabinets instead of moon at Kay. Later this week, I can set her to work varnishing completed pieces before they're installed, and he'll be busy hand-carving my baseboards."

Duke understood. A lover's quarrel, or even quick, clandestine meetings between two critical sets of hands, could effectively delay production. "Got it. Hey, speaking of those reclaimed slats, where in the hell did they all go? There's plenty for the secondary walls, but—"

"Then that's all you need to worry about," she cut in sweetly.

He'd known it. She definitely had something up her sleeve, something she was desperate to keep from him. However, he knew something else, too…pushing Neve was never a good idea, and with a cabin this small, he'd eventually stumble onto her secret.

* * * *

Kay annoyed him so endearingly, Duke didn't have it in him to hold her personality against her. God, she was tiny. Despite his little custody joke about his weekend, but he was pretty sure no less than a few people assumed Kay was his grown daughter. Didn't do a damn thing for his ego. The numbers didn't add up, but he'd look like a crazy person if he explained to every stranger they passed on the street there were only eleven years between him and his young companion.

Tiles and a last-minute order of pizza retrieved, he and Kay were ready to head back to the cabin before they'd passed a full hour in town.

Kay sat in the passenger side with her perpetual smile, hot pizzas in her lap and a steady string of nonsense pouring forth from her gullet like a waterfall. "My parents can't believe it, but they should. I mean, they're who taught me anything can be achieved through hard work and perseverance. Besides, they—hey, look at that!"

Duke snapped his head toward Kay, her sudden exclamation filling him with instant anxiety. He relaxed when he followed the line of her pointing finger to a ramshackle single-story home practically buried beneath a yard full of junk.

"Let's check it out!" Kay already had the pizza boxes shifted from her lap to the seat between them.

Duke peered at the dilapidated house. Faded, peeling, pale yellow paint, white trim, and a side door hanging crooked from its hinges. He couldn't fathom a reason for stopping, but he slowed as they passed. "What for? It's just an old house."

"Don't you see the sign, silly? It's a shop. See there." She pointed again, this time at the picket fence, probably white at one time, with great pieces either missing or broken.

Sure enough, a hand-painted sign hung off a remaining chunk of fence.

"Thrift House. Huh. So, all this junk is for sale?" He was all about some secondhand shopping, but this…he came to a stop when Kay's intent interest showed no sign of waning. She had her seat belt undone and the door open before he set the gears to park.

"Fine," he said to the empty truck cab. "Keep an open mind, Duke." He joined Kay in the yard.

With abandon, she dug and plucked through stacks of boxes and heaps of random household items. Neve might make more of it, picking through the trash in search of treasure, but he had no clue what she'd find appealing or worthwhile. The crystal chandeliers she'd picked up at the flea market last week had thrown him for a loop. He wasn't about to make any assumptions, but Kay probably had a keen idea of Neve's final vision for the cabin.

He stood idly, eyeballing the yard and the wares carelessly, when his gaze landed on a set of French doors. Duke started.

Neve adamantly went against having anything white in the cabin. No white appliances, no white tile, no white sinks, or even dishes. Everything should either match the wood grain or compliment it to invoke and stress the outdoor element.

But these doors were white.

White and utterly perfect.

The panes of glass were set in a standard crosshatch pattern, but not in the usual horizontal and vertical alignment. Rather, they were set at an angle, diamond-shaped, and slightly larger than was typical.

To his trained eye, the glass was original—thin and old. He'd rather die than replace it. Maybe this was what Neve had experienced when she found the chandeliers, because suddenly Duke couldn't imagine any other set of doors in the cabin. The white would offset the pattern against the honey-colored wood. He beckoned Kay with a wave.

Her arms were full of stuff. She had a couple of leather bound books, a handmade clay jar, two brass candlestick holders, a plaque so filthy he couldn't discern the design if there was one, and a small decorative kerosene lamp. She navigated the twists and turns of the random merchandise piled haphazardly across the yard. It seemed like the lackadaisical attempt by the owner to showcase his wares. And the product of years of hoarding. Likely story, the owner woke up one day, painted a sign, and stuck it on his fence to excuse the mess and maybe clear out some of his hoard.

Kay stopped next to Duke, blinking expectantly.

Duke ran his hand across the faded white paint of the French doors. A fresh coat, a little glass cleaner, and they'd be good as new. "Neve has this thing against white, but these doors...am I wrong? Am I crazy? I think they'd work."

Kay set her armload down in the grass. She didn't try to appease Duke or answer out of blind loyalty for Neve's vision. She looked the doors over, front and back, studied the grain and tested the glass panes with quick raps. Then she stood back and smiled appreciatively. "What a find! The design, even the color, is...well, it's like Neve's chandeliers. They're going to work, even if you can't exactly put your finger on the why and the how. Even if they *shouldn't* work. It takes real genius to spot it. The glass panes will be difficult to replace since they're original, but they're all in one piece and sturdy, far as I can tell. A few loose ones at the bottom"—she shrugged—"but that's an easy fix. Good eye, Duke!"

As if he hadn't designed houses the better part of a decade. "Thanks, Kay." Then again, Kay's approval was a nice balm against Neve's ever-present demand for perfection.

A black man, probably in his forties, ambled to the threshold when they approached the side door of the house to make an offer. His yellowed teeth and slight limp didn't speak well of his health. Nor did his greeting, or lack thereof, speak well of his regard toward them.

Kay didn't appear to notice. She made her purchase with a big smile. "There's the weirdest metal doohickey over there. I have no idea what use we'd have for it, but it's neat-looking."

With an eye toward a return trip in the future to dig a little deeper, Duke introduced himself to the proprietor. "I'm Duke Kennicot. This is Kay Bing. We'll probably be back since we're doing some work in the area. You've got some, uh, great stuff here." A lot of junk, too, but the French doors were a real find.

A rheumy eye glared at him through the old screen door that squealed with each small move. The man didn't come outside to make the transaction but stayed behind the protective barrier of the door. Possibly agoraphobic. Finally, he reached out to take their money. His hand quickly disappeared back inside. "Krandall Beels."

Duke blinked. Interesting. "Beels? The cabin we're renovating up the hill is supposedly known around here as Beels Cabin. Any relation?"

A small shrug accompanied Krandall's obvious disinterest. "Supposed to have been my great-granny's or some such. Mebbe further on back than that, but I ain't got no family now, so's don't matter, anyhow. Y'all have a nice day."

Duke shrugged, thanked him for the fair price, and walked with Kay back to the truck. "That's interesting. Florrie's descendant living right down the highway from the cabin. Florrie was Ben's mistress. I wonder…" Duke suddenly recalled whom he was talking to.

Kay's eyes were bright with interest, and she probably wouldn't hesitate to gab to Finn anything Duke said.

He shook his head. "Never mind. Small town, that's all. Come on, I bet they're missing us by now."

Kay expressed her doubt. "Fewer chiefs and all that. I bet things are running as smooth as butter without us."

* * * *

The sudden clamor outside punched through the quiet bubble inside the trailer like a shotgun blast.

Neve scrambled from her desk, where she'd been making a final order for the large appliances, hurried down the steps of her trailer, and pushed Darcy the Pit back inside when she saw the source of the commotion.

Too many people coming too fast and too loud up the road from the cabin. They rushed onto the gravel road quickly, with steely determined faces, their attention centered on a group of five or so men moving together in a huddle. They went slower than the rest of the workmen, who hovered like stirred-up bees around a bear.

Neve went straight to the center of the chaos.

Two of Vince's crew members held him up between them, his arms locked around each of their shoulders. Another man struggled to keep pace slightly ahead of them, bent over and holding up Vince's left leg at the knee while Vince hopped along on his one good foot, leaning heavily on the men around him.

Neve's heart constricted. The foot the crewman held off the ground was a mass of blood—too much for Neve to tell the severity of the injury at a glance.

Questions raced through her mind. Vince headed the deck project. Had he tripped over the wood saw? Someone put a drill through his ankle? She'd seen plenty of injuries on job sites, but the sight of so much blood made her dizzy.

In the distance, a four-wheeler roared, drawing closer.

Tim? Had someone called the rancher for help? But how? Probably the walkie-talkie channel Hux had provided in case they needed to get in touch or had another incident like Duke crashing from the broken stairs.

She didn't use the walkie-talkies, but Vince and his team did. He must've had someone make the call, knowing they didn't have time for the long journey into Red Hill. Nor did their first aid kits have the supplies for an injury such as this.

Duke and Kay pulled into the parking area, gravel crunching and dirt hurling up from the tires as they came to a jerky stop. Duke vaulted from the truck and rushed toward Vince and his entourage.

"What the hell happened?" His shout rose over the confusion of voices.

Someone answered, but Neve didn't catch the explanation.

Duke took over for the man on Vince's left, taking on more weight and easing the burden for the man on Vince's other side.

The four-wheeler finally came into sight. Neve recognized the driver as Miles, Tim's brother. He wasted no time. He stood upright as he arrowed through the parked vehicles and multiple location trailers at a speed that made Neve's skin prickle. He towed an empty flatbed that bounced violently on the gravel. He'd have to go much slower on the way back to the ranch. He parked a few yards from the group of men, shouting and waving frantically. "Two of you on the flatbed with Vince. Let's go! Let's go!"

Duke made sure he was one of them. He shooed away several of Vince's guys who attempted to join them. He and one of the workmen held Vince steady on the flatbed. The old man's face pulled taut with pain, but his eyes fluttered like he'd soon pass out.

Neve didn't interfere. Duke dove into the chaos without hesitation. Easy enough to forget he could run this whole operation blindfolded, that he was a leader, and an act-first kind of man. Yet, he could. He could've had easy command of this whole group, and Vince's guys giving way to Duke's authority without question only proved it.

She'd only be in the way if she jumped in. Instead, she'd hold down the job site.

Chaos reigned. Someone had to take control of Vince's team before every one of them tried to trail the four-wheeler back to Lady Killer Ranch. They moved restlessly, some pacing, some scratching their heads and worrying their hands. She didn't dare leave them idle.

Shaky with adrenaline, she advanced on the group. She ran across Kay, chewing her thumbnail like it was dinner. A concerned frown wrinkled her forehead. Without a word, Neve motioned for her to follow, which she did, seemingly relieved to have a purpose to march toward.

With Kay at her side, she addressed the men. "You two." She pointed at the closest pair. "Get that storage trailer unhitched from Vince's truck. I'm driving it to the ranch, and I'll bring back a progress report for all of you. Tim has people at his ranch who will know what to do, and it shouldn't take them long to discover the extent of his injury. In the meantime, you all have something better to do than rubberneck. Whatever you were working on when the accident occurred, finish it. Vince set up a standing spotlight this morning, obviously intending to work past sunset. Let's go!" she shouted angrily when they didn't move.

Most of them jolted into movement. Some hesitated and gave her resentful stares.

She stared back. "Get to work or get the hell off my job site. You can explain to Vince later why you abandoned his contractual obligations."

One by one, they relented.

She shook her head. *Stubborn idiots.* Stubborn but loyal. Well, she understood how much that counted for. She turned to Kay. "I'm leaving you in charge again. Keep them busy, or they'll be worrisome and jittery. Don't take any shit. If they have a problem, they can leave. For good. If I'm not back by nightfall, make sure Darcy the Pit isn't left outside."

The young woman squared her shoulders, set her jaw, and nodded. A tough little thing. "You've got it, Ms. Harper. I mean Neve. Count on me."

Neve was already headed for the truck Duke had left running. It had the distinction of being one of the only vehicles not entirely blocked in. "I kind of have to."

"Right, of course. I only meant—"

"Go!" She didn't look back to see if Kay followed orders. She heard the scramble of her feet on the rough gravel. Carefully, Neve reversed, mindful of the unhitched storage trailer a yard or so away. It made for tight quarters, but she navigated the space and finally pointed the truck in the direction of Lady Killer Ranch.

Branches scraped and scratched against the truck sides as she tried to maintain speed while not driving like a maniac at the same time. Not the easiest feat.

A sudden familiar bleeping distracted her. She glanced between the seats at Duke's phone and rolled her eyes. She ought to suggest a belt holster. Then again, cell phones were pointless contraptions at the cabin. Most of the workmen, Duke and herself included, began leaving their phones in their trailers where they actually sent and received calls and texts, if spottily.

She ignored the call and put her concentration into not bypassing the entrance to the ranch, veiled behind swells of foliage.

The phone rang a second time.

Neve snatched it up. Same 912 number as before. She shook her head and answered. "Call back and leave a damn message, would you?" Anxiety and adrenaline gave her natural impatience the run of her mouth.

The woman was unfazed by Neve's rudeness. "I've had enough of whoever the hell you are, okay? Give me Duke, *now.*"

Neve's mouth quirked up. A worthy adversary, this one. "It's a damn shame, but he isn't available. However, there's this nifty new invention that might be the answer to your woes. It's called voice mail. Very edgy technology. See, when the robot voice tells you to leave a message, you talk to it, say whatever dire thing you have to say, and then hang up. After that, the real magic happens. Duke will eventually hear the message you gave the robot, and he'll do this thing they call *returning a phone call.* It's all much simpler than it sounds, I promise."

She didn't get the desired effect. Cut from the same cloth as Neve, apparently, the lady hardly reacted. Instead, her voice turned sympathetic. "Oh, honey. You must be another confused little girlfriend."

Neve started, slowing the truck to round a curve in the road. The words *Duke* and *girlfriend* together in a sentence rang wrong on so many levels, Neve didn't know where to start. "Girlfriend, huh?"

"Oh, sweetie. I understand. He's sweet, if a tad boring, and good-looking. But there's one tiny thing he might've failed to mention."

"Um, yeah, like he's gay." Neve pulled to the side of the road for fear she'd drive right past the entrance in her distraction. The mystery lady had some dish on Duke, and Neve was determined to discover it.

Laughter came over the line. Not the mocking type, either. This lady's deep belly laughs were the genuine article. "Really? And he'll pretend you turned him straight or something? Wow. I guess I have to give him points for creativity."

Something tweaked in Neve's chest. *Surely not...* She needed sure footing, not a game of wits. "I'm a colleague of Duke's, not a girlfriend."

A beat of silence. "Why are you taking calls for him?"

"Circumstantial." Neve's short answer gave away her impatience. "Look, we've had an on-site emergency. Duke left his phone in the truck I'm driving. Now, let's make a deal. Tell me your message, and I'll make sure Duke gets it. I delight in tormenting him, so don't hold back."

"He's working again." A note of something like envy tainted the woman's response.

Neve wondered if she'd chosen sides wisely. "Against his will. It's my project. He's consulting."

"Hm." A thoughtful pause. "Okay, fine. I'm Candice Kennicot. I'm Duke's wife, and I'm not signing a damn thing until he returns my call."

Neve's tongue shriveled up and stuck to the roof of her mouth. She worked her jaw until words formed. "Duke, he's...I mean, you're certain he's not gay? You're sure?"

"Did you miss the word *wife* in my introduction? We were together for years. I'd have noticed if he wasn't attracted to me, don't you think?"

Made sense. Still..."Any idea why he'd lie about it?"

Candice sighed in a bored way. "Hell, I don't know. To avoid relationships? I'm not sure how well you know him, but I kind of did a number on the guy. We're not on great terms. But he opened a can of worms by sending me these papers, and I'm not signing anything."

Neve's head swam.

Not gay.

Not gay and *married.* That filthy, rotten, dirty straight *bastard.* Hairy, lying prick. Stupid dirty cretin. The insults tumbled through her head, repeating themselves and growing in fervor.

Every time she'd felt a physical attraction to him and wondered what was wrong with her—her face blazed with heat. *He'll suffer for this. My God, how he'll suffer for this.*

She already knew the perfect punishment. "You want to get your hands on Duke, a phone call won't cut it. Hell, we're almost always down at the renovation site anyway, a hike down the far side of a mountain where there's no cell service."

"What are you saying, hon?"

"Hon is great, but you can call me Neve."

"Fine, Neve. You're suggesting something. What is it?"

Neve smiled. The sweetest revenge her crooked mind could concoct only worked if she got Duke's little wife on board. She had a feeling Candice would be game. "Why, I think you should get some fresh mountain air, don't you? After all, it's hard for a man to ignore what's right in front of his face."

A moment passed. "I'm in Georgia, and that's quite a trip." A pause and a deep breath. "But I hear the Ozarks are beautiful this time of year."

Chapter 8

Duke paced the creaky porch of the ranch house and nervously rubbed his hands together. He'd let the tag-along crew member go in with Vince while Owen and Laurel dug out their veterinarian tools and went to work on Vince's ankle. How much did they really know? Should they have pushed for the doctor in town? Duke might've stopped the bleeding by then. Then again, maybe not. The only options seemed equally risky, but the ranch had been closer.

He recognized Vince's truck crawling down the lane toward the house. He guessed the driver was Neve before she parked and stepped out of the cab.

And he fell into the glacial crevice that was her gaze.

Ice-cold gold-flecked eyes bore into him with a hostility he hadn't seen since...

Since never.

She'd never looked at him the way she was looking now. He swore his nuts shriveled as she stalked past him and tried the front door.

"We're locked out." *Hey, ho, Captain Obvious.* "I let Vince's guy go in with him. He eventually passed out from the pain." He grimaced, only able to imagine. He couldn't claim to have the experience of a pain so intense it robbed him of consciousness.

Neve stayed in front of the door, her nose nearly pressed against it, her head down. With choppy, robotic motions, she went to a rocker, sat, and stared straight ahead.

Frustration built up in Duke's chest. Somehow, over the last four weeks, they'd discovered common ground. They were on solid terms. He'd almost call them friends, except Neve didn't have any those. He took two steps toward her. The memory of her cold glare kept him from getting any closer. "Are you okay?"

"Perfectly fucking fine," she ground out.

"Perfectly fine, huh? That's what you call this Ice Queen routine? Is this because of Gavin?" *Shut up, Duke. Don't poke the bear.* He didn't heed his own advice. "Because if so, your timing is shitty. We could at least survive this crisis before you start taking it out on me that Gavin won't talk to you. I try, Neve, every time. I haven't given up."

With inexplicable ferocity, she snapped at him. "It has nothing to do with Gavin, you idiot." She took in a breath through her nostrils. "And everything to do with Candice Kennicot. Ring a bell? A *wedding* bell, maybe?"

Slowly, her hard gaze met his, watching him like a viper eying a trembling mouse.

Dread roiled in his gut. Candice's name coming from Neve's mouth made everything inside him shrivel up and disintegrate into ash until he was a hollowed out bag of flesh. Stupidly, he gaped at her and said the dumbest thing imaginable. "I can explain."

Neve nodded slowly and turned her face away from him, but not before he caught the pinched edges of her mouth and the half-lidded expression of pained disappointment.

He recalled their talk back at his loft before they ever came out to the cabin. She'd said then he'd never let her down before. And now he had. Regret washed over him like an unforgiving wave. He could fix this, though. He could explain. "Neve, please. It's not—"

Her palm shot out to silence him. "If you say it isn't what it looks like, I'll remove your testicles. Slowly and methodically, I will remove them with the rustiest tool I can find and a smile on my face."

He blinked and licked his lips. He'd been about to say those very words. And they'd have been a lie, too. The circumstances were irrelevant. "Fine. It's exactly what it looks like. I'm not gay."

Another slow nod. Deceptively at ease in the rocker, arms on the armrests, hands lax, she kept her face turned away from him. "And married."

"Divorced, actually." He took the rocker beside Neve's. "We divorced a long time ago. After I did Vale House." His next words were cut off by the front screen door clattering open.

Owen and Vince's guy—Duke seriously needed to get the guy's name—shuffled out looking tired and worried. Neve and Duke scrambled from their rockers to ogle them expectantly.

Laurel came through the door behind them and was the one to speak. Duke's stomach pitched in fear at the blood on her hands.

"Vince's ankle is a mess. It's not life threatening, but the injury isn't small, either. We got the bleeding to stop and cleaned it, but I have to stitch the larger wounds."

Neve took a step toward her. "What do you mean *wounds*? What the hell happened to him?"

Laurel continued like Neve hadn't spoken. "He's in there drinking whiskey right now, said to do whatever I had to do, and adamantly refused to be taken to a hospital. I'm keeping him a few nights, until the risk of infection has passed. We have a wheelchair around here somewhere, from when Tim's daddy was still alive, and a pair of crutches from when Miles broke his leg three summers ago. Vince will need both for a time."

Neve's mouth formed a flat, dangerous line. "Tell me what caused the injury."

Owen offered her a troubled frown. "Steel trap."

Laurel's worried glance at her husband made Duke's skin prickle. They knew something. Guilt framed the edges of her explanation. "It appears your friend stepped on an old trap out by the pump house. He says the men he was with pried it off his ankle with whatever tools they had on hand. That's when the bleeding would've began in earnest."

"Old, huh?" Vince's crewman spoke up for the first time.

They all looked to him.

His arms crossed, openly hostile. "Didn't look old to me. Not a speck of rust on the thing. Gleaming hinges. No, ma'am, not a damn thing old about that trap."

Owen pretended to find something interesting on his shirtfront. Laurel swallowed.

In a phenomenon of epic proportions, Neve didn't erupt in a fiery gush of rage and destruction like Duke expected. But she did take another step forward. Not toward Laurel, the woman, the easy target. Nope, not Neve. She stepped up to Owen, the man who outweighed her by a hundred pounds, and narrowed her eyes. "That's private land. No one has permission to hunt or trap on Gavin's property. Mind telling me how a shiny new trap found its way to our pump house?"

None of them had to guess. The guilt sang from Owen's face, and Laurel's, too.

Neve jabbed Owen in the chest with an angry finger and practically growled. "Where is Hux? He's going to answer for what happened to Vince tonight."

Owen looked away, but Laurel shook her head and answered. "He ain't here. He's gone to auction with some of the cattle, but he'll be back next week. I'll tell him to come see you as soon as he gets back. I swear it."

"Don't worry about it," she snapped, glaring from husband to wife. "He and I have a date."

* * * *

Duke had never considered himself a coward. One day, he'd have to remember to thank Neve for opening his eyes to this overlooked flaw. Though, to be fair, he'd volunteered for the position of Vince's caretaker. For the last week, he'd been Vince's eyes and ears, as well as hands, feet, and mouthpiece. The task had given him little time for a conversation with Neve about his grievous lie, let alone any sort of explanation for it. He hadn't even told her about the French doors he'd found at Thrift House.

He'd get his chance eventually, though. He expected her to track him down any day now, because she didn't avoid confrontation like normal people.

No, siree. She came at it with claws and a sledgehammer, a shotgun strapped across her back and a knife holstered at her ankle, in case the first two didn't sufficiently obliterate her opponent.

Okay, okay. She isn't that *bad.* Her most powerful weapon was a sharp tongue and her skill in wielding it. But she cut deep when she wanted to. And he had a feeling she'd want to when they finally spoke.

He'd love to see Neve's keen mouth up against someone like Candice, who had alligator skin. His ex-wife didn't care enough about others' opinions for them to hit their mark. She chocked it up to poor judgment and moved on.

Neve hadn't let Vince's injury slow production. She kept his team busy with the icynene spray foam insulation, which they'd applied only yesterday. The very second, in fact, that Jake finished wiring the cabin for the propane generator and solar panels, and Andrew completed the plumbing connections.

Vince's crew had also begun sanding the exterior walls of the cabin in preparation for the stain and weather-resistant coating they'd apply two weeks from now—granted they stayed on schedule—and measuring and cutting the slats for the secondary wall Duke would begin constructing tomorrow, day one of week five.

The newly insulated walls waited for Duke, dry and exposed, to build the log profile boarding. Then they'd move on to sanding the inside as well. Already, Finn's cabinets were near completion. He and Kay had begun the sanding yesterday. The custom pieces would be varnished and ready to install as soon as the cabin was ready for them.

After five days of playing nursemaid and getting all his updates secondhand from Neve, Duke looked forward to getting his hands dirty on a real project.

He tugged his work boots on and shook his head at his determined ward. "I'm telling you, Vince. You need to stay off that ankle another week. Your team is working fine without you. Hell, today's the last day of the week, anyway. Might as well take it easy. I'm only making the trek to get a second glance at the measurements. I'm sure they're fine, but never hurts to double-check."

Vince grunted. "Exactly."

Duke pursed his lips. He'd practically made the man's point for him. "Fair enough."

Vince didn't wait for approval. He grabbed the crutches resting against the wall of his trailer, where they'd spent most their time since the injury.

Duke realized the old man already had on his boots and cap. He'd be going down to the cabin today, whether Duke agreed or not. They stood together, and Duke clapped him on the back. "You're sure you feel okay?"

"Hell, Duke, today's the first day I feel normal. That lady kept me high as shit those first few days. I think they gave me horse tranquilizers or something." With the crutch gripped tightly beneath his arm, he ducked his head enough to adjust the dirty ball cap he hardly ever took off. "Besides, my mouth works just fine. I can bark orders good as anyone, crutches or not."

Duke nodded as he moved to help Vince navigate the three steps down from the trailer. *Horse tranquilizers. I knew it.* "Listen, I've got to get the blueprints for the secondary wall from my trailer. Think you can navigate the path down to the cabin?"

Vince's frustrated glare met Duke's gaze. "Crutches. Not a damn wheelchair." He shook his head at what he'd taken as some kind of insult.

Duke grinned. "Okay, then. I'll meet you down there." He watched Vince go then turned toward his trailer. Neve plagued his mind, as usual, since their encounter. He'd really screwed up. At the time, the reasons for his dishonesty seemed legit, despite her dire warning about lying to her. Unfortunately, his explanation would only make things worse.

He'd been lying to her since the day they met.

He retrieved the blueprints, which he lazily scanned as he made his way down to the cabin. Neve really did have an eye for space. He'd die before he'd say it to her face, but he'd probably have swapped the kitchen sink to the far wall of the kitchen. It would've made more sense for the floorplan but also added significantly to the plumbing costs.

The cabin buzzed like a hassled beehive. Kay, who looked more like an eleven-year-old every time he saw her, worked alongside Finn, with her sleeves rolled up to her elbows. Their faces masked, electric sanders blasting through the quiet.

Duke wondered what Neve had ordered for the countertop. Granite seemed like overkill, but laminate wouldn't cross her mind unless they'd blown their budget completely. He imagined quartz or stone. He didn't doubt for a minute she'd already taken the measurements from Finn's completed woodwork and was having it custom built.

Inside the cabin, Duke ran a critical eye over the walls. He'd get to know them intimately in the next week. Braces were installed, the spray foam hardened. He spotted Neve but ignored her and the scurry of workmen to duck his head into the bathroom.

No more of him would've fit with the two men working within. Andrew Bale had completed his job, so plumbing was a go. Pipes stuck out of the wall, patiently waiting for someone to plug in the commode and sink.

The rubber membrane in the shower stall had been applied and a drain hole cut. The miniature concrete mixer Duke had noticed out in front of the cabin likely held the batch ready to go down next. Once the concrete had had time to cure, they'd put in the shower stall and hook up the water. Finally, another team would come in and lay the wall-to-wall tile Duke had picked out at the hardware store.

It's all coming together. He had to smile as he left the men to their task. His grin fell away at Neve's voice, raised and edged with real anger.

Duke joined the gathering and leaned against one of the newly constructed walls.

Neve's ever-present clipboard rested on a jutted hip, a hip hugged by a pair of low-rise jeans. She wore a men's loose white button-up, with the tails knotted at her navel. It was the sort of disheveled professional look many aimed for but few achieved. Her hair was tied back into a loose ponytail, a few wavy strands flying free. Even coming apart, she looked amazing and together. Designer to the core.

She all but growled at Vince. "Dedication is all peaches and cream until it's not. This is a workman's comp issue, Taggart. We're liable. You can't work with your injury. Find Duke and have him drive you to town. If you want to work, it'll be with a doctor's signature stating you're healthy enough."

The old man stood his ground with an equally fierce expression. "All due respect, my ankle's been looked at."

A vein popped out on her neck. "By a *cow* doctor. An *unqualified* cow doctor, I'd add."

Vince shook his head. "I ain't filing no paperwork, and I ain't going anywhere."

A moment of silence passed while Neve studied the determined geezer. She set her jaw. "Fine. You can work under one condition."

The old man grunted and issued a challenge. "Name it."

"You sign a waiver clearing Gavin and myself of all liability. You don't want to play by the rules, that's your call. But don't come looking for the playbook when your ankle sours and you're a damn amputee. Put plainly, there won't be anywhere to send that bill."

Unbelievably, Vince cracked a grin. "Deal." They shook on it, Neve's slender hand engulfed by his larger one.

Neve whirled away from him in a huff, muttering unintelligibly under her breath as she glanced at her clipboard. Her gaze came up and slammed into Duke. "You."

He tried on a meek grin. "Me."

"Good. Walls are ready for you. Since Vince is apparently all better, you're free to get to work. A day early suits me fine, if you've got nothing better to do."

Despite the impatient edge to her voice, Duke said what he'd determined to say. Instead of waiting for Neve to track him down and pry an explanation from his fingers, he'd give it willingly. "Actually, I wanted to talk."

Her disinterested golden gaze swept over him before returning to her clipboard. "I'm not your wife or your mother. As far as I'm concerned, those are the only two women a man should ever explain himself to."

Whoa. This didn't come close to what he'd expected. "But you're my friend, and I hurt your feelings. I feel I owe you something."

The Neve he'd momentarily forgotten existed emerged then. She'd been playing nice, he recalled too late, keeping things light while they worked together. Apparently, that deal was off, Gavin or no Gavin.

She laughed, a light tinkling, mocking giggle, lazily letting her head fall back. Then she gathered herself and placed a pitying hand on his shoulder. "Oh, Duke. We're not friends. Do you recall the conversation we once had about your usefulness? If you can't bear to get your hands dirty, go play fetch with Darcy the Pit or something. Anything, really, so long as you're not underfoot." She laughed again, turning away from him.

The men working around them pretended very hard not to hear every word, but each syllable carried in the small area.

With nothing to lose, Duke caught her arm before she could move away. She'd embarrassed him. So what? Backing down now wouldn't take the blush from his cheeks.

Besides, if Vince had the stones to stand up to her, surely Duke could muster the courage. "Why don't you catch me up on everything? I've been outside the loop for five days now." He'd kept tabs easily enough, but maybe something work related would entice Neve to forget she hated him. At least long enough for him to steer the conversation where he wanted it to go.

Neve tugged her arm free and walked toward the gaping space where they'd eventually install French doors. "Your professional interest warms the hard little nugget in my chest I assume is my heart." She glanced back once, as if to see if he followed, and went through the gap, disappearing outside with a sly smile that made him nervous.

Duke trailed after her and stepped outside.

His head spun as he realized he hadn't stepped down a set of steps into the backyard. He stepped onto a *deck*.

No one had ever mentioned a deck. Not in the blueprints, not in any discussions with Gavin over his wish list. Not even in random talk of all the possibilities for the cabin. It stretched from one end of the cabin to the other with a set of three stairs on the far end, giving yard access, and a simple railing enclosing the space. It was huge, nearly a third of the depth of the cabin itself.

He gaped at Neve.

She rested against the railing with a nonchalance that jabbed, no doubt as she intended.

"What in the hell is this?" He hardly recognized his quiet voice. "Gavin didn't ask for this."

"Of course not." She had the nerve to look at him like he'd lost his mind. "It's a gift."

"A gift?" Indignant, frustrated anger bubbled up. "If you want to surprise a client with a gift, you give him a bottle of fine wine. You definitely don't make expensive changes to his house without asking. Are you fucking insane? Gavin's going to flip his lid."

"Quite sane, thank you. You're the one out of your depth and about to embarrass yourself."

The way she took his anger in stride, coupled with her condescension, made him see red. "Me? Out of *my* depth?"

"Absolutely. Hell, I haven't even told you about the hot tub yet."

She was baiting him. She'd intentionally led him to the deck, which she'd managed to keep secret from him throughout its construction, choosing her weapon with uncanny precision.

But this went beyond some little head game. "You've taken Gavin's money and made an unauthorized change to his property. This isn't your house, your money. Who are you to make a decision like this without consulting anyone? Me, maybe. The consultant, handpicked by Gavin to be his ultimate decision-maker. So tell me, Neve, why the hell wasn't I consulted on a thousand-dollar side project?"

She smiled with no humor and hard eyes. "Because you're an idiot. For starters, Duke, you have no idea why you're here. Just why is it so terribly important to Gavin that you signed on for this?"

Duke might've questioned Gavin's motives once or twice, but it hardly had a thing to do with the topic at hand. However, something in Neve's hard stare told him she might have more of an answer than she offered. "He trusts my judgment. Yet another reason why you should've come to me with this."

"I'm not done, sweetie. Let me answer the rest of your questions." She took a moment to readjust her feet, crossing her ankles, getting comfy. "You've wandered into the part of the story where you embarrass yourself, and I'm nothing if not helpful. You ask who I am to make the decision. The one *paid* to make it. I'm in my element, while you're hell and gone from yours. For the sake of illuminating you, let's spell it out. This isn't a restoration. It's the last time I'll say it, Duke. You work with cemented guidelines. For example, before the late eighteenth century, no one knew what the hell a paisley pattern was, so strike that off the design board. Your choices are made for you. My job, now...I don't think you could handle it. The freedom would undo your feeble little mind. In my world, everything is given up to my whim and interpretation. Gavin isn't paying me for my carpentry skill or my way with a sewing needle, he's paying me for my *style*. You're right, this deck isn't in the schematics. But I'm designing a retreat, and that is what I'll build. Gavin will come home to his cabin after a long day of hiking or birdwatching, or whatever the hell he imagines he's going to do out here, and have a Jacuzzi to slide into. To make this happen, I did this thing with my supplies and my budget called *math*. Obviously, it fits within both time and budget constraints."

Duke rubbed his jaw and worked his brain to deny her point. She was right for the most part. Restorations were strict replications. Little freedom to be found, even in the choosing of patterns and materials. Not if he wanted to perfectly mimic the original.

Still, the deck was an outlandish expense, as was a hot tub. "I'm not an idiot, Neve, but you still don't see how you've taken your authority too far." She snapped then, the cool façade of nonchalance falling away as she stepped toward him. She pointed an angry finger in his face. "You are an idiot, Duke. An idiot and a liar."

Anger surged him forward, and it didn't surprise him when she didn't step back or even widen her eyes at a grown man coming at her. "I wouldn't have lied if you weren't such a horrible person who terrorizes everyone you meet! I lied because your last neighbor warned me against getting involved with you. Now who's the idiot?"

The moment the words escaped him, he wanted to suck them right back into his mouth with a vacuum hose and pretend they'd never passed his lips. They were the truth, but a hurtful one he hadn't intended to dish out in anger. His stomach flipped and his throat went dry.

"Now who's the idiot?" Neve quietly posed the question like she truly wondered at the answer, head cocked slightly. Her hands were on her hips, and she swayed idly from side to side. The perfect blankness of her expression unsettled him. Then she met his gaze squarely. "Still you. Because only an idiot walks around with half a story in his pocket and thinks he owns the library."

He struggled with a reply as she strode past him, down the steps and into the yard, where she disappeared around the side of the cabin. Duke cursed, hung his head, and pinched the bridge of his nose.

A big hand came down on his shoulder. Duke glanced up into Vince's disapproving green eyes. "She's right. You're the idiot."

"Of course. Neve's never an idiot."

"She's tough." Vince's gaze swung toward where Neve had disappeared from sight. "Tougher than spit. But she didn't deserve that. Now, I don't much give a damn about whatever personal business is between the two of you, but I know it ain't got no place out here." He paused and squeezed Duke's shoulder. "Besides, if you gotta dig that deep for ammo, boy, it's because you done lost the fight."

* * * *

Son of a bitch.

Neve didn't know if she wanted to thank Duke for finally answering the question burning in her mind since discovering he was straight, or gut him for doing it in front of an audience.

She sighed, disgusted with herself and the scene they'd caused. She had to strong-arm respect from the men, especially Vince's team while he was laid up with his injury. Every inch was gained with a pint of sweat and buckets of well-aimed barbs that made them think twice about questioning her authority. She couldn't do the job without authority. And it wasn't something people handed out—it was something she had to take. Always, every time, at every job.

How much had she lost with Duke's little confession? How many loogies would she have to spit to gain that respect back?

At least she finally had the honesty she wanted. Late, but unshaded by niceties. She couldn't be upset by what Duke had said, only the time and place he'd chosen to say it. He had no right to tell her how to do her job, but the bit about her being a horrible person...well, she hadn't come this far in life by being delusional.

She'd pushed Austin away with her attitude. Hell, Gavin had probably been as straight as a west Texas highway until the day he'd met her. No, she wouldn't be upset with Duke for calling her out on her personality flaws.

But her history with Ernie was something else. If Duke had bothered to get her side of the story, he could've saved himself two years of trouble.

The guy who'd been her neighbor before Duke had been a smooth player who'd talked Neve into a committed relationship—her last, actually. She'd agreed to be exclusive. Ernie hadn't kept his end of the deal, continuing to see a few tarts on the side. He'd deserved everything she'd thrown at him in the aftermath. But for all everyone's opinions about her, all she'd ever had in her arsenal were words. She'd never brought home guys to make Ernie jealous, hadn't scorched his clothes, slashed his tires, thrown pots and pans at his head. She had her spiked tongue, a vibrant, extensive vocabulary, and a knack for keying in on weak spots.

But that was all. It was all she'd ever had. Who the hell was anyone to begrudge Neve her armor?

What had been the cost for Duke to pretend he was gay for years for the sake of avoiding her? What could Ernie have possibly said to him?

Watch it, she's mean. Yeah, she'll call you names. Better steer clear, pal.

Amazing. Utterly amazing. Two years, and she'd never questioned. She'd taken him at face-value. At his word. Damn. Just when she'd thought she'd learned her lesson about trusting people.

"Neve, wait!"

She squeezed her eyes shut. No matter how calmly she wished to confront Duke, the fury simmering in her belly flared at the sound of his voice. She knew herself. She knew her caustic insults came from a deep well of resentment. She'd annihilate him. Whether she willed it or not, her mouth would take over, and she'd shred him into ribbons without ever laying a finger on him. He needed to go away, and he needed to do so for both their sakes.

"Neve, please. Let me apologize."

She kept walking. "An apology won't save you, Duke. The deal's off. By this time tomorrow, you'll be so fucking miserable you'll run home on foot."

"Please." He caught her hand, forcing her to a sudden stop.

Neve almost tripped but caught her balance in time. She whirled on Duke and shoved against his chest with both hands.

With eyes almost comically wide, he fell onto his ass in the dirt and grass. He gazed up at her in astonishment.

"I'm like a museum exhibit, Duke. Look, don't touch, and try to keep your voice down." She strode away from him, resisting the urge to kick dirt in his stupid face. Why did men think a simple word fixed everything? An apology didn't unsay a biting insult—she should know—anymore than it could un-screw a girl at the gym. She didn't often bother with them. She took care to say exactly what she meant and mean every word she said. That was exactly the problem. If she blew up, every syllable she uttered would be utterly, painfully true.

"Neve, stop."

With gritted teeth, she did. "I swear, if you say you're sorry, I'm going to hit you right in your colossally hairy mouth."

He came around to stand in her path, this time careful to avoid touching her. "Please, listen. What I said, it's only partially true. Yes, Ernie told me about what happened between you two after you broke up and warned me to avoid you. But I swear, you weren't the reason I played the gay card. At least, not to begin with. Ernie brought his sister along when he showed me the loft. She kept eyeballing me, and I was still hung up on Candice. I told them both I was gay. Ernie laughed and quit telling me horror stories about you, and his sister rolled her eyes at me." He shrugged like the whole story confused him. "I've been gay ever since. It seemed, at the time, like the answer to staying single and out of the market, avoiding getting too close to anyone."

Neve puffed out her cheeks. "You're still married, Duke. Candice called herself your wife and said she wasn't signing any papers."

Duke's grin had an edge she knew wasn't for her. "Oh, we're divorced, all right, no matter how creative Candice wants to get with her introductions. The papers I sent—"

She didn't care. She couldn't care. Even if he had his reasons, she was talking to a man who'd invested astounding diligence and perseverance into the pursuit of his deceit. Two years. She couldn't wrap her head around it. Every joke about his clothes, every stupid comment about turning him straight—she burned with mortification. "Isn't this exactly the sort of involvement you pretended to be gay to avoid?"

He glanced at his feet and toed a spot on the ground. Then his dark blue gaze met hers. "I'm sorry for what I said."

"And I hope you sleep better. Now, get out of my way. I have somewhere important to be." She stepped around him. She'd wasted enough time caring about Duke, and more than enough wishing he was straight, only to have it come true and mean nothing, anyway.

He followed with an apparent death wish. "Where are you going?"

"Well, Chief, I figure since you're so goddamned smart, you can take care of things here while I find me a rancher to chew up and spit out. Timothy Hux should be back from his well-timed hiatus, and he's going to answer for that trap. If he won't talk to me, he can talk to Red Hill's sheriff."

"You shouldn't go alone. I'll come with you."

She stopped and turned on Duke. "I'm glad you got your feelings about me off your chest. But even horrible people like to feel wanted every now and then. Oddly, Yosemite actually seems to enjoy my company. Maybe he's horrible, too, and it takes one to appreciate one. Either way, it's the sort of change in scenery I need at the moment. And you have a wall to build."

The metaphor wasn't lost on her, but she wouldn't prolong the conversation with a pointless show of wit. This time, when she walked away, Duke stayed put. She ignored the tiny niggle of disappointment and focused instead on her new target.

Tim Hux had a surprise coming, and not the good kind.

* * * *

Yosemite proved easy to find, lounging in a rocker on the front porch when she arrived. High noon. Cowboy lunch hour. He tipped his hat toward her and grinned before biting into a green apple. He took his time chewing, his eyes only landing on her when she crossed the path of his gaze.

She joined him, taking the rocker to his right. "Afternoon, cowboy."

He nodded but didn't turn his gaze from the view of his land in front of him. "Ma'am."

"We need to have a little chat, you and I."

"Sure do. I need to know what you want for supper tonight."

"Tonight, huh?" She was pretty sure she'd been given power over when their dinner date was to occur.

"Well, sure. You're here in the middle of the day. Can't be too much going on at the cabin. I hear your plumbing and electricity is all primed to go."

"You hear a lot."

"Wise choice, the propane generator. But maybe I ought to look into some of them sun panels. Gets hot down here in the valley."

"Actually, I think we should discuss property lines before we start planning a menu. Yours and mine."

Finally, he turned his head and peered at her through eyes squinted against the bright sun. "Is this one of them 'personal space' talks? I'm not the type to force myself on a woman, so's you know." The gleam in his hazel eyes beneath the wide brim of his ten-gallon hat gave him away. He knew what she meant.

But she could spell the situation out for him, too. "I'm talking about the steel trap Vince walked into last week. A brand-spanking-new steel trap. Now, if you want, you can deny the thing belongs to you. I can go into town and come back with the sheriff."

Was it her imagination, or did the rancher blanch? Nope, definitely not her imagination. He went as pale as the moon in full daylight. *Interesting.* Far from evidence, but it fit in nicely with her theory something shady was going on at Lady Killer Ranch. The rancher was hiding something. Maybe a marijuana grove on the property somewhere. Not totally unheard of in these climes.

She continued with an air of benevolence. "Or you can explain to me why the trap was on Gavin's property, and we can sort this out ourselves."

Tim rocked forward and spit a chunk of apple over the porch rail. "I hunt the property. No one's lived in that cabin for decades. I've been hunting the land so long I've forgotten it ain't mine to hunt."

"Not hunting. Poaching."

He lifted a shoulder, nonchalant. "I'll go over the property lines with my crew. Won't happen again. Tell your man I'm sorry and to send his bills my way."

Neve nodded. Seemed fair enough to her. "I'll do that. As for that dinner, I think we can forget about it and call ourselves square."

"Ha." He grinned. "Don't go getting your bargains confused, girly. Less you want to bring me back every last piece of the hayloft you carted off my ranch, dinner's still on. And it's tonight."

Damn it. Well, it'd been worth a shot.

Besides, any man who got away with calling her *girly* with his balls still attached to his body was probably someone she should spend more time with. Neve relaxed into the rocker. "In that case, I want steak. And lobster. And cake for dessert. I won't eat if there isn't cake."

This time, Tim laughed out loud. He rested back in his rocker until they reclined side by side. "I'm glad you like fried chicken and blackberry pie. They're my favorites, too."

Chapter 9

For six days, Duke worked on constructing the secondary walls, a thin layer of log profile boarding to cover the insulation they put in, one board at a time. Over the dry insulation, he hung up sheets of plastic and nailed them down taut to create a barrier. Then each board was measured and nailed to the braces in a brickwork pattern Neve preferred over the straight horizontal alignment. It meant more work, as Vince had to put a team on cutting the sanded wood slats to size to fit the design as Duke measured and marked, but he agreed the design looked better in the space.

The cement in the bathroom had cured and awaited the shower stall. Neve's surprise Jacuzzi had come in, and she'd talked Hux into letting her stash the bulky surprise at the ranch in case Gavin visited the cabin, which he'd threatened once or twice, but hadn't made any hard and fast plans to come check up on them. Duke assumed he'd wait until they were closer to completion.

Most of the interior had been sanded and awaited the final step, a refinishing with varnish to protect and beautify the wood. They remained miraculously ahead of schedule. Even Finn's custom built-ins were stained to match the natural wood inside the cabin and ready for installation. The glass and frame for the front window had arrived and been fitted into place, replacing the tarp material they'd covered the hole with. The window had a darker oak grain than the rest of the cabin, but Neve said she liked the contrast.

Everyone else, including Vince, worked to complete sanding the deck and cutting down the rest of the wood supply from the ranch into baseboards and trim for the interior. They were a purely aesthetic feature to cover the unsightly gaps left between the floor and the wall to allow for seasonal expansion of the wood.

So far, they were a day or two ahead of schedule, despite everything— Vince's injury, Neve and Duke's inability to speak more than two words to each other at a time, and even Neve's new penchant for disappearing nightly to visit Tim Hux at Lady Killer Ranch.

Maybe that was what had kept Duke from showing Neve the French doors. Then again, maybe it had been the mounting depression dragging him into a hole of despair.

Candice refused to sign the papers. His heart grew heavier every time he thought about it. There was nothing he could do. He had no leverage, no means to force her hand.

He hammered the last board into place and stroked his beard as he stood back and studied the final product. A clean job, looked just about the same as it had before, less the few inches the insulation had taken up in the floorplan. Slight enough not to endanger space, and well worth if it Gavin ever used the cabin during the winter.

Neve would be pleased with his work.

Duke ran a hand through his loose hair and sighed. Guilt oozed from his pores every time he looked at her.

She'd warned him. In no uncertain terms, she told him, before the job even began, exactly how she felt about liars. Taking this into account, he knew Neve would never extend an olive branch. If they were ever going to move past this, he'd have to be the one to do the work.

Was she worth the abuse to make it up to her?

Duke tugged the heavy work gloves from his hands and went outside, where the sky had purpled with twilight. In the eastern clearing, Kay, Finn, and a handful of Vince's men continued to work. They chatted and laughed.

A pinprick of envy found its mark as Duke turned away from them and headed up the path toward the road. He wished he had nothing more than the completion of the cabin weighing on him. Hell, or even just a friend, someone to laugh at his stupidity alongside him.

Realizing Neve had provided his only companionship up to this point, he made up his mind. He strode up the path with renewed determination.

Inside their trailer, Neve had her boots on and bent over to nuzzle Darcy the Pit's face.

Saying good-bye, he surmised. "You headed to the ranch?"

Her gaze sprang to his from the sheer force of her surprise. He hadn't said a single word to her in nearly a week, so the reaction was warranted. She stood up straight and moved as though to go right by him without an answer.

He took a step to the side, blocking her path. "Can I have a minute before you go? It's work-related, if that eases the abrasiveness of my request." A hint of bitterness seeped into his voice. Her avoidance was worse than her cutting remarks. "Come with me to the storage trailer. I never showed you what I found." Come to think of it, he hadn't told her about Krandall Beels, either. "Or who I met," he added, watching her carefully for a spark of interest.

Neve had on her poker face. "Hurry up."

Despite the command, he took the time to drop his work gloves on Neve's desk and take a heavy-duty flashlight from one of the drawers.

She waited by the door without comment.

He led her outside, around the three other location trailers parked at the road's end. Two housed Vince and his team, and Kay had solo possession of the last one. For whatever reason, no one had suggested Neve move in with Kay. Judging by Kay's hyperactive tendencies, the arrangement wouldn't have gone over smoothly.

The storage trailer sat where the men had unhitched it the day of Vince's injury. Duke held out a hand for the key to the padlock, which Neve kept in her pocket.

She fished it out, handed the silver key over. Still expressionless.

Where was the angry impatience? The snappy rebukes? Duke checked a sigh and undid the latch. He pulled the heavy door open to reveal the purchases from Thrift House. The door had been placed flat and wrapped in travel blankets for protection. He yanked back the blankets and stepped away for Neve to inspect his offering, shining the beam of the flashlight down on the glass-paned French doors.

She inched closer. Duke didn't have a view of her inspection nor could he see her expression. Several minutes crawled by before she stepped back and stared at him in the near dark. He kept the flashlight's beam pointed downward, even though he was dying to know what her face might give away. He had to force the muscles in his back and shoulders to relax.

"The wood is white." She said it with all the emotion of a toaster.

"I realize it's exactly what you didn't want, but something about the style, the age." He shrugged. He couldn't explain it. "It seems like they belong. I don't know if you've ordered another set of doors—"

"I haven't."

"Okay. Well, if you don't want them, I'll find some use for them. For what it's worth, Kay agreed with me. I probably wouldn't have bought them if she hadn't approved."

"Duke, I almost hate to say this, but they're perfect. The white will add the touch of contrast I've been searching for. The countertops I ordered are a local stone. They're a burnished gray color that will probably blend seamlessly into the cabin. I'm still mad as hell, and I don't consider you a friend, but I guess you're an okay designer. Good call."

Duke grinned into the darkness. He'd take it. At least they were speaking. Sure, her tone was monotonous and devoid of any emotion despite her praise, but they were talking. She was talking. And he wasn't done yet. "Interested in who I met?"

She sighed. "I can't imagine it's anyone too special."

"His name is Krandall Beels. The proprietor of Thrift House."

Silence met him. Neve's feet shuffled, and gravel scuffed beneath her boots. "Beels, huh? That's strange."

"I thought so. Krandall doesn't have any family, and he doesn't seem to know much about Florrie, but he recalls she supposedly owned Beels Cabin at some point. He's not the social type, so the conversation was short and to the point." Duke stuck his head in the storage unit and pulled the protective blanket back over the French doors. He closed the trailer door and shined the flashlight on the lock while Neve re-latched it.

He thought she'd leave then. He didn't have anything to add, but Neve surprised him. When she spoke, they might not have been fighting at all. He could almost pretend things were back to normal.

"Think about it, Duke. Florrie died in that cabin at the hands of Lulu Hux. What are the odds she met another man and had his child? If Florrie had a baby before her death while living at the cabin, the kid had to have been Ben's."

Duke scratched his cheek. "Makes sense. Why suddenly move his mistress onto his property, build her a house, and deed the place over to her unless an heir was involved? It'd be the only way his illegitimate kid would inherit part of the ranch. Sort of puts events in a different light."

"Not only Ben's actions." Neve's breath caught on her realization. "Lulu Hux. She must not have known about the pregnancy."

"I kind of thought that must be the case, too. Krandall's existence suggests Lulu didn't know about the pregnancy. I mean, if Lulu was going to go nuts and murder Florrie, why not kill her before she gave birth?"

Neve's voice lowered. "Maybe infanticide was going too far? Could explain what pushed Lulu over the edge. Maybe she caught sight of Florrie with her baby and puzzled things out. Either way, she'd have easily discovered the land and cabin had been cut from the inheritance due her legitimate kids. That could've been the catalyst."

Her theory made perfect sense but left one burning question. "So, what happened to the baby? Obviously, the baby lived, or Krandall Beels wouldn't exist. It's got to be a succession of boys, or the name would've changed by now. Krandall's grandfather or great-grandfather would have to be the missing baby, right?"

"The baby who lived." Neve snorted. "What in the hell have we stumbled into, Duke? And why do I feel like the locked chest has something to do with all this?"

The chest. He'd forgotten about it. "I still have a meeting scheduled with Cherish Rancourt from the Historical Society. We may learn something yet."

Neve was quiet for a moment. "Do you think it has something to do with the land? Yosemite says the ranch has been sold off in bits and pieces, but the land the cabin sits on belonged to Florrie. So, how did the cabin even end up in circulation? Shouldn't it belong to Krandall?"

"Not if his grandfather sold it."

Her voice went flat with sarcasm. "You think Florrie's baby returned as a grown man to the cabin where his mother was murdered and demanded the deed from Tim's granddaddy so he could sell the place?"

"You got me there." Duke had no clue how land titles and deeds worked. His experience ended with buying his loft, which the realtor had pretty much handled. "I guess we'll never know."

"We might if we get that box open."

A tiny spool of excitement unfurled in Duke's chest. Neve was talking like they were a team again. And the chest might do more than unlock some old, small town mystery—it might bridge the gap he'd put between himself and Neve with his mistake.

Neve sniffed, cleared her throat, and when she spoke again, the dry, emotionless tone returned. "Yosemite is expecting me. If I don't hurry, he'll send Owen up the road on a four-wheeler to check on me." She paused, a hitched breath caught on unsaid words, but released the air without uttering a thing.

Duke wanted to say that suited him fine. They were in a rocky place, but he'd made some headway. Besides, he had plans for the night that had everything and nothing to do with Neve. But what he really wanted was for her to give him something. Throw him a bone. Tell him they'd talk more later. Tell him he was the one liar she'd give another chance. If he were tougher, or more confident he could talk her into it, he might've tried to get her to go back to the trailer with him, and lay all their cards on the table. He couldn't stand how she'd dusted him off her hands like dirt.

But he wasn't confident. Not even a little. He couldn't explain why she brought him so low with her dismissal, or why it mattered that they fixed whatever broke between them. "I don't know how good your night vision is, but the rental car is parked about eight yards south from here. See you later, Neve."

She might've raised a hand in farewell. Maybe not. The darkness gave nothing away.

Duke turned back toward the trailers and tried not to rub his hands together. The bottle of whiskey he normally reserved for a completed renovation beckoned like a sultry dancer, promising things it wouldn't deliver. When he awoke tomorrow, his ex-wife would still be refusing to sign the papers, and Neve would still hate him, but at least he'd have a hangover to excuse his misery.

* * * *

Neve returned from the ranch late that night, stuffed like a primo sausage. Not once in her life, not even as a child, had she had pie made from scratch set before her by the same hands that had produced it.

Her mother was the head of the Psychology Department at Colorado State University in Denver. She didn't bake pies, nor do much of anything else in the kitchen besides reach for the silverware when Dad came home with takeout. Ever since Neve's first taste of Timothy's homemade blackberry pie, she couldn't seem to quit the habit. Tonight, Laurel had made blueberry cobbler from their very own blueberry patch. Neve had almost cried into her dish.

Sobbing delicious, the latest in culinary descriptive terms.

Despite the distinctly shady side to her little rancher buddy, Neve had a hard time saying no to Hux's invitations. Being wanted somewhere felt good, and spending time with a man who appeared to enjoy her company and liked to ask her questions about her job, like what inspired her and what drove her creative process, felt even better. He laughed off her snarky, barb-wired tongue like a fly buzzing in his ear. She'd have to dig pretty damn deep to offend Yosemite, and that knowledge set her at ease.

She hoped Duke would be passed out so she could slip inside with the late hour of her return unnoticed. But as she came closer, she took note of the lights glowing from within. Smothering a groan, Neve went inside and nearly shrieked at the stranger sitting on Duke's cot.

Except...

Except not *a stranger.* Duke.

Neve approached him. He stank and his eyes were unfocused. "You're drunk." She glanced around the room and spotted the half-empty whiskey bottle next to the small steel sink. "You got drunk and shaved your beard clean off. I can't believe it." His long, grizzled beard gone, like it never existed. She stepped closer. "Are those..."

No. Surely not. She inched closer, reached out with a timid forefinger and touched one. Goddamn dimples. "You've had dimples this whole time."

He stared at her with eyes that seemed to change from dark blue to black but offered no response.

"Why did you do this?"

His lips moved. Lips she could really see now, set on a wide jaw.

She'd imagined how he'd look without his beard a thousand different ways, but always secretly suspected he'd been hiding a weak chin or an unsightly skin condition. But no. The bastard had been hiding dimples and Brad Pitt's jaw the whole time. She regarded him with undisguised interest in his weakened state.

She should kiss him now and get it out of her system. When he squealed in horror and backed away, it'd be the final peg in his rejection, and probably enough to cure her of her stupid crush.

"You shouldn't look at me like that." His voice came out raspy and an octave deeper than usual.

Her skin broke out in goose bumps. She stepped away, dropping her hand abruptly.

His expression went from blank to despondent, almost beaten. His eyes were red-rimmed like he'd been fighting back tears. Then he spoke, saying all the things Neve had no desire to hear. But she didn't stop him, either.

"She left me for our widowed neighbor. My fault, really. Vale House took every minute of my day. I was never home. No kids. Just the dogs to keep her busy. She was alone all the time. And Jon, well, he's a good guy. I'm not that drunk, actually. I poured out the first drink. But not the second or third."

"Or fourth or fifth," she muttered.

A grin ghosted over his mouth. His eyelids drooped. He sat back with the slow, tired motion of someone on the downswing of a hard buzz.

She'd looked forward to going straight to bed, but she couldn't leave Duke like this. "Come on, let's get your boots off." She crouched and began to untie his laces.

"Neve, why are you the way you are? What did your parents do to make you like that?"

She stiffened, then decided the question was a fair one. Not that she gave much credit to psychoanalysis. "Nothing, Duke. They did nothing. They were honest with each other, always, and honest with me. When I went to college, the number of liars I met astounded me. Girls who pretended they liked me when they didn't. Boys who thought talking about the universe would make them seem smart and get them in my panties. There are no excuses for who I am, or what I choose to accept in this life. I choose not to accept liars. The rest is just my personality, and we all have to deal with it." She allowed herself a wry grin. "Even me."

He didn't reply but leaned over and helped her untie and remove the second boot. When he sat up again, he patted the spot next to him.

Neve sat. Part of her was still spellbound by his clean-shaven face. She couldn't help herself. She traced her fingers across his jaw. "Why'd you do this?"

He started as though he'd forgotten, and rubbed his face with fervor when she drew her hand away. "Because I'm not getting her back. I quit shaving the day I left, but there's no homecoming. Because Candice..." He came back with renewed energy seconds later. "Whatever your parents did, I'd like to hire them to raise my kids. If I have any."

Stunned, Neve stared at him as he blinked lazily at the far wall and spoke mostly to himself.

"There's something pretty fucking great about knowing where you stand with a woman. No guessing games, no undertones I can't understand for the life of me. Neve Harper doesn't tell a man she's fine if she isn't fine. No, not Neve. Neve spells out the problem in glowing letters before a guy has the chance to ask what's wrong. It's great. If Candice had been anything like that, we might still be married, you know it? No, really. She could've *said* something. But no, she suffered in silence. Slunk off with the neighbor. And then took everything that mattered to me." A lengthy pause lapsed before Duke continued on his tangent. "That's why I quit the job. Something in my personal life goes to hell every time I get involved in a project. I think I'm cursed." He shocked her once again by sliding away from her then laying down until his head rested in her lap. "You have incredible legs. I have to pretend to tie my shoe for an excuse to stare at the ground when you wear that one skirt. You know the one? It's green and looks like crushed velvet. It's not fair to walk around with material a man is dying to touch wrapped across your ass."

Neve's mouth fell open.

Duke closed his eyes. "Oh, God, and that stupid fucking bra. The yellow one you made me fix. Just burn it, please. I can't stand it. I have dreams about that damn bra. It kills me. You joked all the time about converting me, but you never even tried. I wouldn't have lasted a second if you'd ever put any real effort into it, I swear. I'd have fallen on my knees and begged for it with the right word."

He kept talking, the words coming slower and less coherent as he rambled on.

Neve didn't interrupt. She stroked his shoulder and listened as nonsense bubbled up from his whiskey haze, and tried to reconcile the gibberish with the man she thought she knew.

"Glass-topped stoves. The worst. Everyone hates those. Ban them. She liked it. I hate that stove. Fuck her. I'm gonna fight. Neve…I'm gonna fight. I'll get her back. I'm gonna get her back…"

Neve's stomach tied itself into knots as Duke passed out in her lap. She should be used to the feeling by now. Still, it crushed her. Always did, when she knew a man liked what they saw, but hated what was underneath the wrapper. So, Duke was attracted to her. Big deal. Sex was easy, uncomplicated. Maybe it said more about him, that'd he have sex with a woman he didn't even like, than it did about her—that she wouldn't hesitate to give into a man who didn't like her.

* * * *

Neve didn't recognize the shiny black Ford when she pulled up, but the Georgia license plate gave away Candice's arrival.

Had to be something. The sixth week of renovation had passed without a single hitch. It'd gone so perfectly according to plan, Neve had taken a day to herself and gone into town for ice cream and a trip to Thrift House, where she'd met the tight-lipped Krandall Beels. She learned nothing more than what Duke had already told her. Now she'd returned only to find the day was about to get marginally more difficult.

If the vehicle hadn't given it away, the raised voices from within the trailer would have. Neve didn't bother announcing herself or pretending Duke had any right to privacy in their shared living space. She opened the door, expecting to garner the immediate attention of Candice and Duke.

Instead, she stepped inside and gasped.

The biggest dog she'd ever seen sat on the sofa. Actually *sat* on the sofa, its front paws reaching easily to the floor. A Great Dane. *The* greatest *Dane, by the look of her.* Certainly female with her ten saggy teats drooping onto the sofa.

Poor Darcy the Pit had her ears back and her tail tucked between her legs in supplication. Her tail thumped against the floor when she spotted Neve in the doorway, and she wriggled toward her master.

Neve scratched her behind the ears and tutted. *If anyone knew what a wimp you are, you'd wipe out the unfair reputation of your breed overnight.* She cooed and instructed Darcy the Pit to lie down, which sent her scrambling toward Neve's room at the rear of the trailer.

It left Neve facing the giant sitting pooch, a high-strung Duke, and an angry woman with a headful of frizzy red hair a gorgeous copper color Neve suspected was the real deal, not courtesy of a colorist. Her suspicions were confirmed by Candice's finely plucked copper eyebrows over pale green eyes. Sea-foam green, were they a paint card.

Candice Kennicot was a looker. Were Neve the envious type, she might be tempted to wish she had Candice's full mouth, perky nose, or porcelain skin. Instead, she decided personality counted for a lot, and Candice's screwed-up face did little to make her attractive.

They both stared at Neve like she owed them an explanation for her presence. Which, naturally, pissed her off. "I live here, you know. Nice to meet you, Candice."

Candice's features relaxed. "You're Neve."

"I am." She didn't offer her hand, because she doubted Candice would uncross her arms to take it. Instead, she nodded toward the elephant in the room. "Could one of you explain the horse sitting on my sofa?" She didn't wait for an answer to offer her hand to the dog for a good sniffing.

Duke spoke up to introduce them at the same time the dog's massive tongue unrolled from its maw to run across the back of Neve's hand in canine acceptance. "This is Hannah. She's a retired show dog." He shot his wife an icy glare. "She's recently retired from breeding as well."

Candice met his gaze squarely. "The hell she is, Duke. She's eight and can safely breed until she's ten."

"Look at her, Candice! She's fucking exhausted, having fewer and fewer live pups with each litter. Hell, you've got three four-week-old pups at home. Instead of prepping them for show, how about you start grooming Hannah's replacement?"

The desperate anger in Duke's outburst surprised Neve. She stared at him. *I'm going to fight for her.*

He'd been talking about a damn dog all along. She almost laughed out loud.

She rubbed Hannah's muzzle and begrudgingly accepted her esteem for Duke as it rose beyond what she ever expected to feel for him. She liked him. He was easy on the eyes. He made her laugh. He took her attitude in stride most of the time, stood up for himself when it mattered. He was a hell of a designer, but now...well, now, he had Neve's respect as a man. "So, you are divorced."

His wild eyes snapped to her. "What? Of course I am. I told you. Had I known Hannah would be taken advantage of to such degree, I would've never left without her."

Candice jabbed a finger toward him. "Bullshit, Duke. You're sick of paying the vet bills. Admit it. You're trying to get out of the alimony."

Neve looked from one to the other. "Seriously? Alimony payment? For a dog?"

Duke sighed wearily as his anger seemed to leave him. He rubbed his forehead. "Hannah isn't just some dog. Her lineage is unparalleled. Her papers go back further than any other Great Dane in the circuits these days, and she's been winning dog shows since she was born. There's money in it, but it also costs a fortune." He pinned Candice with another hot stare. "We agreed to retire Hannah from showing after another year, which a judge decided I'd be financially responsible for since Candice was awarded custody."

"You're serious?" Who'd ever heard of such a thing? "You had an actual custody hearing for Hannah?"

Duke's glare swung to her, lit with challenge. "You wouldn't fight for Darcy?"

She'd never thought about it. But, yeah. Hell yeah, she would. She'd go to insane lengths for Darcy the Pit. Impractical, insane lengths. *Like a custody trial.* She looked at Duke, and something warm and terrible spread through her…something more than respect.

Duke pressed on, his anger growing again as he spoke. "Hannah's worth money, but her pups are worth more. See, Candice got clever after the hearing. She retired Hannah from shows but has continued breeding her. I'm required to pay the showing costs of one pup per litter. I think you've milked it long enough, Candice. Hannah deserves to retire."

Neve chewed her lip and worked over Hannah's great big ears. A tongue like a flank steak rolled out of her giant mouth.

"She's how old? Eight, you said?"

Candice and Duke both eyed her.

Candice spoke first. "This is a perfectly healthy dog. Do you have any clue what her pups are worth?"

"Enough to pay vet bills," Duke snapped. "And showing fees."

Candice flushed but kept her attention on Neve.

Neve imagined what she'd do if this were Darcy the Pit. Hot anger flared, along with a sudden urge to flatten Candice. "Let me tell you what I think. I think Duke would gain from taking you back to court. Unless you get a judge who hates animals, they'll side with him."

Candice's jaw set. "Am I mistaken, or are you inadvertently saying I hate animals because I'm still breeding her?"

Neve tilted her head and let her eyebrows come together in puzzlement. "It was hardly inadvertent. But you being a terrible dog owner isn't the issue here. The issue is how you're making twice the income the judge awarded you. You're taking Duke's alimony payments, but I'd wager you're not showing Hannah's pups. You're selling them."

Candice's deep flush matched her hair.

Duke's voice dropped to a confused murmur. "Not showing them? But their papers, their bloodline, it's...wait." His head snapped up. "Forget twice the income. You're making thrice the income."

Neve nodded. "Basically, yeah. Your alimony for Hannah, plus the money for the cost of imaginary dog shows, and finally, her additional income from selling off the purebred Great Danes. Given the lineage you bragged about, I'd definitely make this a court issue."

Duke shook his head at Candice. "I should've known you'd find some new way to screw me over."

"I can't afford the shows anymore, Duke. Jon's life insurance policy from his wife's death is spent, and he's having a hard time finding work. And with Hannah getting older, the vet bills to keep her healthy enough to breed have grown. I need the money."

Neve let herself blend into the background and watched the proceedings like a tennis match.

Duke's steady gaze didn't waver from his ex-wife. "You know, Candice, a long time ago, I would've died before I'd admit to anyone I missed my dog more than I missed you after you left me. Now, it makes perfect sense. You're going to sign the papers. You're going to give Hannah back to me, and then you're going to leave. You're going to do it, or I'm going to take you to court."

She studied him and chewed her lip. "So, what am I supposed to do for money? Married for five years, and what do I get out of it?"

"No more than what you've already taken," he growled. "You're Jon's problem. Not mine."

Neve patted the top of Hannah's head and moved to stand beside Duke in a show of support. Then, she drove the final nail. "Don't be so kind, Duke. Take her to court regardless. Not only will you be reimbursed financially, I bet you can get custody of the last litter as well. Judges are kind of like cops in that they hate being lied to. They especially hate when people find loopholes in their judgments."

Candice didn't quiver or back down from Neve's commanding stare. But she knew when she was beaten. She met Duke's gaze with something like begrudging acceptance. "I'll sign the papers, Duke. Under one condition."

Neve grinned and didn't wait for Duke to ask. "You want to keep the last litter."

Candice looked at her. "You're an insufferable person. Someone ought to tell you if you've never heard it."

"Not normally to my face. I appreciate it."

She ignored Neve and switched her attention back to Duke, whose face registered disbelief. "You're right, Duke. I'm no concern of yours. No more than I was when we were actually married."

Duke squared his shoulders. "I guess there's no better way to learn exactly where you stand with a man than giving him an ultimatum. It doesn't say much about you that I chose Vale House."

Candice glowered. Neve didn't detect any hurt in her pale green eyes, but plenty of ire. "It says a great deal about you, though. I hope like hell you do *her* better than you did me."

It took Neve a second to realize Candice meant her.

"She doesn't strike me as the type to sit by idly while her man loves something more than he loves her, whether it's a house or a damn dog. But then, I didn't suspect such low self-respect from myself, either. You spent five years on Vale House. It took me four to figure it out." Candice stalked toward the door and glanced back over her shoulder. "You keep Hannah. You'll need her when another woman refuses to come second to your other passions. I didn't bring the paperwork along. You'll have to trust I'll mail it."

In the silence that followed Candice's exit, Duke's gaze seemed to alight on every available spot in the room except Neve's.

And on the inside, she burned.

Everything inside her was on fire. The good kind and the bad kind, twirling together in a miserable tango. Her heart tripped over itself in her chest as she thought back to every time Duke had suffered her company just to see Darcy the Pit. She thought of Duke last week, drunk and fighting back tears over a dog. A fucking dog.

Nothing else in the world could have done it. Nothing else could have made her realize her feelings for him were deeper than she'd ever let on. She remembered meeting Austin for drinks after firing Ruby that day. She'd sat there, a young, handsome playmate at her side, but her mind on Duke. Every minute with him since had just been digging the hole deeper.

Fury swept into the heady mix of emotions in her breast. He'd fired an arrow into her weak spot without even realizing it, and she'd be the one to pay for it.

I'm falling for someone who's already rejected me. Well, fuck you, Duke Kennicot. I'm going to get what I want from you, and then I'm going to give you what you want.

Neve stepped close to him. Well within his personal space. His gaze landed on hers, only to slide from her face. Perhaps it'd be easier for him to stomach if he avoided eye contact.

She let her anger and hurt drive each small, painful movement. From the fingers that gripped his collar, to her mouth as she tilted her head and pressed it against his, hard and desperate.

A flash of hot energy shocked her when he gripped her hips and pulled her tight against his body. Heat pooled between her legs when he moved his mouth to her throat, hot breaths on her neck, sending chills down her back.

"Don't fuck with me, Neve." Like a threat, his left hand slid between her legs. His thumb smoothed over her and applied pressure. Enough to take the breath from her lungs when he found his mark. "I told you, I wouldn't hesitate."

She refused to submit control. Neve moved her hips against his hand, giving consent while demanding more. Let him make no mistake about who would do the taking tonight. She ran one hand through his hair, wrapping strands around her fists. The other slid down to tease the ridge of his erection. She licked the side of his neck until her lips reached his earlobe.

"I've always wondered if you were the generous type," she breathed, flicking her tongue over his skin, and rode his hand with smooth, deliberate undulations. "Are you generous, Duke?"

His breathing turned ragged, his answer choked. "Yes. Hell yes."

She bit his earlobe, released his hair, and covered his hand with hers, pressing him harder into the sweet spot between her legs. "Show me."

Chapter 10

Duke's brain, instantly searching for Neve's voice, came awake at a glacial pace. By the time he rubbed the sleep from his eyes, he registered he was alone.

Alone in Neve's bed.

He turned the fact over in his head and let it settle. What the hell had he been thinking?

He wanted to berate himself, but he dug deep and couldn't find an ounce of regret. Despite everything, he'd been fantasizing about last night for two years. He didn't consider himself a weak man, but when temptation came knocking—and biting and licking and touching—he didn't have the strength to deny himself.

Duke ran through the renovation schedule to take his mind from Neve for a second. His body might be purring with satisfaction, but his head and his chest were at war, and he wasn't quite sure what they were fighting about.

Today marked the first day of their seventh week. The interior walls would get their coats of varnish, and the custom cabinets would be installed. All the baseboards and trimmings Finn and Kay had painstakingly carved, sanded, and stained would go in. Neve would want to put in the French doors immediately, as they were one of the only things they were behind on. The stone countertops Neve had ordered should arrive sometime this week, along with every major appliance. A separate team would work to stain the exterior cabin walls and add a layer of weatherproofing.

He scratched his chin, momentarily startled by the lack of rough beard. He ran a hand over the foreign smoothness.

Anxiety rode him hard. He should find Neve. She wasn't some girl he met at a bar. She probably hadn't forgiven him entirely for the massive lie he'd told, but last night had happened. More than ever, she had a reason to talk to him.

Shit. Last night made things more complicated than ever. He was still trying to repair their friendship. What did sleeping together do to that? Help or hurt? It was just sex—it was always just sex with Neve. Why was he so worried she'd want more than that?

He sat up and swung his legs over the side of the bed, only to find Hannah curled up on the floor. He grinned, his feet hovering over her. He tucked them back onto the bed and leaned over on his stomach to rub the Dane's massive head. He also owed Neve the world's longest, wordiest thank-you note.

Finally, he hauled himself from bed and gulped the last of the cooled coffee from the carafe. He paused in taking the last sip when the front door slammed open with the hurricane-force winds.

Ah. Not a hurricane. Just Neve. She stood battle-ready in worn low-rise jeans and a loose gray T-shirt smudged with dirt. She had a strange glow in her amber eyes.

They reminded him of the vibrant yellow and gold of autumn leaves. He'd confronted the idea of talking to Neve with a bravery and confidence he no longer felt. "Hey."

Seriously? The morning after, and all I got is "hey"?

Her gaze roamed from his bare feet, over his form-fitting boxer briefs, and came to rest on his face. Hard, unyielding.

Duke had a bad feeling. Unease settled over him like a fine mist.

"I'm here to give you a progress report to pass on to Gavin when he calls today, which he will."

"You've been keeping track of his calls?"

She blinked. "He's the client. Of course."

It took him a second to register the perfect blankness of her features. Intense but giving nothing away. No small smile to acknowledge what had passed between them. Not even a twinkle in her eyes. Like it never happened. The sting of it caught him off guard. They were right back at square one.

From her desk, she snatched up a pad of yellow legal paper and a red pen, and tossed them at Duke.

He caught them against his chest, the pen clumsily clutched against the pad.

Neve didn't hesitate but began her report immediately. "Sanding has been completed on interior walls, and the varnish process has begun. Shower stall's in, and the bathroom is complete, with the obvious exception of baseboards and trim, which will go in today. I need to make a final buying trip in order to purchase basic necessities, such as towels, bedding, and additional small kitchen essentials, most of which I expect will be available at the hardware store in Red Hill. The last of the reclaimed wood from Hux's ranch is being made into a shelving unit to use in place of a headboard. Mattresses will arrive along with our large appliances. The refrigerator, stove, and dishwasher are all stainless steel, overlaid with burnished copper accents I had custom-ordered. Another tiny surprise for Gavin." Finally, her expression changed. Unfortunately, it was for the worse as her thin lips spread into a sardonic smile. "Gee, I'm sorry. Once again, I failed to get your approval before making a decision. Apologies."

He stared. Couldn't think of a single thing to say.

"In the meantime, the French doors have been installed," she continued. "Vince is sealing them. The deck has been sanded, but I've decided against staining it to match the exterior. We'll finish the surface but leave the natural color of the old barn. It'll contrast nicely."

Well, he had to hand it to her; like the inside of the cabin, there was a certain feel from the old wood. To look at it, and see its age and flaws.

"As you well know, the staining process is one of the most finicky, difficult undertakings on this project. Six days of meticulous work and care to properly stain the outside of the cabin. If you deign to join us anytime soon, there's a need for extra hands. But don't stress yourself. I certainly don't mean to impose on your morning off."

He struggled to come up with something, anything, to show he had his head in the game, as much a part of the project as Neve or Vince. "You're sure about the dark brown for the exterior? The cabin's got a hint of red in it. I thought you might go with a cherry finish."

"Ah, back to the whole 'too much freedom' thing. The sheer amount of options I have is overwhelming, but here's a free lesson in restraint. It's all about the blend. Like a woman's rouge. Too much would gaudy up the place. The exterior deserves the same finesse we've put into the inside, and the dark tone will contrast beautifully with the light natural wood of the steps and decking. The red highlights will come through if we dial back on the number of coats we apply, and they'll be just that—highlights." She turned, an abrupt about-face, and exited the trailer as swiftly as she'd entered.

Duke reeled.

It was one thing for her to ignore what happened between them. But this wasn't dismissal or avoidance. The absence of warmth struck him as almost cruel. It snuck up on him, a slow dawning; he hadn't been worried that Neve would expect more now they'd slept together. He was worried she'd want less. Less than he wanted.

Duke glanced at the pad still clutched to his chest with the sense of having survived a small natural disaster. He hadn't written a single thing.

* * * *

Duke picked up on the sound of gravel in the distance the minute he stepped outside. Maybe Tim coming over from the ranch, or a few of Vince's guys returning from Red Hill with additional supplies. It seemed like they were forever in need of something. Extra screws, replacement bulbs for the electric lanterns they hung inside the cabin at night to illuminate the workspace.

Darcy the Pit took off running down the path toward the cabin. Hannah bounded after her, slower, but easily making up the distance with her longer strides.

Duke let them go and waited to greet the new arrival. Besides, he was in no hurry to spend the day tiptoeing around Neve. His little revelation back in the trailer effectively put the brakes on his desire for a heart-to-heart.

To his surprise, the dogs came loping back up the hill, Neve a short distance behind them. At the same time, the vehicle came into view and parked near the end of the cul-de-sac.

It shouldn't have shocked Duke when Gavin alighted from the passenger side, and a female version of him exited from the driver's side. He glanced back at Neve. She wasn't going to like this. He hitched his chin toward her in greeting and nodded toward their visitors.

Neve reached him, her mouth a grim line as Gavin and his sister approached. "You knew about this? And who's this he's brought along? Has Gavin got a secret wife, too?"

"Hell no, I didn't know he was coming. And that's Terri, his sister." Duke had met Terri once. She and Gavin weren't twins, but they should've been. They had a similar manner, bobbing and nodding their heads as they spoke, and resembled each other in both their blond hair, pale blue eyes, and friendly, confident personalities.

Neve's irritation etched itself plainly onto her face, but Duke didn't have an opportunity to say anything before Terri and Gavin reached them, all big smiles. She took point after brisk introductions were made and guided them as a group down to the cabin.

Gavin didn't seem particularly interested in anything. Not the cabin, not the work being done, and not the property lines Neve pointed out as they walked around the acreage. Neve also made a point to inform Gavin of his neighbor, Tim.

"Oh, he sounds friendly," Terri chimed in as she ran a bored gaze over their surroundings.

Duke scratched his bare skin where shaving had left him irritated. Bored. That was it. Gavin and Terri were both bored out of their minds.

"Oh, he is *delightful.* And handsome to boot." Neve jumped into acting her part with a little too much relish, and no small edge of something dangerous lurking on the edges of her words.

Last night had been a surreal thing, unlike anything Duke had experienced. Angry sex made him think of whips and handcuffs. If someone had told him there was such a thing as *emotionally* angry sex, he'd have doubted it. Now, he knew better. Heat spread up from his neck. Probably hadn't been a healthy thing, but the urgency, the hunger, the taking…God help him, it turned him on.

Today, Neve wore the same anger on her shoulders, only the emotion had had time to marinate overnight, apparently, growing fiercer and heavier.

Something like dread settled in Duke's gut, despite his vivid memories of last night. If his instincts were on point, this trip of Gavin's might have a few ugly surprises for them all.

Finally, Neve led them to the rear of the cabin.

Duke swallowed when the brand new deck came into sight.

Gavin's dropped jaw and bugged out eyes only gave away his astonishment at what Neve had done. A few taut seconds passed where Duke could hardly breathe, and Neve waited with challenge in the lift of her chin. Terri idly glanced around, unaware of the subtle suspension of time.

The moment of truth arrived on Gavin's cry as he found words. "How fantastic! Wow, Duke." He shook his head in awe. "What a fabulous idea. I knew I had to hire you. I just knew it."

Neve flipped her hair and stared, her expression giving nothing away.

Duke cleared his throat and prepared to eat crow. "Neve's idea, actually. Not mine. And you're right, it was a good one."

Neve wouldn't meet his gaze. It'd be too much like thanking him for what was clearly her due.

Gavin ignored her still and wagged a finger in Duke's direction. "Ah, I should've known. Duke here is a traditionalist, of course. Still, I must give credit where it's due." He slid a hand onto Duke's shoulder. "Hiring Neve was genius. She's exactly what this place needed, don't you think? Listen, I have an idea. Let's take a day off, huh? The four of us. You ladies can go into town and do some shopping and have lunch. Duke and I will stay here and talk shop."

Terri nodded eagerly, her smile bright. She might not be so excited once she saw the slim pickings in Red Hill. And she didn't strike Duke as one to enjoy a flea market.

Neve's face settled into a stony glare, and Duke realized what Gavin had done. He was dismissing Neve like she were an extra stagehand. But she was the director.

And by the look of it, Neve wasn't going to take it on the chin. "That's not happening," she intoned in a low voice. She managed a small apologetic smile for Terri, whose face fell. "I'm in the middle of heading a renovation. I'll be free this evening, if you'd like to get dinner, but, in the meantime, I'm afraid Duke is the only person here with nothing to do."

Gavin came uncomfortably close to scoffing. "Oh, come on, Neve."

Her stance changed. Hip cocked, arms crossed, chin hitched. Then a bazooka shot from her mouth, and none of them were prepared for it. "Mr. Chambers, I understand you'd like some alone time with Duke, but entertaining your sister isn't on my agenda. Frankly, I'm offended you assume it would be."

Alone time...what the hell is she talking about?

Even behind his tanned face, a deep flush of red welled up from Gavin's neck to take over his face. Terri seemed to struggle with something in her throat.

Duke stared at Neve, waiting for an explanation of some kind.

She didn't give one, but had a glare laden with meaning for Gavin before uncrossing her arms and giving them all a jaunty little wave as she made to leave them. "I'm glad you like the deck, Gavin."

She left the three of them in strained silence.

* * * *

"This," Neve breathed, running a hand over the scarred, paint-flecked white door with the perfect diamond panes of old, aged glass, "is so perfect. How can Duke be so stupid and smart at the same time?"

To her surprise, Kay didn't jump into a long diatribe in an attempt to answer the question. The girl was focused entirely on the task at hand. Two of Vince's men held up the cabinet structure, while Kay drilled through the back, mounting it to the cabin's wall. Her short hair had grown some since her arrival, and the few inches of pale strands stuck up at odd angles, creating something of a manic look about her. It worked well with her personality.

Neve had to admit she liked this more sober side to Kay.

Kay pulled her head out from the cabinet and passed the drill down to Finn, who waited behind her with a measuring tape and the shelving supports, which he dropped into her waiting palm. Her eyes never left her work. "On this end, there are no space issues. However, in the corner, I had to get creative."

Oh, boy. Neve couldn't complain much about whatever solution Kay had rendered, given they were her own weakness. She had to trust her assistant. For the next hour, Neve watched her command the guys at her disposal, issuing short, terse directives with single-minded concentration. She measured and set steel support pieces, slid the gleaming wooden shelves into their slots, and moved on to the next installation in an unbroken flow of movement.

Finally, they moved to the corner. The sink had been installed against the new wall, leaving an odd length of counter on either side.

Kay grinned as Finn left and came back with a tiered shelf split in half and reconnected at a ninety-degree angle to set into the corner. The base started out wide, each shelf narrowing until the top had but a small ledge, large enough to hold the tiniest of trinkets. Kay hammered nails through the strategically placed pre-drilled holes. Once mounted, she stood back to study her handiwork, then dug in her pocket.

She pulled out a small white stone. Quartz. "I found this outside in the dirt. I kept it for a souvenir, but when Finn and I came up with this design, I realized this last tiny shelf needed something special." She smiled at Neve and placed the small mineral rock on the last ledge, where it perched like the star on a Christmas tree.

Neve found herself nodding. "Well done."

Actually, everything was well done. The cabinets and counters had been built in sections, so each drawer and storage area had been designed specifically for the space it inhabited. No wasted space, no false drawers.

"Seriously, well done."

Kay beamed, and Finn grinned at her with pride. They made quite the team.

A spark ignited in the back of Neve's mind. She shook hands with Kay and Finn and congratulated them both on their successful project. "Now, let's hope you didn't screw up the measurements for the fridge and stove. Know where I can find Vince?"

* * * *

Vince had his team unloading the large appliances from one of the stationery storage trailers. Large woven belts with heavy-duty fasteners were tossed over the appliances, still wrapped in their protective plastic sheets from the manufacturer and secured to dollies maneuvered by two men. The fridge, electric range, and shower stall were all ready for installation. As soon as Gavin got out of the way, they'd get the hot tub plugged in as well.

Vince had the look of a man about to be released from a debt.

Neve supposed he was. Once the big stuff was handled, he and his team would move on. She punched his shoulder. "You look awfully smug."

He grunted. "I'm pleased." He lifted one shoulder. "I didn't know if you could save this dump. Now I'm not convinced it's the same cabin."

"Yeah, well, it's a bit too soon for me to rock back on my heels and congratulate myself. You, however, deserve a cold beer." She gave him a sideways glance. "You get to Little Rock often?"

Vince couldn't quite hide his grin. "Couple times a year, maybe."

"You know, before I took this job, I'd been hunting for a new team."

"Yeah?" He met her gaze. "What happened to your old one?"

"Mutiny." She shrugged. It didn't bother her so much now. "I was due for an upgrade anyway. I've decided I'm going to keep Kay, if she wants the job permanently." Since it wasn't in her nature to beat around the bush, Neve got to the point. "I like you, Taggart. And Kay likes Finn. We'd make a nice little family. Don't you think? There's the part where you'd have to relocate to Little Rock, but there's never a shortage of work. I mean, unless you really *love* working on cabins—"

"I hate cabins."

She nodded. "I'll admit to being somewhat indifferent before this job."

"And now?"

"Now I can't wait to do my next inner-city loft."

Vince's grunt was different this time. A little bit disappointed with a pinch of hopeful. "I ain't no use in a loft, and neither are my men. We build houses."

Neve lifted an eyebrow, sensing more. "And…"

"And you design them, don't you? Seems to me the math is pretty damn simple. You want a minute to work it out?"

She understood well enough but bobbed her head anyway. She didn't need to do the math, only decide if she liked what the equation added up to.

Vince silently withdrew from her side, leaving her to ponder the noisy men shouting orders and grunting from their physical efforts.

Up until this cabin, she'd only ever moved walls to suit her design purposes—redefined space. She'd never imagined a house from the studs on up. What could she do with a blank template on an empty lot of land and a hearty, capable team at her fingertips? Duke's experience would come in handy.

Neve bit her lip. Or would it? Did she only think so for an excuse to ask him to join their team? A professional reason to ask him to stay near, to stay in her life, despite how she shoved him away. She wiped sweat from her brow. It was the dumbest thing ever, but the big, stupid dog had done her in. She'd been waiting for a reason to love Duke, and he'd given her the only one in the world that could've accomplished the feat of tearing down that last wall of reserve.

The whole *gay* thing…well, what had he done, really? Lied about who he was attracted to. But he hadn't changed since she'd discovered the truth. He hadn't faked his personality, his love for Darcy the Pit, or his patience and cool temperament that were a perfect foible to her trigger-happy temper and sharp-edged personality. He hadn't pretended to be someone else. She'd liked him when he was gay, had wished many times he were straight. How could she like him any less now?

She liked Duke but hated the lie. Hated the rejection. And she'd be damned if she'd sit through his "It's not you, it's me" speech. She already knew. She didn't need the facts painfully reiterated, but Duke would naturally feel obligated to explain last night had been physical, not emotional.

So, she'd beat him to the punch. She'd be cold and distant. She'd make it apparent she had no attachments, no emotional stake in what had happened between them.

And Duke would never suspect her darkness was nothing but a shadow cast by a bright light she refused to let him see. Eventually, with enough time, it would dim into nothing but a memory.

* * * *

Duke approached her from the path, eyes down, hands curled into loose fists at his side. He glanced up when she cleared her throat. "There you are. Gavin wants to see you. He's in our trailer."

She'd seen that coming. She nodded. Duke turned back up the way he'd come, and she followed. They walked in silence.

Duke obviously had something on his mind, and she had a clue as to what it might be. If he hadn't figured out how the pieces fit by the time they were done with Gavin, she'd happily show him. She'd waited long enough to clear the air. The whole lot of them were approaching soap opera territory, all because she'd kept her mouth shut.

Inside their trailer, Gavin sat at the dinette table, his lips pressed together in a universal expression of disappointment, and his hands folded neatly on the tabletop. "Neve," he stated simply by way of greeting.

"Gavin." She matched his tone. His lips pressed tighter together. She chose to remain standing. She crossed her arms and rested her hip against the counter. Duke took his usual spot on the sofa bed.

Gavin addressed her after a deep sigh. "Neve, I'd like to discuss with you the sort of etiquette I expect from my employees. I was rudely shocked by your behavior this morning."

Neve pursed her lips and squinted at him. "I wasn't aware you hired me for my good behavior."

"Well, of course, I hired you for your skill, but—"

"Then it shouldn't surprise you when I say I was rudely shocked by *your* behavior this morning. Nor do you seem to realize the insult you paid me. You don't show up on a work site and start calling shots and going over my head. You want to come check on what your time and money is becoming, that's well within your rights, but you should do it with some semblance of respect for the people out here doing their jobs. I've worked for weeks now to earn the respect of these men, a difficult task to begin with, being female. Now, recall your backhanded, sexist suggestion that I leave my site to enjoy the utterly useless and almost strictly feminine pastime of shopping for fun, and you'll see the breech in etiquette was yours. Not mine. If you doubt it, ask yourself if you'd have made the same suggestion to Vince Taggart if he were heading the project."

Gavin's face turned red all over a second time. He cast a helpless glance at Duke, who only shrugged. He blinked rapidly before stuttering over an answer. "I assumed the men followed Duke's lead. He's the one with the experience."

"He's a consultant, which amounts to very little. I'm the one who makes the decisions and gives direction. An example is the deck you like so much. Duke had no idea I even ordered it built. Now, for my part, I apologize for my tone this morning. I might've had more tact in my decline of your invitation."

Duke's eyebrows went up.

She glared at him. He didn't think she could say sorry when a situation called for it? Showed what he knew.

"There's one other thing you should know, Gavin." Neve inhaled deeply. "I wondered if you were aware that our mutual friend here"—she swung her hands to Duke, as though he were a shiny new car on a gameshow floor—"is as straight as a landing strip."

Duke's dark blue gaze slammed into her. His jaw clenched. Unexpectedly, he grabbed Neve by her elbow with a fierce grip and excused them from Gavin's presence. He practically manhandled her outside the trailer, tugging her until they were several yards away.

She let him because she'd provoked him intentionally. *Let him know what I think about secrets—and the harm they can do.*

He let go of her and paced a few steps away, his hands curled into fists. His breathing came deep and labored. "You have such nerve. Gavin has been good to me, but how much do you think he'll trust me now he knows I've been lying my ass off for years? How could you do this? *Why* would you do this? What makes you such a miserable fucking person?" His expression morphed from angry to pleading. The lack of ire somehow made the words more hurtful.

Neve ignored the pinprick of pain in her chest and bit her lip. "You won't like it when I tell you."

"Since there's not much I happen to like right now, I doubt one more thing is going to matter."

"Fine, have it your way. Gavin's in love with you."

Duke froze, his eyes gone wide with terror and disbelief.

"You looked scared. You're not a homophobe, are you, Duke? Because the irony would kill me dead."

"But Gavin…no, Gavin's straight. He's totally straight."

"About as straight as a crazy straw."

"You're sure?"

"Yes. You've been inadvertently leading him on for the last two years. Have you noticed his marked lack of interest in the cabin? The weird fact he'd only speak to you when he called? I put it out there because Gavin deserves to know the truth. He's pining away for a relationship that has no future. I can relate."

"Oh, I see. So, you're suddenly the empathetic type?"

She wanted to smack the derision off his smooth face. Instead, she lowered her voice. "You don't know me, Duke. Did you see Gavin's face? He's shocked. And probably mortified. Oh, and likely hurt. Because it sucks to be lied to. He's been pursuing, however quietly, a straight man for over a year because you don't have the stones to be honest. But, by all means, let's feel sorry for you." She shook her head, disgusted with him and herself. "Gavin's refusal to deal through me in regards to the cabin was an issue born of his desire to get close to you. Just like I took the job to get close to him. It's unfair to him and to you. Hell, and to me. Has it crossed your mind he's not the only one disillusioned?"

Duke's eyes narrowed. "That's why you gave up trying to get Gavin to talk to you. That's why you let him deal through me. How long have you known?"

"Since the look on his face five minutes ago. But I've suspected for a while. The cabin…" She waved her arms, indicating everything around them. "I don't think any of this means much to him."

The veins in Duke's neck stood out. He swallowed. "You think…you're saying all this…the renovation, the work, all because…"

"Because he's in love with you."

Duke seemed to wilt and buried his face in his open hands. "Fuck me."

"Pass. Now, not so miserable, am I? I made the right call." Surely, he understood now. She was honest, brutally so, but she was never cruel for the sake of being cruel. She'd spoken up to break the cycle of lies and misconceptions, a cycle Duke had created and perpetrated with one single, powerful lie.

"No, you're still miserable."

She'd expected a joke, or for him to at least line the remark with a soft buffer of sarcasm, but there was granite beneath the words and his gaze. Neve smirked, determined not to let the depth of the cutting remark show.

"There's something to be said for tact, Neve. Empathy matters to us mortals, no matter how difficult it may be for someone with a stone heart to comprehend. Had you taken me aside and explained it, I'd have addressed it. I would've confessed to Gavin on my own terms and apologized for misleading him. I could've done some damage control. Instead, you made a harsh public display of both our secrets. I don't know how he and I are going to face each other after this." He shook his head at her like he'd never known a bigger disappointment. "You're an asshole, Neve. Does it truly help you sleep at night to tell yourself at least you're an *honest* asshole?" He stepped around her, not waiting for an answer.

Neve didn't know what shook her more. That she'd so easily found the cold, heartless approach she'd been going for, or that she'd finally discovered Duke's breaking point.

Chapter 11

Duke felt pretty useless walking around the cabin.

They were rounding the corner into the final week, but Gavin's cabin already had the unmistakable glow of a high-end retreat. The stone countertops were a smooth, deep gray, and as Neve had expected, they blended well into the warm space. The doors had arrived, both the front door with its elaborate inlaid glass design Neve had cleverly chosen to compliment the French doors in the rear, and a much plainer one for the bathroom. The tiles had gone down, a wonderful pearlescent amber that glimmered in the low light of the bathroom.

Before departing, Vince and his guys had hauled the hot tub from Tim's ranch and hooked it up. A small covered structure hugged the wall of the cabin between the back doors and the hot tub. Already cut logs were stacked and waiting for the first fire. Neve would probably have one burning when Gavin came to see the final masterpiece next week.

It hadn't surprised Duke when Gavin and Terri announced their immediate departure, but it did offer a huge measure of relief. He didn't have the guts to face Gavin. Not yet. How the hell was he supposed to work with the guy now? Did it qualify as a triangle if he had stirrings for Neve, who had her eyes on Gavin, who was in love with Duke? Somehow, he had to not only apologize, but do so without making the situation worse.

He blamed Neve. It was all Neve's fault.

The lie that had snowballed and started this whole mess, her fault.

The shocked, hurt look on Gavin's face when she artlessly threw out Duke's secret, her fault.

Her distant anger in response to their lovemaking.

Yep. All her fault.

Easier said than believed. Duke left the cabin without bothering to remind Neve of his appointment with Cherish Rancourt, the head of the Red Hill Historical Society, this afternoon. After all, he was but a mere consultant, unlikely to be needed, let alone missed.

* * * *

The wide cracked sidewalks lined with trees and tiger lilies showed care in the landscaping, if not the maintenance. Alas, flowers were cheaper than concrete and labor.

Duke entered the historical society's museum. The building's overpowering musty smell hadn't dissipated since his last visit. He hitched a man purse higher on his shoulder. He didn't like carrying the strange box out in the open, in case he ran into that sly old fox, Hux.

The receptionist waved him toward the back, where he finally met Cherish.

No younger than seventy, she was an African American with her black hair shorn close to her head, the tiny black curls greased down into perfect swirls against her scalp, and no taller than four foot three. She wore oversized gold-framed bifocals that matched the rest of her thick gold jewelry and a dress suit, blazer, and flared calf-length skirt in the rich deep purple of good red wine.

Cherish had style and proved to be the epitome of the ever-so-famous southern hospitality. She smiled wide at Duke, welcoming him warmly with an offered hand. Her other closed over his as they shook. "Mr. Kennicot, is it? Am I saying that right? I'm so sorry, I hate to have to ask."

"That's right. You did fine," he assured her. He took the seat she indicated. "Nice to meet you, Miss Rancourt."

Instead of sitting behind her desk, she sat in the guest chair next to his and gathered her hands in her lap. "Oh, please, hon. You call me Cherish." Best friends already.

Would Cherish be willing to give Neve personality lessons? "Yes, ma'am, but only if you'll call me Duke."

A small laugh. "Fair enough. It's nice to meet you as well. What is it you'd like to know about Red Hill, Duke?"

Duke placed his bag on the floor at his feet and settled back into his chair. He could bask in Cherish's friendly company all day long. Beat going back to the cabin and facing Neve's stone-cold façade. "Well, Cherish, I've got some questions about the cabin we're renovating up near Timothy Hux's ranch."

At the mention of the ranch, her mouth turned down. "Hm. Yep, I know the place. It's one of the more colorful stories you'll find in our little town. It's not registered as a historical landmark, but I couldn't tell you why. The cabin is called Beels Cabin after the woman who lived there. Or rather, for whom the cabin was built in the first place."

"Florrie Beels," Duke cut in. "We learned some from Tim Hux. He also claimed the place is haunted by Florrie's ghost. Lulu's, too."

Cherish readjusted her heavy gold frames, the smile vanished from her features. Duke regretted seeing it go.

She seemed to chew on her next words before finally launching into a slow, thoughtful telling. "I suppose the beginning is a fair place to start. Benjamin Hux is the main character, really. His daddy homesteaded that land up there back in the 1860s. At the time, the idea seemed crazy because of the way the valley sits up there so high. Back then, the ranch was called Huxley Ranch. Ben Huxley was born Benjamin Arthur Huxley in 1883 and, for some reason none of us can account for, shortened the name to Hux." She held up a finger. "*But*...most people don't recall he didn't change it till long after he married Lulu. Lulu was Lulu Huxley, but all the boys were Hux boys. The minor change didn't take long to stick, I guess, what with how people tend to like shortened names. But the reason why is lost to us. Now, Ben and Lulu's boys were all born between 1908 and 1912. Three of them, all within a year or so of each other. And they went on to run the ranch together. Between them, only one brother produced an heir, which, of course, was Tim's daddy in 1945, I believe, and he ended up the sole heir. He has the distinction of buying back about half of what Ben sold off in his time."

Duke recalled Ben's gambling addiction.

She waved her hands as if brushing away a fly. "Not that you care none for that. We'll go back to Ben, Tim's great-granddaddy. Now, Ben wasn't a likeable man to begin with. He had a reputation in town, and the only woman ever could tolerate him was Lulu Basker, who had a harsh family life and an abusive father. She grew up poor, and so Ben's offer was like a platter of gold and, of course, her parents greedily accepted the match. But she married Ben and cut ties, so her mama and daddy never got anything out of it. Well, that didn't hurt Ben's feelings none, you can imagine. He married Lulu under pressure from his daddy to produce heirs. For Lulu's part, Ben had been a knight in shining armor. Despite his drinking and..." She paused and dipped her chin, apologetic but frank. "Whoring is what they called it then. Lulu didn't care. 'Course, that behavior was somewhat more acceptable a hundred years ago. He'd saved her from a terrible life. She had money, comfort, and three healthy boys who'd inherit a profitable ranch. Life was good."

"It didn't stay good, though, did it?" Duke asked, though he knew the answer.

Cherish gave him a sad smile. "Unfortunately not. Ben Huxley didn't marry for love, understand. So, when he met and fell for Florrie, well, it fairly rocked this town. Relations were had. That much wasn't uncommon. But Ben didn't do anything halfway. He built Florrie that cabin on the very same land where he lived with his wife and boys. We guess this happened when his oldest was about twelve. So around 1920 or thereabouts. Ben was thirty-seven, possibly thirty-eight, and Florrie couldn't have been more than nineteen. So, Ben had more than one mark against him. Mistresses, even black ones, weren't uncommon, but you didn't park them next door to your family."

Duke chewed his lip. He and Neve hadn't considered a relationship of love. He leaned forward. "So, he didn't build her the cabin because he got her pregnant? My partner and I just assumed. I mean, why else build her a house on his land?"

Cherish's hand splayed across her chest and she blinked at him. "How did you know about the child?"

"I met Krandall Beels. He doesn't know much about his history, but he knows the cabin was in his family at one time."

A wry grin spread over Cherish's wrinkled lips and she relaxed. "Well, you're right, but not many folks know it. Right about the baby, not about their relationship. Florrie took up residence at the cabin, along with the deed from Ben, in 1920, same year they met. Florrie didn't have her baby until near the end of '22. She was murdered in the summer of '23, when the baby was nearly six months old. So, we can reckon on a winter delivery, but don't have an exact date for the baby's birth."

"Okay, okay." Duke nodded, trying to work out the math. "So, given how young Florrie was, Krandall might actually be her grandson. His father is the missing baby. Neve and I, we can't fathom what happened to the baby after Florrie died. He lived, or Krandall wouldn't exist."

Cherish took a good look at Duke for the first time. "May I ask why the interest in all of this? It happened so long ago."

"Actually, that was my next question." Duke bent over and wrested the strange box from his bag. Gingerly, he held it out for Cherish. "Do you recognize this? Can you tell me anything about it, like what it is, where it came from, or who may have designed it?"

Her brow furrowed. Before taking the box, she removed her glasses. She turned the chest over in her hands, and Duke's heart fell long before she shook her little old head and gave him an apologetic shrug. "I'm so sorry, but I couldn't tell you anything at all."

Duke took it back and sighed. "We think it's a lockbox. Someone buried at the cabin, and we wondered if it didn't have anything to do with the history, given the aging of the container. There's no telling what's inside. And no finding out until we locate the key. You can't think of a metalworker from these parts that might've used the same material or design?"

Cherish returned her bifocals to their perch on her rounded nose and shook her head. "I'm sorry, hon. I wish I could help. I've never seen anything like that contraption there."

Duke shrugged, smiled at her, and returned the box to his man purse. "It's no big deal. Though, I'm a little surprised after talking with you. You sure do know your history. Tim Hux doesn't seem to know much beyond the story of Florrie and Lulu's ghosts supposedly haunting the cabin."

Her mouth turned into that funny little frown again. "He knows more than he lets on. That Hux boy went to school with Krandall Beels. They were born the same year. Obviously, he must know there was a child. Florrie had no brothers."

"But...well, why isn't the baby a Hux? Why'd Florrie's name get passed on?"

"You can't imagine any of Ben's boys would've tolerated the poor thing. Someone would've smothered the babe while he slept. I always reckoned some friend of Florrie's, maybe even one of the girls she worked with, had the baby when Lulu murdered Florrie. Because there was never no talk of a fourth heir to the ranch, and one of the older women raised herself a son named Paul Beels, which some folks thought was her way of honoring her murdered friend, because not everybody knew Florrie had given birth. Some did, though, or put the pieces together. As for Ben, he seemed to give up on life after Florrie passed. He'd already quit the boozing and whoring. He lived the rest of his days on the ranch. Almost a recluse till the day he passed away, and his boys took over the family business. By then, the cabin had already been claimed by the...uh, well, the brothel Florrie worked for. Wasn't no secret Ben had deeded it to her. And the Hux boys didn't fight it. Most folks think they were happy to have it officially broken off from the ranch. But that didn't stop the new name from spreading like wildfire. Lady Killer Ranch."

Chills broke out on Duke's skin. "Cherish, how do you know so much about what happened? You tell an awfully detailed story for standard recordkeeping."

"Oh, hon." She put a friendly hand over his and smiled, a knowing grin behind which were secrets beyond what she'd shared. "I know it because it's my family history. Krandall Beels is my son. And his daddy was Florrie's missing baby. I heard the story firsthand from the woman who raised him."

* * * *

Lightning might as well have been shooting from her fingertips.

In a good way, for once.

Neve hated to celebrate too soon, but she'd done it. She'd truly done it. Eight weeks and one defunct cabin later, and she had *this* to show for it. Seven weeks and five days—two days ahead of scheduled completion.

A merry fire crackled in the unblocked fireplace. The old chimney stones had been scrubbed clean, and the firelight danced off the natural dips and ancient marks, like history itself. Nearly everything was in place. She'd even nicked a roll of toilet paper from her trailer. The dishes she'd picked out were strategically placed on the made-up table, which she'd had stained the same dark mahogany as the front window frame. The thick forest-green canvas curtains were swept back from the small window to allow dappled sunlight to splash across the cabin's interior, along with a special glow and refraction pattern from the diamond panes of the French doors.

Rustic and clean, ancient and new, sleek and cozy. The perfect balance.

Just one last touch. The sprinkle of brown sugar atop a muffin. The hint of cocoa in homemade chili.

Okay, so the glass chandeliers weren't as subtle as that. They would, however, be the element that took it over the top—from perfect to *wow*.

She opened up the ladder at the same time Kay bounded in holding one of the chandeliers. The tapered end draped over one arm. How the hell she managed to bound and keep her grip on ten pounds of metal and gems was a question for science. The biceps on her tiny arms bulged, but she maneuvered herself effortlessly and smiled hugely at Neve.

"This is incredible. The task seemed so impossible when I first arrived. I mean, I've seen some major transformations in school and stuff. But this place..." Her eyes went wide as though there was nothing left to say.

Neve supposed there wasn't. She climbed to the top of the ladder and held herself steady against the crossbeam with the fixture base attached. She planted her feet and kept her balance while Kay handed up the chandelier.

They repeated the process until the two glittering pieces hung side by side, just as Neve had envisioned. Together, she and Kay backed up to the entrance and surveyed the finished project.

Kay sighed in her adoring way. "This is why I want to work for you so desperately. This morning, I was so upset about Finn leaving—" She stopped abruptly and turned big eyes to Neve.

Neve grinned wryly. "Was it supposed to be a secret?"

"Well, no. Not exactly. I mean, professionally speaking, having a crush on one of the crew members is probably a bad thing, right? They didn't cover that in design school."

If a crush was bad, knowing how Neve felt about Duke would rock Kay's world.

She didn't like thinking about Duke. She still caught herself reeling whenever she played over the scene with Gavin and realized Duke had been right. She owed them both an apology but had no clue where to even start.

At the beginning, for dragging Duke into this in the first place? For not telling Duke her suspicions about Gavin when they occurred to her? For taking her anger out on Duke in such a sexually perverse manner? Although, he seemed to have enjoyed it at the time.

"Anyway, the whole Finn thing had me down. Even though he gave me his number. I should've called it while he was still here, huh? Because I'm thinking it's not his real number, and he was just being nice. But right now, I'm standing in the presidential suite of cabins, and I can't feel anything but proud. And blown away. And kind of intimidated."

Neve patted Kay on the shoulder. "It's my rigid, unyielding belief that lying is cowardice in its rawest form. For what it's worth, Finn didn't strike me as the dishonest type."

Kay sighed in her small, happy way. "You know, everyone wants the truth. But there are times…well, let's say I've always figured it's what we do with the truth that matters."

The simple insight hit Neve like a slap.

Miserable. Horrible. You nailed me in more ways than one, Duke.

Neve forced a quick smile for Kay's sake. She couldn't let the toothy beam on the girl's face go unanswered. "I'm sure you're right. I like you, Kay. You should come to work for me on a permanent basis. Vince seems to think we can make a go of designing houses from the ground up." She glanced at Kay. "Your face is going to split in half if you don't give that crazy smile a rest."

"I know!" She issued an excited squeal and danced on her toes. "It hurts, but I can't stop. You mean it? For real? For, like, *real* real?"

Neve bit her lip. "We might have to work something into your contract about caffeine restrictions. Have your pediatrician call me." She let herself smile at Kay's soft snort. Then she sighed. "Okay, I can't put it off any longer. I haven't talked to Duke since yesterday, but we need his stamp of approval before we call Gavin back here to see the finished product. Do you mind fetching him for me?"

Kay's smile faltered. "Sure thing, Boss." She paused in the act of taking a step toward the exit and tilted her head. "Are you guys okay? How do you avoid someone you live with in an eight-by-ten can?"

"For your information, it's an eight-by-thirty. And two determined adults can do anything they put their minds to."

Kay accepted the dismissal, leaving Neve alone with her masterpiece. Alone, alone, alone. *As per usual.* Even Darcy the Pit had abandoned her almost entirely in favor of Hannah's company. Being a few years older, she napped quite a lot. Darcy was more than happy to go along with that plan. Besides, the days were hot and long.

Neve turned around and gasped. Her hands instinctively fisted in front of her chest. "Goddamn it, Yosemite! Is there something you have against *not* scaring the shit out of people?"

He paused at the threshold and scanned the cabin's interior with an unreadable gaze.

She didn't overly care about his opinion, either way. She loved the cabin, and in a way, that mattered more than if the client loved it. Yet, she wouldn't deny a certain curiosity. She shifted her fists to her hips and cocked one for good measure. "Lay it on me, Hux. I know you've got something brewing under that hat of yours."

He removed his hat. Underneath, bland light brown hair rested on its side, like his mother had fixed it for him that morning. He blinked up at the chandeliers. "Wow."

"Really?" She stroked her chin thoughtfully. "Doesn't seem your style."

His gaze traveled from the over-the-top light fixtures to the gleaming custom cabinets and stone countertops of the kitchen. "I didn't know you could do stuff like this."

She'd truly consider taking offense with anyone else. "My confidence just jettisoned into the next layer of the atmosphere. Did you see it? Like a shooting star."

He grinned wryly as his gaze finally found hers. His eyes were open wider than usual and shining with newfound wonder and respect. "That ain't no lip, city girl. When you said you were gonna fix this place up, I thought you meant making it inhabitable again. Back to normal. This here ain't normal." His eyebrows rose with conviction. "Definitely not normal for any cabin I've ever laid eyes on, anyhow."

Neve shook her head. Backwoods as they came. "You ever want to put a spit-shine on that ranch house of yours, you know who to call."

He shook his head. "Only city boys like Gavin and old money can afford stuff like this." He looked around again, still taking it in. His attention landed on the bed, sitting out in the open, not three feet from where two chairs cozied up to the fireplace. He scratched his head but didn't say a word.

He definitely hadn't spent much time in a city. Or a studio apartment.

Neve paced to the end of the bed and relaxed against the post, tucking her thumbs through her front belt loops. Damn, Yosemite must be growing on her. "Actually, this was a remarkably affordable job. Thanks to you, we came in a mile under budget. We built these two walls here to create the bathroom and put up secondary walls after adding spray-foam insulation. All with the supply from Lady Killer. The rest is the original wood, polished and coated with sealant. Hell, even the custom kitchen came from your old hayloft. Not much I can do about having to buy new appliances—the shower stall, fridge and stove—but the furniture I refurbished. Every piece is secondhand."

"And these?" He pointed up, doubting her chandeliers.

Oh, but they were stunning. She'd been right about them, if not about anything else. "Those were a gift from Providence. Dumb kid at the flea market thought they were glass. They were filthy. Had he cleaned them, he might've noticed the colors. Only crystal reflects a rainbow back at you. If Gavin were real, real smart, he'd have them suckers appraised. They may be worth far more than even I realized."

Tim huffed and stared at her. "And you stuck them inside a dirty old cabin in the middle of nowhere?"

She shrugged. "That's what they pay me for."

He grunted, half in disbelief. The other half was definitely envy.

She never did find out what Timothy had going on at his ranch. It troubled her, but no more than realizing she'd miss his easy company. She'd finally met a guy who made her comfortable with herself, and it had to be a shady rancher in the middle of nowhere with some truly creepy family history.

"So, to what do I owe the pleasure of your company, cowboy?" Duke would be here any minute, and she'd have to endure one of those hooded looks he always gave Tim then pinned on her like she was hiding something, too.

Tim mimicked her stance, thumbs through belt loops. "I came to invite you to dinner. If my calendar ain't broke, this is your last week." He swept another openly impressed gaze around the room. "And clearly, someone ought to pour you a glass of bubbly and make a toast. To you. It's really something else."

A sweet warmth spread through Neve's chest like a tulip opening up for the sun. Normally, when a team finished a job, someone threw up a *hoorah!* and they were on to the next project. Occasionally, clients made special gestures for Neve and her team. But few times in her life had someone outside of a project suggested she deserved kudos for her handiwork beyond her paycheck. Most people acted like it all came with some kind of manual, when in fact she pieced together one day at a time with meticulous planning and—as in the case of the crystal chandeliers—a little bit of luck.

She pushed away from the bedpost and swung an arm around Tim's broad shoulders. Not as broad as Duke's, but not bad. Somewhere along the way she'd forgotten to flirt, and the sexual tinge between them had faded into the ether. That was fine with her. She didn't need any more visitors to her bed, but she could damn sure use a friend. "Dinner it is. Just as soon as my useless partner puts his meaningless stamp on my finished product."

Chapter 12

Darcy the Pit and Hannah were heaped together in a tangled mass of fur, giant paws, and wet dog snores that Duke tried to ignore in his deep concentration, a study that so far had led him nowhere. The locked box wouldn't give up its well-guarded secrets no matter how often he fondled it. He bit back a sigh and turned the chest over in his hands. He ran his fingers over the strange lock. The strange little box couldn't possibly be the only one in existence. Someone somewhere had to know where it came from and who'd made it. Maybe they'd have to branch out.

They?

Did Neve even remember their mystery box existed at this point? He didn't mind going solo. After all, he'd been the one to discover Krandall and learn Florrie's story from Cherish. Duke hadn't bothered to fill Neve in on the details. They'd done a splendid job of avoiding each other since their last confrontation.

He should've felt as smug as shit over it. He was probably one of the only people on the planet who'd ever seen Neve's face overcome with shame. So, why did he feel guilty? All he'd done was point out the obvious. Neve's love of honesty blinded her to courtesy. In Duke's opinion, there was room for both in any circumstance. To ignore one in favor of the other was ignorance at best. Cruelty at worst.

She hardly managed eye contact lately, let alone full sentences. As for his excuse, he wasn't the type to harp. He'd made his point. She understood. If Neve had the pair of balls she loved to claim, she'd apologize to Gavin at some point. After the way Duke had lied to her, he didn't expect one for himself.

Neve was still *Neve,* after all.

The trailer door swung open in a sudden *whoosh.*

Duke startled, nearly dropping the chest. The act of keeping the box from flying from his grasp took place of what would've otherwise been a furtive, if futile, attempt to hide it. He was left cradling the box in full view of Kay's inquisitive stare.

"Hey!" She pointed and strode straight at him, little blond head cocked. "That's interesting. What is it?"

Duke set it beside him and attempted to ignore it. "Oh, it's nothing. What can I do for you, Kay?"

"Neve sent me. That cabin's done, and we need the final seal of approval from Gavin's in-house man, which, of course, would be you." She stopped and seemed to consider him. "Okay, so this is maybe not *super* professional of me, and might even be kind of, um…traitorous?"

Whatever it was, Duke already disliked it. "Kay, I—"

"It's Neve. You guys are friends, right? She's happy with the cabin. Proud like she ought to be. But she's kind of down, too. Off. And I just haven't known her long enough to know how to help. Or what to say. But you guys are neighbors, and she needs a friend, I think. Something's weighing on her, and I can't help."

"Huh." He chewed the inside of his cheek and ran a hand through his loose hair. "Neve and I aren't on *super* good terms right now. I'm probably not the best person to talk to her." He smirked. "You might want to try the rancher. She and Tim have been spending quite a bit of time together."

Kay wrung her hands. "Maybe. Well, I tried." Then she fixed him with a canny stare. "May I see the box you're trying to hide? It seems familiar." Without waiting for permission, she moved to Duke's other side and plucked the box from its failed hiding spot.

With a word like *familiar,* Duke didn't dare stop her.

Kay's brow furrowed as she traced a finger over the starburst design of the lock. "So strange. I swear, I saw something like this…" She worried her lip.

Duke waited with air trapped in his chest, afraid to exhale.

Then Kay's pale eyebrows shot toward the ceiling, and her bright, excited gaze swung to him. "Oh, my! Of course! The place where we found the door. Thrift House. Do you recall I mentioned seeing a strange metal thingy?"

"I believe you called it a doo-hickey."

"Yes! That metal piece had this exact same design, except not attached to a chest. Like, if this lock were a single piece."

Duke's heart skipped a beat. *The key. It's got to be the key.* "You're sure?"

Her brow furrowed, this time accompanied with pursed lips. "Someone around here obviously hasn't noticed my extreme attention to detail. Look,

I'm telling you, it's the same metal, and a strikingly similar design. I assumed it was some kind of weird local art. I mean, part of why I love the Ozarks so much—"

Duke stood and swiped the chest from Kay's hands in one smooth motion. "Listen, I can't check on the cabin. I don't have time. Tell Neve…" Tell her what, exactly? "You know what, tell her I'm not here. I'll check on the cabin later. Promise." Then he recalled the deck he'd been so terrified of, and how happy it had made Gavin. Neve was the last person in the world who needed a nose over her shoulder. "Actually, you know what? Tell her I approve. If she says the cabin is done, it's done, and Gavin's gonna love every inch of the place."

Kay stared at him with her mouth slightly open. "I can't lie and say you weren't here, but I can let her know you're leaving. Trust is one of those things you shouldn't mettle with." She tapped her chin. "Funny, Neve and I were discussing a closely related topic a few minutes ago. Actually, I might've overstepped myself when I asked if everything is okay between you two."

"What did she say? I mean, we're okay. I just…did she say?"

"Not exactly."

Of course not. "Okay, well, by the time you get back down to the cabin, it won't be a lie. I'll be long gone. Besides, my opinion doesn't matter. Hasn't the whole time I've been here. Seriously, have you ever seen a more useless consultant?"

A pained expression crossed her delicate features.

"And anyway, she has Yosemite to keep her company." He sighed. "It's okay. I won't ask you to lie to me, either. But you see my point. Neve doesn't need me, and this can't wait."

Reluctantly, Kay left.

Duke snatched the rental car keys from the kitchen counter and caught the morose stares of Darcy and Hannah. "Oh, stop," he said, crouching and scratching them each behind the ears in turn. "Don't judge me. I'm loyal when it's warranted. You know that, Hannah."

Darcy let out a muffled sneeze and laid her head back down.

Hannah continued to stare at him.

"You think I'm jealous, don't you? I know that look. But I'm not. And anyway, I bet Tim Hux's brain isn't much bigger than his shiny, oversized belt buckle."

Hannah blinked.

Duke bit his lip and switched his attention to her chin, aiming for the spot just beneath her collar. "You're right, that was low. I take it back.

He's probably a smart guy. After all, most weedy, sly people are. Now, that I won't take back, because it's true, and you can't puppy-shame me into believing otherwise."

Hannah seemed to give up on him, yawning in his face and flopping back down to snuggle into Darcy's side.

By the time he arrived at Thrift House, so had an unexpected sprinkling of rain and a cover of dark blue clouds that promised more. He parked the car parallel to the rickety old fence and jumped from the vehicle. The rain picked up speed, and Duke tucked the chest under his arm in an attempt to keep it dry.

Thrift House's shutters were closed. No exterior lights offered aid as Duke weaved through the piles of junk, squinting past the raindrops smattering across his face as he searched for the key in the unhelpful twilight.

From stack to stack, desperately trying to recall where Kay had been the day she'd found the key, Duke searched. The rain became a force as the clouds rolled directly overhead. It soaked through his shirt and weighed down his hair. With his free hand he pulled it back and behind his shoulders, but every time he bent to inspect another item in the near darkness, it draped forward, despite him, wet strands sticking to his cheeks.

"Damn it. C'mon." On to another stack. And another.

Maybe Kay is mistaken. There's nothing here. But between the rain and the lack of light, Duke couldn't be sure he'd checked every pile, every stack. Plus, it couldn't be much bigger than the palm of his hand. Shit, what if someone bought it? He clenched his fists. The storm brought with it a strange sense of urgency. He forced himself to take a breath—and take stock of himself.

Acting like a madman. Looking for a mystery in a storm so he could unlock some kid's candy stash from 1890. He ran his hand through wet strands and cursed. He turned toward the car.

That was when he saw it. Tucked up against the side of a wooden crate nestled in the mud, he'd never have noticed, relying on color to guide him. The tapered spines of the starburst design stuck out like a hand taking hold of the crate. Creepy but noticeable.

Duke rushed for it, again with a sense of urgency he couldn't begin to explain. Excitement swelled. Giddy with it, he snatched up the key and laughed. Holy shit, he'd found it. Right here in the dirt all this time. He didn't bother breaking down Krandall's door to purchase the piece. Hell, if it opened the damn box, he'd leave the box and key behind once he had his hands on the secret within.

He folded himself into the dry car. The quiet interior lent a somberness to the act of opening the chest, a marked contrast from his fevered search in the pouring rain, heart pounding. He set the chest facing upward on his lap. He didn't need to study the strange lock. He practically had the design memorized.

He turned over the key. Exactly as Kay had described it. As though the lock mechanism from the chest had come apart from it. Same material, same design, only inverted. Where a piece on the lock was long, the key had a corresponding prong, shorter and likely meant to slide together. He slid his finger along a spire and found one side slightly flattened. Same for the key.

With trembling fingers, Duke positioned the key over the lock in his best estimation of how they fit together, and pressed. Gently at first, then with more force. A give beneath his fingers made his pulse skip.

The prongs seemed to melt together, forming a single three-dimensional starburst. At the connection, some hidden lever made a faint *click.*

Stunned, Duke lifted the lid, from which lock and key broke off and stayed attached to the front of the chest. Duke saw, finally, why they were unable to devise a way to break in. A false hinge. The box didn't open at the obvious crease, but a different internal hinge, accessed only when the prongs from the key applied pressure against the metal pieces, altered their arrangement, and allowed for leverage. To attempt to open the chest at the false hinge, in turn, put pressure on the *actual* hinge and made opening it an impossibility.

It's the Chinese finger trap of treasure chests. Someone had a lot of time on their hands. And a hell of a secret.

His heart thrumming in his chest, Duke reached inside and retrieved a wax envelope. Inside, papers of every shape and size. Some were small, just patches folded in half. Others were multiples. The paper was old, yellowed, and crumbling away at the corners. Letters, he realized, scanning one of the short notes. He scoured the pages. His heartrate increased with every word.

A minute later, Duke pounded on Krandall's front door. The rain battered him, ran down his face unchecked, his hair like a wet curtain on either side of his head. He hardly noticed. He lifted his fist to the door. "Krandall! Krandall Beels, open up!"

The porch light turned on, dim in the wild night.

Slowly, the weathered door creaked open, revealing one of Krandall's eyes as it roved over Duke. "You a madman or what? Take this nonsense someplace else. Thrift House is closed."

Duke held out his hands. "Wait! Wait. Krandall, listen. I know who you are. This is important. Trust me, please. I need to know where I can find your mom. I have to talk to Cherish. And I need to do it *now.*"

* * * *

"What do you mean he isn't coming?"

Kay bit her lip, eyes wide. "Uh, well, he's...not coming. He left. He didn't say to where, but something about—"

Neve cut her off with a raised hand. She closed her eyes and took a deep breath. "Forget it. Forget him. Besides, the cabin's done, isn't it? Gavin will love it or hate it, and Duke's opinion has small bearing on the outcome."

Kay scrunched her nose. "That's basically what he said."

Neve glanced out the window. What had she expected? Duke to come see her spectacular finish and give her credit? She forced down the tiny part of her awash in disappointment. His approval shouldn't matter. "It's nearly dark, anyway. Let's call it a day. If Duke's not too busy tomorrow, he can make the call to Gavin. The sooner the better. I can't wait to get the hell out of here." A small smile for Tim. "No offense."

He only smiled back.

Neve put a hand on Kay's shoulder. "I'm going to the ranch for dinner. Do me a favor and check on the dogs, will you?"

"Sure! Aren't they freaking *cute?* They're like best friends! So cuddly. Who knew pit bulls were so cuddly?"

Neve raised her eyebrows. "I did. I've owned a few different breeds and never met one more affectionate than a pittie. They're loyal to a fault, too, which is the quality that makes them so easily exploited by douche bags everywhere. But raised properly, you'll have a cuddle buddy for life."

"I'm more of a Heeler man myself," Tim intoned.

"Want to talk about a vicious breed."

He grinned, a predatory thing. "Precisely why I like them."

She shrugged. Different strokes. She waved good night to Kay, trusting her to close up the cabin for the night, and took off for the path at Tim's side.

"Snazzy timing, Yosemite." Neve pointed through the trees at dark clouds gathering in the direction of Red Hill.

Tim took a cursory glance. "Might move off to the south. That happens a lot. Seems like the storms can't be bothered to climb the mountain sometimes."

Neve grunted. "I can empathize."

* * * *

Neve couldn't put her finger on it.

The rancher said the right things, made the gentlemanly gestures she'd become accustomed to—doors opened, chairs pulled out. But something different—something subtle—settled onto his features. Like a mask. Or, perhaps, the absence of one. She'd always known he had a shady side. A charge in the air and a strange quality to Tim's manner suggested she might soon find out what he kept hidden. She calculated how long it would take her to jog back to the cabin if his secret turned out to be *really* dark. Like, murdering hitchhikers or something. With Tim, anything seemed possible. The guy had a poker face like a stone wall.

She appreciated the challenge while, at the same time, missing Duke's easy unguardedness. He could obviously keep a secret, but he also had an honesty to his face. She'd never been able to read Duke as easily as she read the college twerps she dated, but he didn't hide his feelings. Or maybe she just plain missed Duke. He was there every day, on the job, but they might've been a thousand miles apart. It was her own doing, but it didn't stop the sudden desire for his familiar company.

Tim, on the other hand, kept everything buttoned down nice and tight. Neve had a hard time reading anything beyond amusement on that rugged face. They sat together over cold beers at the eat-in table in the far corner of the long galley kitchen.

Neve liked the space for its original charm, but also desperately wanted to open it up. "You know, if you'd just let me take down this wall here, you'd have a huge kitchen. I'd make up for the storage with a real snazzy island. Hell, I could even have Finn make it out of the wood from the walls we tear down." She sipped from the cold bottle and lifted a daring brow at Yosemite.

He chewed the inside of his cheek and sighed.

Not the response she'd expected.

"I'm half kidding. But I'm also half serious."

He leaned back and studied her.

Here we go. Yosemite had something in his maw, and she was about to find out what. "Go on," she pushed. "Spill whatever the hell it is you're chewing on."

A slight smile. "You're perceptive."

"Yeah, well, eye for detail and all that. Every now and then I apply my skills to humans."

That unnerving stare again. "You know, we had Vince holed up here for a week. A lot of time Laurel and Owen had him on some pretty good painkillers. By nature, he ain't the talkative type. Or so I gathered."

The direction he'd gone baffled her. Vince? What did Vince have to do with anything? "A fair assumption. He's more of a doer."

Yosemite sat forward slowly and rested his elbows on the table. "He mentioned an odd thing one evening. Not to me. To Miles, my brother. They got to talking about you and the work you were doing. To hear Miles tell it, Vince could hardly get a breath in from singing your praises. He's mighty impressed with you. The work you do. Your design ideas and such."

Neve didn't check her grin. Count pride among her flaws. She affected mock modesty. "Yeah, well, greatness will recognize greatness."

"And," Tim added with an odd gleam in his hazel eyes, "the strange little box where you keep your inspiration."

The sharp turn in the conversation sent Neve careening. The locked chest. He knew about it. By the look in his eyes, he knew more than she did. On the heels of one realization came another. Every dinner invitation and show of friendship had served a purpose. *God, I'm an idiot. People don't like me. How could I forget that?* She should've known Tim's supposed interest harbored some underlying agenda. Of fucking course.

Hadn't she been the one to say Tim Hux didn't do anything without a reason?

Neve sipped her beer and let Tim talk. She forced herself to take short, even breaths. But that sense of a mask falling away wouldn't leave her. The feeling that the rancher had a secret had never seemed more ominous.

"I was out of town, you recall," Tim went on. "And with a ranch to run, Miles forgot about the mention of such a strange box until recently." His eyebrows furrowed, as though he were truly confused. "When I realized what he'd described, why, I ain't been so confounded since high school calculus." Tim stood from the table, slow and deliberate as was his style, and left the room.

Neve didn't move. No sense in bolting now. She was inches from finding out Tim's big secret and something about the lockbox. She changed her mind about wanting to stick around when he came back with the chest in one hand and a small caliber pistol in the other. She was on her feet before the thought to run had fully registered.

Tim shook his head. "We ain't done yet, Neve. I don't intend to use this anymore than I intend to let you leave without telling me where the box is."

The sheer fucking nerve. The threat to her person choked her with incredulity. That anyone, anywhere, anytime would force her to bend her will made her see red. She stayed standing, despite the tiny barrel pointed at the lower half of her body. "Oh, we're done, you psychopath. You *have* the box, right there in your hands. You're clearly out of your ever-loving mind, and I'm walking out before something insane happens."

With speed that belied his easy movements, Tim moved his arm, aiming the pistol to Neve's left, and fired.

Searing pain like nothing she'd ever known shot through her arm. Her right hand instantly went to the screaming flesh of her arm and came away wet and sticky with blood. Shock took her feet from under her, and she sank to her knees. Her vision swam, but Tim's boots were clear enough as he stepped up to her.

"A flesh wound," he said without inflection. Like mentioning the storm earlier. "I'm a hell of a shot, I ever tell you that? The bullet grazed your arm. Enough to hurt like hell and offer you some incentive to play along, but nothing a few stitches won't put right. I'll give you a minute. Then, I think you ought to take your seat. Finish that drink. Hot beer ain't any good."

Neve's senses might've gone into shock, but her mouth apparently reverted to instinct in a time of crisis. "I've at least earned a finger or two of whiskey."

Tim issued a low rumble of laughter.

He's insane. What do I do? Where's Duke?

Her cell phone was in her pocket. Her heart leaped. She had cell service at the ranch. If she'd known Tim was going to come back with a firearm, she'd have used her spare moment to text Duke. In the meantime, she had to find a way to mute the stupid thing before someone called or texted and gave away her only hope of reaching out for rescue.

Where were Laurel and Owen? Miles? Were they in on this, or would they help her? Jesus Christ, had she stumbled across the Southern edition of the Manson family?

Wheels turned and her vision cleared. The shock faded as the pain in her arm, which she could now pinpoint to one burning spot on her bicep, grew. She craned her neck to check it. A graze, like Tim said, but as hot as the heart of a raging fire and seeping blood. It flowed down to her elbow, where it gathered and dripped onto Tim's wooden floor.

She cursed herself for not realizing he'd left until she looked up to see him walk into the room with a tumbler of dark brown liquid.

Sweet Jesus, he actually brought me whiskey. "You're a swell guy, Tim." Her legs trembled and shook as she forced herself to stand enough to crawl back into the chair.

The thick-bottomed glass landed with a *thud* in front of her, and she hardly waited for Tim's hand to pull away before snatching it and slamming back the whiskey like it was the elixir of life. In sixth grade, she'd broken her arm playing a rather violent game of football with the neighborhood boys one summer. She hadn't felt pain like it since or before, until now. She turned a flat stare to Tim, refusing to plead or show an ounce of the desperation growing in her breast. "Be a pal, Yosemite, and hit me again. With whiskey," she added, eying the pistol he held loose at his side with distrust.

He didn't smile this time. His patience waned, evident in the hard line of his mouth and absence of amusement in his hazel gaze. Still, at the far end of the galley, he grabbed the whiskey decanter, this time bringing the whole thing to the table. He poured another smaller shot and sat down, waiting for Neve to toss it back.

She did, not bothering to savor it. The faster the liquor hit, the sooner it would start numbing the incredible pain in her arm. She didn't wait for Tim to restart the interview. "You have the chest. I don't get what you want from me."

He leaned back. He'd set the chest on the table, off to the side. Now, he pulled it to the center and looked at Neve over the top of the intricate lock. "This ain't your box, sweetheart. This one is mine."

Neve blew out air from puffed cheeks. "Whatever. Okay, so two boxes. So what? I can't open the one I have. Is that what you want, the key? Because I don't have it. I found the box, and it's locked and impossible to open without destroying whatever could be inside." She refrained from mentioning Duke was involved. Didn't seem wise to tell the maniac with the gun every little detail.

Tim smiled, the same predatory grin he'd showed her once already tonight. His true smile, if she had to peg it. "Key's not what's important. It's what's inside that I want. Or rather, what I don't want seeing the light of day in my lifetime. There are some secrets that need to be kept buried. It's funny. You and your aversion to lies, while my whole way of life and everything I hold dear depends on them. I reckon it's a simple matter of perspective."

Did she dare ask? Did she want to know? "What's in the chest, Tim?"

"I'm not a villain in some movie, city girl. I want the box. That's all. I sent Miles to your trailer while I kept you busy at the cabin, and he couldn't find it. Does your boy Duke have it, then? Miles watched him leave with a bag, but his instructions were to search the trailer."

Well, that answered her question about Tim's cohorts. Definitely in on it. As for Duke, no telling. He could be following up a lead, or Miles was very bad at hide and seek. "Duke and I haven't exactly been on speaking terms lately. If he took it somewhere, he didn't tell me."

Tim leaned forward, serious again. "Tell me where the box is, Neve. If hurting you doesn't work, there's always your assistant. Then again, your regard for human beings seems a little lacking. Now, I'm an animal lover, but I'll do what I've got to."

The implied threat to Darcy the Pit sent chills down her spine and froze the very air in her lungs. "I'll murder you in your sleep if you touch a single fucking whisker on my dog," she managed to say on a breathy exhale.

Tim didn't seem to register the threat. Nor did he respond when the shrill ring of Neve's cell phone cut through the silence between them, adding a new flavor to the tension-filled atmosphere.

Neve's heart filled with dread. She swallowed the lump rising in her throat. "You want me to get that?"

"I sure do. And if it's your partner, invite him on over. With the box, of course."

With her uninjured arm, Neve twisted to her side, dug her phone from her pocket, and used her thumb to slide the answer button. "Duke. Where are you?"

"I'm with Cherish. There's no time to explain." His excitement hummed over the line. "Listen to me carefully, Neve. Stay away from Lady Killer Ranch. Timothy Hux has been after the chest. You won't believe what's in here."

She bit her lip. Shit. Duke not only had the chest but had accessed whatever Tim had shot a woman in order to contain. "Uh…" Too late now. "Tell me more."

Tim waited with his head cocked to one side. He crossed his arms, the pistol still gripped in one hand.

Duke's discovery had left him near breathless. "They're letters. Neve, you won't believe…letters between Ben and Florrie. Letters from Florrie to the woman who ended up raising Florrie's baby. It's all here, the whole history. I took everything to Cherish Rancourt to confirm. I'm with her now, and it's all legit, Neve."

"What's legit, Duke? You're all over the place."

He groaned with frustration. "Ben told Florrie everything in his letters. Lulu *did* know about the baby. His name was Paul, and his birth wasn't the tipping point that set Lulu off. He was six months old when Florrie was killed, so that didn't make sense, anyway."

"Wait, when did we learn that?"

Duke ignored her. "Somehow, Lulu must've found out what Ben planned to do, but Florrie knew what was coming and had Paul taken away. And Lulu didn't kill herself. She was murdered, too. By Ben."

Neve nearly forgot Tim was sitting across from her. "What are you talking about? None of this makes sense. Why would he do that? And why wasn't he able to protect Florrie if he was there when it all happened?"

"Ben did something drastic, and when Lulu found out, she planned to kill Paul. Only Paul was gone, and in a rage, she killed Florrie. Ben came upon the scene. He knew the baby was safe, but he says in his final letter, the one accompanying his living will, he felt Paul was better off raised without him. He'd always be at risk. Where Lulu had failed, one of her sons might one day succeed. Better they believe the baby had died. He must've hidden the box away so one day someone like you would find it and his proper heir would be recognized. Then Ben avenged Florrie."

"By killing Lulu. What did Ben do to set her off, anyway, if not have another kid?"

"That's the part where Tim Hux comes in. Ben left everything—the ranch, the land, all of it—to Florrie and her baby. He writes in one of the letters to Florrie that he found out none of Lulu's boys were his. The timing had never added up. Just like he hadn't married for love, neither had Lulu. She'd married for security. She didn't care about Ben's mistress. But when he found out Lulu's children didn't belong to him, he had his will rewritten. Instead, he deeded the ranch to the child he knew for certain was his. Paul Huxley. That's when the name changed. Lulu's boys weren't true Huxleys. Ben shortened the name, going so far as to rename the ranch they'd inherit, in a subtle declaration of the truth. It's all right here, Neve. Tim has no claim to Lady Killer Ranch."

"Florrie's baby," Neve whispered. She raised her eyes to Tim.

He had the gun pointed right at her. "I caught the gist of it. Tell your friend to bring the box to the ranch, or I'm going to give you a bigger hole to worry over."

She tried to laugh, but it came out strangled. "Tim, it's over. There's evidence you're not the legal owner of this property." Her mouth fell open as it hit her. "Krandall Beels is."

On the other end of the line, Duke concurred. "Cherish was Paul's wife. And Krandall is their son, and yes, the rightful owner of Lady Killer Ranch. Tim's known the evidence existed this whole time."

"I know," she said. "I'm with him now. And he wants the box and all the documents brought here. Or he's going to shoot me again, Duke."

"And his dog, too." Tim smiled. "Better mention that. Especially if he thinks about bringing the local sheriff along. "

Miles walked in then, Darcy the Pit and Hannah trailing behind him on their leashes.

Chapter 13

Tim poured her another shot of whiskey. He'd laid the gun down on the table. The barrel still faced Neve like the staring black eyeball of a demon, but at least no finger rested on the trigger.

This time, she sipped the strong liquor, mindful it may be her last joyful thing in this life. What she'd give for Darcy the Pit to come through on that badass reputation right about now, instead of lolling her tongue around, simply excited to be on an adventure. Until some overt act of violence took place, the dog wouldn't react. Neve didn't know Hannah well enough to say what she'd do if one of the men attacked, but she, too, appeared serene, if not outright bored, by it all.

"Tell me about the chests, Yosemite." Now the cards were on the table, she saw no point in keeping secrets. "Duke and I searched everywhere for the key. I still can't tell you where the hell he found it. No one in town has seen anything like the metal-locking mechanism. We even tried the historical society."

A glint of pride rippled over his features. "Family heirloom, you might say. My great-granny Lulu learned metal-smithing from my great-grandpa. And no, I don't mean old Ben. I mean the real one, of course. Only child Ben ever sired was missing-presumed-dead baby Paul. Alive after all."

"If you didn't know Paul lived, why did you need the letters so desperately?"

He settled back and let out a small sigh. At some point, he'd poured himself a whiskey, too. Half of what he'd poured for Neve.

Of course, he's not the one with a gunshot wound.

"I've always known the ranch wasn't mine. Just like my daddy knew. And my granddaddy. And Krandall, me and him, we schooled together.

Beels or not, he can't make no claim to my ranch. He doesn't know a thing. How could he? But Lulu didn't keep no secrets from her boys. Ben was never nothing more than a means to survive. She wrote everything in a letter, along with her plans for that little nigger baby of Ben's. I had no idea about the chest you had until Miles mentioned Vince babbling on about your strange little box. And how remarkably similar it sounded to one I happen to have." He put a hand on top of the chest. "Lulu would hardly have hidden anything at the cursed cabin, but easy enough for Ben to get his hands on one of Lulu's chests and stash proof—proof we've kept hidden for generations."

"Proof this land belongs to Krandall."

"Like hell." Steel flashed behind his gaze. "See, Granddaddy found Lulu's letters in her workshop after Ben passed away, letters explaining everything she'd done. Ben had kept the space barred, closed up tight after he murdered Lulu in cold blood."

"She killed the woman he loved after failing to murder his only legitimate child. I'd call it a crime of passion."

"I'd call it hypocrisy. You think life on a ranch is easy? Lulu put her life into this land. She didn't do nothing worse than what Ben did, carrying on publicly the way he did. With a whore, no less. A black whore. A mark of shame for his whole family. Lulu deserved better. She deserved to see her children taken care of."

In a way, Neve sort of agreed. Ben had been a real piece of work. She'd say it ran in the family, except Tim's insanity had apparently come down from Lulu. "Fine. Whatever. Say you're right, you deserve the ranch and Krandall doesn't. First of all, the law doesn't take into account what one deserves. It's a simple matter of ownership. What's your plan, Yosemite? You going to shoot everyone who knows the truth? Because that's three charges of murder in the first degree. Paul's wife is with Duke. Cherish Rancourt is the one who verified the letters."

"When I burn the evidence, it's a matter of word. Yours versus mine. And possession is nine-tenths. Duke gives me the documents, and y'all scamper on home. This gun won't exist by the time you get any authorities out this far. Ain't nobody got time to search hundreds upon hundreds of acres for a weapon that may or may not exist."

Neve wanted to make a joke, but the throbbing pain in her arm reminded her of the seriousness of the situation. Some part of her still seemed convinced she'd get herself out of this. But even if she ran for it, Tim Hux was psychotic enough, judging by the graze on her arm, that he wouldn't hesitate to put a bullet through both of the stupid happy dogs, now practically sitting on each other at Miles's feet.

He hadn't uttered a word since entering with the dogs. Bunch of coldhearted fuckers, these Hux boys.

She resigned herself to the role of damsel. It chafed. She'd done things solo her whole life, but there was no getting herself out of this pickle alive—and with two healthy dogs—without a cavalry arriving to save the day.

Duke would deliver. He had to. If not for her, he'd do it for Hannah. Somehow, that gave her more faith than if she were his sole motivation. All else aside, the dude really loved his dog.

* * * *

Duke had never attempted a daring rescue mission before.

Cherish and Krandall weren't exactly helping. Cherish tittered after Duke, and Krandall didn't seem to have a care for what happened next. He'd already made it clear as day he had no interest in the ranch. After Cherish had ridden with Duke back to Thrift House to wake Krandall again and show him the proof of his inheritance, he only tagged along to look after his mother, who insisted remaining by Duke's side until the ordeal was over.

Somehow, Duke doubted Tim would take much confidence in Krandall's disinterest. He wanted the documents, and he'd have them.

He'd also have a new hole to match Neve's if he wanted to make things any more difficult than that. Duke held up the Beretta and gave it a distrustful once-over. He was a rifle man. The pistol didn't sit right in his hand. But he still knew how to pull the trigger. Would, if it came to that. Fear, cold and heavy, settled into his gut like a boulder when Neve told him about the gunshot wound on her arm. He'd hardly even registered Tim's other hostages, Darcy and Hannah. They were secondary. He couldn't save them without first getting Neve out of that house.

"Listen, Krandall, I appreciate the, uh, weapon."

Krandall's unhappy expression didn't change. All just a big old inconvenience, this.

Cherish worried her hands. They sat together on the sofa in the location trailer. "Duke, please. Sheriff Walsh could be here in five minutes. Let him handle this."

"I'm sorry, Cherish, but I told you. Tim will shoot the dogs. Not only do I believe he'll do it. He's got it in him to shoot a woman he's become something of friends with, but I also happen to know, with absolute conviction, Neve won't forgive me if I let anything happen to Darcy the Pit."

Huh. The full name did sort of roll off the tongue once he got used to it.

"He won't expect me to be armed. And while I don't have much use for guns these days, I grew up hunting with my dad. Never aimed at a human before, but there's probably no end to the shit we're each capable of with the proper motivation."

He stopped, sat up straight, and blinked at the wall.

"Shit," he breathed, realization dawning like a new day. A new, unwanted, unbidden day. "I love her. That's what this is. I'm not worried for a friend. I'm terrified down to my bones that I might lose her." He swallowed hard. "She's...I can't lose her. It'd kill me. God, she's so awful, how did this happen?"

He didn't expect an answer, but Cherish offered one. "Well, you're a nice man. She must be a sweet girl."

"If a granite wall were a person, that'd be Neve. Hard, unyielding, bossy, angry." The list really did go on.

"Oh." The old woman shrugged. "Well, the heart wants what the heart wants and all that."

He rubbed his forehead with the hand not holding the loaded gun. When she'd said Tim had shot her, everything inside him fell like a scattered pile of Legos, all corners and edges, and none of it fitting together. Before the cabin, before the anger and the arguing, they'd been friends. For two years, he'd been Neve's neighbor and confidant. And while he'd gone to Hell and back to avoid her temper, he also loved her fierceness. He loved that she was solid. She had a mouth, but she backed up everything that came out of it. She lived her credo of honesty, even when it was the kind that hurt. Neve taught him lies didn't hurt less if they sat behind good intentions. It all hurt the same. So, maybe she was right. Better brutal honesty than honeyed deception.

He shook his head.

His plan was crazy, Cherish had that much right. But Duke's gut said a few minutes without police interference might save a couple of canine lives. He refused to acknowledge the trade put his own at further risk. "Shit. All right, I'm going to get Neve. Cherish, you can go to the sheriff when you get back into Red Hill if you want. All I need is a head start. By the time anyone arrives, I'll have either pulled this off, or we'll all be riddled with bullet holes, anyway, and it won't matter."

She sighed and readjusted her gold frames. "Some optimism wouldn't hurt your cause none."

The trailer door swung open. Kay marched in with a small pistol pointed toward the ceiling. "You're out of your mind if you think you're going in alone. And yes, I heard everything. I may have a small eavesdropping habit, but don't tell Neve. It's just I'm small and quiet, and I tend to sneak up on people."

Duke gawked. "What the...? Am I the only person not armed by default?"

She cocked a little blond eyebrow. "Have you read the crime statistics in Little Rock lately? I have a license to carry concealed. You would, too, if you were a hundred-pound, five-foot-nothing female who lives alone. Relax, I'm trained." She hitched her chin toward Krandall and Cherish, who didn't look nearly as surprised as Duke felt. "Y'all go on and get the sheriff. We'll want him here when we subdue Tim."

Duke blinked at her. Subdue Tim. Right. Okay. Sure. They were totally going to do that.

Kay drove the rental car at a crawl with only the parking lights on and the windows down to listen for any noise, such as the whir of a four-wheeler engine coming from the ranch.

Duke snuck a side-glance at Kay. Unflinching gaze at the road, jaw set. Determined and one hundred percent on game. That was good. He couldn't afford to doubt his partner.

He checked the small pistol Krandall had handed him with three bullets, safety on. Duke would keep it on as long as possible. After all, he'd brought the goods. The chest in his lap weighed a thousand pounds—or at least as much as the lives of Neve and their dogs. It had every letter, every incriminating note, and necessary documentation, including Paul Beel's birth certificate confirming Ben Huxley was his father. And, of course, the real treasure: the living will Ben Hux had drafted and notarized after Florrie's murder, the one naming his legitimate heir.

Kay kept the headlights off as they approached the ranch. Made no difference. Their arrival didn't go unnoticed. Miles met them at the front door, weirdly friendly, considering the circumstances. He didn't have the dogs with him.

Duke held tight to the lockbox, the pistol tucked into the back of his jeans and hidden by his shirttails. "Well? How do we do this? I can't claim a working knowledge of hostage negotiations, unless you count bad eighties movies. But maybe you and Tim have this down, huh? Don't tell me it's your first time. I mean, I'm nervous enough." He impressed himself, keeping his sense of humor. Neve would be proud. She was probably in there now, hurling zingers at Tim and the gun pointed in her face.

Kay frowned, as if offended he'd flirt with the enemy. Then she amazed him by taking up the reins. "The dogs, Miles. A fair trade. You give the dogs to me, and Duke hands you the chest. Then Tim can let Neve go. She needs medical treatment if he actually shot her."

A subtle attempt at information gathering. And it worked. Miles's sober attitude matched the occasion. He tucked his hands into his pockets and nodded, almost guiltily. "It's a flesh wound, but she might need a few stitches. Nothing serious, though. Tim wouldn't really hurt Neve." He hooked a thumb behind him at the front door. "Let me get the dogs, okay? I'll be right back."

Duke shook his head. "That easy? What about Neve?"

Kay didn't waste time. The second Miles disappeared inside, she withdrew the gun from her back and clicked off the safety, then returned it. "Tim won't need her when he has the box."

"Won't need her? As in she's expendable, or he'll have no reason to keep a gun trained on her?" He ran a hand through his hair. "You're planning something. I don't think you should do anything crazy, Kay. Remember, Cherish will have the sheriff headed this way as soon as they reach Red Hill. We only have to maintain the situation, not get slaughtered trying to be heroes."

She pinned him with a hard gaze, her childlike countenance making it goddamn eerie. "If you want to run the risk of Tim actually getting away with this, go sit in the car. As for me, I'll be giving Tim a taste of his own sour medicine. And it's like you told Cherish. They don't expect us to be armed. Certainly they don't expect us to try anything."

"You should consider joining the armed forces."

"Daddy's a cop."

"That does answer a question or two."

She grinned. "Here he comes. Relax, okay?"

"Sure, Boss, I'll get right on that." Contrary to the sarcastic claim, his heart jumped from his chest as Miles exploded through the screen door with Darcy the Pit and Hannah on leashes, tangled up and excited from the buzz of human emotion clogging the air. They had to sense the tension, the heady anticipation.

The dogs tugged against Miles, who smiled at their enthusiasm and struggled with all his body weight to keep them from bounding to Duke when they saw him. Miles let out a small laugh like they were all good pals and came close enough to hand the leashes over to Duke. At the same time, Duke held out the box.

The swap successfully made, they both turned at the sound of a *click* from behind Miles.

Kay had her pistol trained on him. Pointed right at his face, actually, with the hammer cocked.

"Wow," Duke breathed. "You're not fucking around." He looked at Miles and ignored the dogs as they sniffed and snorted at his feet, happy and excited to see him. "She's not fucking around."

Kay didn't take her eyes off Miles. "Put the dogs in the car, Duke. And get the box back."

Duke followed orders. He had no idea what kind of games Kay had played growing up, but he got the impression she hadn't been a big Barbie fan. He opened the back door of the rental car and settled the dogs inside. Almost immediately they melted into a mingled mass of fur and paws. Then he took the box back from Miles, without an ounce of resistance, and locked it in the trunk of the car.

Miles chewed his lip and eyed the barrel of Kay's gun with a respectfully fearful gaze. "I just want you guys to know I don't hold this against you. Tim's kind of lost it. If we have to sign the deed for the ranch over to Krandall, we won't know what to do with ourselves. We'll have nothing. I think we could manage, you know, but Tim's convinced the world's gonna end or something."

Duke shook his head. The violence, the threats, all so unnecessary. "You know, it could've been a really simple thing. Krandall isn't interested. He'd have probably signed over the deed to you with nothing more than an impatient grunt. As it stands, your brother is going down. What do you think, Kay? Is shooting Neve assault with a deadly weapon or attempted murder?"

Her face didn't move, not so much as a tic in her jaw. "Assault and kidnapping."

"For taking the dogs?"

She sighed, but still her gaze stayed set on her hostage. "Neve is here against her will."

"Oh, right." Whatever. Duke withdrew the gun at his back and clicked off the safety but kept his finger well away from the trigger. He held it in both hands and waited for Kay to tell him the next move. Her plan, after all.

She nodded approvingly at his readied weapon. "Let's go get Neve. Where's everybody else, Miles? Owen and Laurel. Are they inside with Tim?"

Miles shook his head. "Tim gave them the night off, sent them into town. I don't think they have a clue what's going on."

Duke believed him. He looked to Kay.

She cocked her chin toward the front door. "Lead the way, Miles. But remember, the hammer's back, and I'll put a bullet in your ass cheek without hesitation. Try me if you want, but first, consider how much you like being able to walk."

Did Neve know her assistant was a badass? If not, Duke would write a letter of recommendation himself, because *damn.* "Where can I get one of you?"

He caught a small dimple creasing the left side of Kay's mouth, as close to a smile as he'd get from her in this situation.

Miles led them up the creaky wooden steps and into the house.

Duke let the screen door slap loudly against the frame. The lack of the telltale noise would give them away quicker than anything. Old houses and longtime residents were like elderly married folks. They knew the groans and moans by heart. Duke had his parents to thank for this small insight. If the furnace didn't whine when it kicked on, his mother noticed without fail and proclaimed it on its last leg.

They entered the dining room, where Tim and Neve sat facing one another, tumblers of dark brown liquid in hand. Whiskey, Duke guessed. That shouldn't surprise him, but it seemed to him only Neve would end up on the drinking end of a hostage negotiation. Gentle conversation flowed until they caught sight of Miles with a gun to his head.

Tim blinked rapidly, pushing himself back in his chair. He groped for his own piece, but Duke was quicker.

He raised his gun and aimed for Tim. Neve's pale face and the bloodied rags next to her glass of liquor made him weak in the knees. His hands shook as he leveled the barrel at Tim's chest, instinct and fear thumbing back the hammer. "I fucking dare you, old man."

"Thank *God,*" Neve cried, coming to her feet. "I'm going to pass out. Someone needs to get me to a doctor." Despite the claim, she made neat work of retrieving Tim's gun from the table as she stood.

Duke had hardly considered what to do next when the explosion sent his vision tumbling.

Smoke curled from the barrel of the gun in Neve's hand, and Tim's cry of animal pain registered seconds before Duke realized she'd shot him. She stood unsteadily, the gun still aimed at the rancher. "I'm a hell of a shot. I ever tell you that? Just a flesh wound. Nobody ever bled out from losing a toe. Or two."

Tim was on the ground and grimacing as he held his foot. The bullet had gone clean through his cowboy boots.

"Your next pair ought to be steel-toed." Duke shook his head. What was he doing? He swung his head, gaped at Neve. "You shot him."

"Self-defense," she rasped, her grip on the weapon slipping. She glared at Tim with malice even Duke had never seen. "He shot me first."

"I'll back that up," Kay chirped. She dug the barrel of her gun into Mile's neck.

"Yup, me too," he said hurriedly.

Duke didn't get a chance to add anything.

A cacophony of shouts and barked commands came from every direction at once, roaring voices demanding they lower their firearms. Uniformed officers swarmed from the front and the back of the old ranch house.

Kay, Neve, and Duke immediately put up their hands, fingers off triggers. Kay took a half a second to safely lower the hammer so no one accidently got shot while taking possession of all three guns, which officers did while two others took Tim and Miles into custody, cuffing them and leading them away without explanation or remark.

The three of them were instructed to make their way to the front of the house. Neve put an arm around Kay's offered shoulder but swayed, despite the support.

Duke tried to get a look at her wound, but she had it covered with a bandage. "Did you lose that much blood? Cherish will have told the sheriff Tim shot you. There's probably an ambulance outside. Or some kind of medical staff they brought from town."

She smiled with narrowed eyes, as though the light hurt. "The bullet hole's just dandy. The whiskey's what's kicking my ass."

* * * *

Neve still couldn't look at Duke. Not without all sorts of weird feelings rising to the surface and threatening to verbalize themselves without her full consent.

For his part, he said nothing. His glassy dark blue eyes were focused somewhere far away, not quite steady on the task of helping Neve onto the sofa, where he untied her work boots and slid them from her feet in slow, mechanical motions. Without his beard blocking the view, his mouth gave away much of his emotions, but Neve had no idea what the grim line of his pressed lips meant.

Anger? Was he upset with her for getting involved with Tim? Or still pissed about how she mishandled Gavin's visit to the cabin?

She didn't know. She was afraid to ask. It would take one wrong word to knock her over at this point. The whiskey, the pain of her bandaged arm, the lengthy interrogation from Red Hill's finest, the fear of sitting at the smoking end of Tim's gun…Neve was hard. Real hard, she told herself. She could handle anything. But she wasn't completely immune to the events of the last several hours. Shooting Tim didn't bother her. He'd deserved it. The cops hadn't hardly asked what had happened. Pretty much took the group's vague self-defense explanation at face value. But she'd almost lost her life. Her dog.

Then there'd been Duke, Kay at his side, waltzing in and daring Tim to make a move. It was like a movie. She'd been rescued by a raven-haired Fabio, who had something hard inside him—hard enough to aim a loaded gun at another man, and by the look on his face, hard enough to pull the trigger.

Hard enough to handle a woman like Neve, if he wanted to. There he'd been, all along, the one guy who could deal, and he didn't even want her. How had she managed to dance through life assuming the choice would always be hers at the end of the day? Finding him didn't mean she got to keep him.

Vulnerable and hurting in more ways than one, she put a firm hand on Duke's bicep as he tried to move away, still crouched at her feet. She swallowed and lowered her eyes, hating how she shook with anticipation, hating the fear in her chest, but knowing she'd ask anyway. "Stay with me."

He moved to sit beside her. "I'm not going anywhere." He gathered her hands into his.

"No." She made herself meet his eyes. It wasn't easy. "Stay with me. Tonight. I need to feel safe. I need something cleansing and honest to wash off this feeling. I'm not—" She stopped and tried to make sense of what she needed. She was unnerved to realize the pinpricks of tears stung the outer edges of her eyes. "It won't be like last time. I'm not angry. But in a way, it is like last time, because I want to take something from you." She waited for the glimmer of pained apology, the pulling away. But like last time, rejection never came.

Duke held her gaze as he brought her hand to his mouth and kissed her knuckles, causing something in her chest to flip over on itself. "Whatever it is, it's yours for the taking. Every time."

He might've taken a needle to a balloon. *Pop.* His generosity undid her. She didn't deserve it. "I'm so sorry. For everything. For what I did to you and Gavin. I'm so ashamed of myself." She dropped her hand. "I don't know when it happened. I told you I'm honest but not cruel, and I lied. Somewhere along the way, the lines blurred, and I always had the perfect justification."

He smiled and pulled her into his arms, wrapping them around her, while being mindful of her injury. His mouth rested near her ear. He lowered his voice. The murmur rumbled through her, and she shivered despite the warmth. "You were right. I would've tiptoed around the issue. Maybe even decided Gavin would be better off if I kept up the lie. You did what I didn't have the balls to do."

"I owe you both an apology."

"So apologize." He leaned away from her.

Her breath caught when he cradled her face in his hands and let his deep blue gaze roam over her face.

"But don't let go of yourself, Neve. You scare me, but there's something utterly wonderful about it. I'd take your painful honesty over a comfortable lie any day."

She closed her eyes. Looking at him hurt. She didn't have the courage to believe his earnest gaze was trying to tell her. She covered his hands with hers. "Maybe this is a bad idea. Maybe I should sleep alone. I keep getting these weird feelings around you. Guilty, and sad, and warm." She inhaled and forced her eyes open, forced herself to look at him. "I know what they mean, but it's not something I can walk into and then step away from. It's a door I won't open. I'm sorry." She tried to push his hands away.

He only allowed it so far. He gripped her and leaned forward to steal the breath from her lungs with a kiss. A fierce sensual pressure swept her senses clean away. The intensity remained without any of the anger, and it hit her. He'd meant it—he'd give it away so she never had to take a thing.

She broke away and squeezed her eyes shut. "Shit. This can't be happening."

"That's what I said. It's fucked up. I'm gay."

The laugh that bubbled up from her surprised them both. "And I'm horrible."

"It's going to explode in our faces, isn't it?"

She kissed him back, amazed by his eagerness and the way he leaned into it with a gleam in his heavy-lidded gaze. "Probably."

"You know, you're not so bad when you're doped up on a painkillers."

"I turned down the paramedic's offer of meds, actually. This is pure aftershock and immensely latent sexual desire."

His smile came slowly, a gradual overtaking that rattled her.

God, she'd imagined him looking at her like this for so long. How odd and gratifying. And stimulating. She bit her lip. "I'm not moving into your place."

"It's okay. Your place is nicer."

With that, the relationship talk was over, and Neve was happy to move on to more fundamental discoveries.

Chapter 14

Inside the cabin, Duke and Gavin each occupied a plush chair facing the cold fireplace. Krandall and Cherish sat on dining chairs turned to face the rest of the group. Neve sat on the edge of the bed next to Kay.

Miles remained standing. He had to be the only person more uncomfortable than Neve.

A week later, her gunshot wound—okay, *graze*—was healing nicely, and Tim sat in county lockup awaiting trial. The charges officially came down to kidnapping and assault with a deadly weapon, no set bail. Miles had come off incredibly lucky after agreeing to testify against his brother. He'd face no charges for his part in the ordeal, which amounted to little more than taking the dogs from Neve and Duke's trailer at Tim's command. Just toeing big brother's line, as he'd spent his life doing.

And no charges were mentioned, concerning Neve's small revenge. She'd heard Tim had kept all his toes.

Cherish shifted in her chair and cleared her throat. "I'm glad we're all able to come together like this. I think it's best we clear the air once and for all."

Krandall raised his hand like they were in a classroom, his lips twisted sardonically to one side. "Can't I just sign whatever I need to sign and be done with it?" He relaxed, but his hands went up in a helpless gesture. "Look, I don't want any of this. And you, Mama, what're you gonna do with some ranch you ain't got no mind to run? I don't care what some old man's piece of paper says. It's Hux Ranch, and I don't want it. Neither do you."

She blinked worriedly, sadness in the slope of her shoulders and the way her gaze traveled between her hands and the floor. "I don't know, Kran. I feel like your daddy's life would've been so different had Florrie lived. Or if Ben had taken him in. The ranch represents what could've been. Where the timeline split off. We could put it to rights."

Miles coughed politely and smiled awkwardly when Cherish and Krandall looked at him expectantly. His booted feet shuffled. "It ain't got to be so cut and dried as all that. I mean, I could teach you to run the ranch. I guess what I'm trying to say is you own Lady Killer Ranch." He indicated Ben's papers piled high on the table with the sweep of one hand. "Whether you want it or not. But it's been my home my whole life. I love it. I understand if you ain't interested, what with our family's history, but I can run it for you and teach you how it's done as I go along. If you were amenable to keeping us on, at any rate. 'Course, I mean Owen and Laurel, too. They had no inkling of what Tim was up to, and they're dedicated."

The hope on Cherish's wrinkled face lit Neve up on the inside. Could it really be so easy?

Krandall chewed his lip and studied his mama's hopeful expression.

"What about the cabin?" Duke cut into the moment unapologetically.

What happened with Lady Killer had no bearing on them personally, but the cabin's ownership was something of a conundrum.

Miles rubbed his cheek, eyebrows raised in question. "I don't really know. My dad sold this land, whether he actually had the right or not. After all, while everyone knew Ben had deeded it to Florrie, no actual paperwork existed to prove it."

Until now, of course. The deed with Florrie Beels's name printed neatly had been in the locked chest.

So, which had legal weight? The original deed, which meant Krandall owned the cabin along with the rest of Lady Killer Ranch, or the falsified documents Tim's father had created in order to sell land he didn't own, which had later on been rightfully bought and paid for by Gavin?

Krandall scoffed and reached for Ben's stack of papers, taking one in particular. "Look here." He showed them the cabin's deed. Then ripped it straight down the middle.

Cherish's high-pitched gasp filled the spacious cabin, and everyone else stared wide-eyed and silent.

He patted his mama's shoulder. "There, there. History and all that, I know. But look here, we're making our own. I know the past is important to you, but it's all such high drama. They were young and stupid. And heartless! And I can't bring myself to care too much for what none of them wanted." He turned his attention to Miles. "I suppose we all need to talk about Lady Killer Ranch, then. I'll tell you what, though, first thing's first, we're changing that awful name."

* * * *

Neve kicked a pebble and locked her hands behind her back. Should she go first?

Gavin smiled. "I'm glad the cabin's mine."

Oh, goodie. He'd be diplomatically polite and make her impending apology easy to stomach. "Me too. After all, it was designed for you."

"It really was. And fantastically so. Really, it bowls me over. Don't tell Duke I said this, but while he's a master of refurbishing, I can't think he holds a candle to you stylistically."

She fanned herself playfully. "Oh, stop. You'll make blush, and my face will explode. I haven't blushed since I lost my virginity."

He cast her a sidelong glance. "You know, I actually believe that. You're not exactly the bashful type." His lips thinned.

It took little to figure out where his mind had hobbled off to, because hers followed. She inhaled deeply and mustered her infamous inner nutsack. "Gavin, I owe you an apology." He started to speak, but she cut him off. "No, come on. Let's be straight. I was a jerk. I won't pretend I wasn't offended, nor will I pretend that's anything more than a handy excuse. I caught on to your..." Had it been attraction? Love? "...feelings for Duke. I suspected, anyway. This before I knew he was straight. So I said nothing, because maybe you two were, I don't know, like, gonna figure it out or something. But when I found out the truth, I should've been a lot, uh, neater with my delivery."

He matched her body language, hands clasped behind his back, and didn't meet her gaze. He nibbled his lip and let the silence between them linger a fraction too long.

"Seriously, I'm sorry." She rushed the words. She had no idea how to make him believe her or know the depth of her sincerity. "Truly. I told myself I'd done you guys some big favor, spewing out Duke's secret like projectile vomit, but I should've taken you aside and explained."

He nodded and finally looked at her with a wry smile. "It would've saved me a little face, if nothing else."

She closed her eyes. *God, I'm such an asshole.* "Or even allowed Duke to tell you on his own terms."

He grimaced. "Talk about awkward." A small laugh escaped him. "Look, Neve, I'm a fair proponent of honesty, so I won't insult you by saying it wasn't a little on the harsh side. Or by pretending I didn't run away with my tail tucked between my legs, wanting to die of mortification. However, I won't fault you for being who you are. We all have those things we struggle with. Me, I'm too upbeat. I grate on people. Duke, he's a people-pleaser. Even what he did with you, pretending to be unobtainable, was in the interest of avoiding hurt feelings and discomfort later on. He just wants everyone to have what they need and be happy. We need people like you to balance us out. It's why you and Duke are going to make such a fabulous couple. Him and all his peacemaking, you with your snarky aversion to bullshit. And what is peacemaking but spewing bullshit to appease everyone at the same time? You're total opposites. Also, I think it's fair I be the best man, don't you?"

Neve's jaw had come unhinged about two-thirds of the way through his monologue. She'd stopped walking and gaped at Gavin. "Wow. You're remarkably observant."

"Eh." He shrugged. "I'm a people person."

"Okay, well, except you missed the mark on the whole marriage thing. Duke and I have discussed…stuff. Like, feelings. But this calls for baby steps." She laughed softly. "Gah, marriage? If we last long enough for that to be an issue, I'll be shocked. We're talking *years* before that's even a thing."

"Well, the cabin will still stand, I'm sure, even if it takes the two of you a decade of beating around the bush."

"Hmm." She squinted at Gavin's perfectly round baby blues. "And that's supposed to mean…"

He smiled his big, dimpled smile. "That I'm giving it to you. A wedding gift. Early, belated, whatever." He sighed, and a wistful expression took over his face. "I had this little fantasy, you might call it. The moment I met Duke, he seemed so cool and confident but not aloof. God, men think that's such a great affectation. But it sucks. People want someone who cares. And Dukes so obviously cares. It's just who he is, and I think I picked up on that from him instantly and decided he must be the one. Why else would I notice him so completely, and his most perfect, glaring quality be one I desperately looked for in a companion?"

Oh, my, this sounds oddly familiar…

"Anyway, the cabin, the reno. It's stupid, but I only wanted him to work for me so I'd have an excuse to get to know him personally. Spend some off-the-clock time with him. Of course, had I known he flew straight, I'd have never entertained such nonsense. You can't convert a straight man, no matter what the media says." A totally fabulous eye roll accompanied the statement.

The depth of her empathy astounded her. She could quite accurately say she knew *exactly* how he'd felt.

Maybe I'm not a sociopath, after all. I just have super-stingy sympathy.

Neve slipped an arm around his shoulders, cementing what she now felt was the beginning of an undeniable bond. "Oh, Gavin, I think we understand each other better than you know." Not that she'd be sharing how she'd felt about *him* at one point. Some secrets needed to stay secrets. Or simply be forgotten altogether, lost to the alums of time. "As for the cabin, your offer is most gracious. I'll ask Duke what he thinks before I promise anything, though."

* * * *

Duke never got tired of the way Neve tucked her body against his just so and subtly kept the remote from his reach with one hand while making tidy work of yogurt-covered pretzels with the other. At least he could put it on the car channel now. Not often since Neve hadn't lost her penchant for crappy television, but maybe, in time, she'd grow careless and leave the remote where he could snatch it up before she had to a chance to stop him.

His heart warmed when the weight of Hannah's huge head settled onto his thigh on his other side. And on Neve's opposite side, Darcy curled into a half-moon mound under Neve's elbow like a damn cat.

Neve wriggled against him. "So, what'd you tell Gavin? It's such a nice place."

"You're right. Those antique furnishing are something else."

"Yep. And did you notice how the appliances fit within the color scheme?"

"Sure did. How about that hot tub, huh?"

"I know. Plus those lovely vaulted ceilings."

He sighed, content, and prepared to have the same argument a third time. "I told him *hell no*, just like last time he tried to pawn that awful cabin off on us."

Neve groaned. "How can you describe any place I designed as awful?"

"Easy. It's in the middle of nowhere. I have to hike a quarter mile to reach the front door. Plus, we have some history with the neighbors."

"Oh, shut up. Cherish and Miles are our friends."

"I still don't want the cabin."

She tilted her head back to blink at him with her molten lava eyes. "Not even for our honeymoon?"

He kissed her forehead and grinned. "*Especially* not for our honeymoon."

"Were you at least nice this time?"

"Of course I was." He squirmed. *Kinda* nice. Not that Gavin had taken offense. He was extremely motivated to sell, and no one in the area seemed interested.

"Goddamn it, Duke." She struggled into an upright position and swiveled her upper body to face him. It turned her small breasts out at an angle a man could appreciate. "When are you going to learn to stop lying? Gavin called me. You yelled."

Duke held up a contrary finger. "I raised my voice. A little. But I did not yell. But seriously, I'm over it at this point. I don't want the stupid cabin."

"Well, lucky for you, he called to inform me he found a buyer. And no, it's not going back to High Mountain Ranch. Kay and Finn decided they want it for a summer retreat. I think they felt sorry for Gavin."

"Huh." The new name they'd settled on for the ranch didn't have the same cadence as its old moniker, but it certainly made for a better first impression. "Good for them. Heck, we shouldn't have to hear from any of them again until the wedding, right?"

Neve laughed and settled back into the crook of his arm. "I understand how you feel, Duke, but would it kill you to have a little tact?"

THE END

Rumor has it, she can't resist…

MEN LIKE THIS
A Long Shot Romance

Roxanne Smith

Can she trust a man who pretends for a living?

Horror author Quinn Buzzly knows all about the dark side, but when she meets actor Jack Decker, she's moved to explore something completely different—at least on paper. With his sexy good looks, intriguing manner, and charming Irish-tinged English accent, Jack is the perfect model for her next hero. Quinn decides to spend one year in London writing a historical romance inspired by him. Until real life butts in…

Jack's jealous ex-fiancée sparks a media storm when she accuses him and Quinn of having an affair. But Jack knows how to play this game. At his insistence, Quinn agrees to go along with the faux romance until the chatter subsides. Then they'll stage a quiet breakup and go their separate ways. Yet Jack is a shameless—and irresistibly convincing—flirt, and Quinn has to remind herself it's an act. Or is it? If Jack means business, he'll have to find the words to convince a wordsmith that their love is the real thing…

Chapter 1

Quinn gaped at Richard as if he'd grown an extra appendage in front of her eyes. He might as well have. He was alien to her, despite having known him for many years. "I'm giving you about three seconds to explain."

He had the nerve to smile. It showed off the large glaringly white teeth inside his too-perfect mouth on his too-perfect face. "You don't like it?" His dark gaze wandered, his approval apparent. "I really thought you would."

They were at a nightclub called Sabini's in Hollywood—Quinn deplored Hollywood. A small treasure of a private bar hid deep in the bowels of the rowdy club: quiet, classy, and far from the maddening *wump-wump-wump* of the dance floor down the hall. Yes, she liked it.

No, she wasn't going to admit it.

She crossed her bare arms, partly from the chill but mostly to show Richard she meant business. "Our relationship demands trust. Why would you lie to me, Richard?"

He spared a quick glance at her defensive posture. "Cold?" When she didn't respond, he waved off her concern. "All I've done is taken you out. Is that so bad?"

A jolt of agitation shot through her. Had he lost his mind? Had one too many cocktails earlier? "Yes, I'd say it was! You dragged me across a nasty dance floor wearing a silk ball gown and diamond brooch worth more than your house. You said my sister planned this. I want an explanation, and I want it now."

Richard continued to scan the bar, unruffled by her outburst. "I brought you through the front because I left my key to the private entrance at home. I apologize." He sat on one of the backless cowhide bar stools and lifted a hand for the bartender. "Bottle of champagne, please. Two glasses."

The busty young woman who could've still been driving on a learner's permit smiled. Her gaze roamed freely over Richard before she dashed off to fulfill his glamorous request.

Quinn fought the urge to stick her finger down her throat. Champagne? Who was he kidding?

He turned back to her and patted the seat beside him as if beckoning her to join him like she were some wayward, spoiled child. "Your feet must hurt." His eyes were kind, and his smile knowing. "Angie has excellent fashion sense, but you shouldn't have let her talk you into those heels."

He spoke the truth.

Quinn's feet throbbed from the towering stilettos she had no business wearing. She planned to set fire to the outrageous instruments of torture the very day they lifted the burn ban in L.A. and fight harder for the ballet flats next time.

She scowled at Richard for being right but sat anyway. The blood rushing back into her feet made her woozy with relief. With some effort, she refocused on Richard. "Quit stalling and tell me what we're doing here, or I'm walking out. If I have to call a cab to get home, I swear, I'm taking my next project to someone else."

Richard's dark and impeccably shaped eyebrows shot up. His mouth fell open. Finally, a dent in his smooth surface. "You wouldn't."

He didn't sound so certain.

Quinn smiled at having the upper hand. "I damn sure would. Like I said, this is a trust thing. It was odd when you told me Emily wanted to get together in Hollywood, but I told myself you wouldn't do anything weird. Then you go and order champagne. It keeps getting weirder, and you refuse to tell me what's really going on. You don't own a white windowless van, do you? Or have duct tape in your suit pocket?"

He didn't appear amused. In fact, he managed to appear unaffected, his impenetrable feathers were back in place. Her show of humor must've left him with the incorrect impression she'd be easily managed.

"You're over thinking this. We had a successful night at the fund-raiser. You're gorgeous. I wanted to have an after-party drink with my favorite client. There's nothing *weird* about wanting to prolong a nice evening with a friend."

He couldn't have mocked her any clearer.

She couldn't have cared any less. "Except for your conniving, I'd agree. Why didn't you simply ask?"

"I wanted to surprise you." He smiled his horse-toothed smile. It ruined everything he had going for his face. "Surprise."

The champagne arrived. He handed her a dainty flute. "Drink this." The sweet condescension in his voice nearly undid the frail threads holding Quinn's temper in check, but she kept her grip on the reins—until she glanced at her glass.

It practically brimmed over with the sparkly wine. A sudden burst of insight hit her. "You're trying to get me drunk."

"Now, Quinn—"

"You used my sister to lure me here knowing I'd never come willingly. Real classy." Quinn came out of her seat, disgusted and angry. She growled at the sharp jabs of pain shooting through the soles of her feet.

Richard must've taken the growl as meant for him. "Quinn, calm down, please. Yes, I'm attracted to you. Yes, I thought this was the only way I'd ever get a date with you."

"This is not a date!" Despite her pain, she stamped her foot. The small *click* of her heel failed to make the desired impact.

Richard placed a hand on her arm. "Obviously."

Her fingernails dug into her palms as her hands formed angry little fists at her sides.

Richard didn't notice. His primary concern seemed to have shifted from her to their audience. "You're causing a scene. You asked for an explanation, now allow me to give one before you get us kicked out."

Quinn seethed but didn't interrupt this time. A lift of her brow invited him to continue.

He cleared his throat and straightened his black silk bowtie. Since they'd come from the prestigious city fund-raiser, he was in a tuxedo jacket and slacks.

They'd been a striking pair. Quinn wore a black strapless gown and styled her long blond hair into an elegant chignon that displayed the diamond drops in her lobes. They matched the cluster pinned to the front of her gown.

In this casual setting, they looked like a bad joke. Overdressed and ill behaved. "You have to understand, Quinn. We work together closely. We talk every day. It's not strange I'm attracted to you. Asking you out seemed unprofessional."

Quinn nearly choked on her unspoken reply. This *wasn't* unprofessional? Her jaw practically unhinged at Richard's startling lack of self-awareness.

"I figured if we went out casually and had a few drinks, things might take their natural course."

A shrug accompanied the statement to show how big of a deal it wasn't, but Quinn saw red. She jabbed at his shoulder with an accusing finger. "I'm not stupid, Richard. You celebrate with a glass of champagne. There are completely different motives at play when you order an entire bottle. You weren't hoping for slightly tipsy. You were going for totally sloshed. Then what? You'd take me back to your place and pretend it got out of hand?"

"No, I'd never—"

Quinn turned away. She braced her hands against the bar in an effort to stay on her bruised feet and tried to breathe. "You sure as hell would. After what Blake did, there's nothing I'd put past a man."

He had the audacity to scoff. "Blake is an idiot."

The comment acted like flame to tinder—instant ignition.

She whirled on him. He was no better. He was probably no worse, but at the least, he and Blake were exactly the same. "Oh, and you're some genius? Do you even realize what you've done? I should fire you." She shook her head to dislodge some of her anger, but it wasn't going anywhere. She trembled. "Get away from me. Leave, now."

"Leave?" He repeated the word slowly. "I'm not going anywhere. I brought you here. I'm responsible for you."

Quinn pinned him with every ounce of fire in her green eyes. They flashed when she was angry. They must be crackling like hot coals now. "Do you really expect me to get back in your car? I'll take a cab home. I don't need your protection. What I need is for someone to protect me from *you*."

He looked like he might refuse again.

She hit him with the final blow. "Our contract is riding on how fast you can get away from me. I mean it, Richard."

Their surroundings seemed to come back to them simultaneously. Everyone stared at Richard as they waited in dead silence for his reaction. Even the bartender watched their exchange with rapt attention. Richard's face flushed a dull red. He stood in a deliberate fashion as if it were his idea to leave. "This is foolish."

His clenched jaw and piercing glare labeled him furious, but Quinn had her own store of ire to draw from. She slipped into the most condescending tone she possessed. "You need to go home and think about what you've done."

He recoiled like she'd slapped him, but she'd wager his reaction was nothing more than embarrassment at getting dressed down in a room full of strangers. Maybe now he'd understand how she felt—mortified and belittled. He'd tricked her into coming here and attempted to ply her with drink for the sake of getting her in bed. She couldn't have done anything more insulting than that.

Richard stormed toward the exit. She hoped the staring eyes of the audience, hers included, burned holes in his back as he went.

Her shoulders fell the moment he disappeared from sight. Her rage fled. She wasn't built for dramatics. She frowned at the two untouched glass flutes on the bar. One sat empty while the other comically full. She'd never much cared for champagne hangovers.

Quinn wiggled her fingers in a girlish wave at the bartender still watching her with round eyes. "Can I get a beer?"

Quinn waited until she almost finished her first drink to call Angie, her best friend, the same demon responsible for her miserable, dejected feet. She plucked her cell phone from the hidden pocket inside the bodice of her gown. She wasn't totally stupid. She'd have never let Richard leave without a backup plan up her sleeve.

Or down her dress, as it were.

Angie answered on the first ring. She sounded unfazed, like she'd expected Quinn's late-night call. "How did the fund-raiser go?"

Oh, that's right. She'd done something fun tonight. "I had a great time. In fact, I wish we were still there."

"Oh, I'm sure you'll have others." Angie sounded slightly distracted. Quinn imagined her painting her toenails or watching television. "What time did you get home?"

Quinn cleared her throat. It wasn't her fault. She shouldn't feel stupid, but for whatever reason she did. Must be some kind of male superpower. "Would it be weird if Richard wanted to sleep with me?"

"Of course not. It'd be weird if he didn't." Angie didn't seem distracted anymore. "Did something happen? Oh my God, did you go home with him?" Her voice dropped to a dramatic whisper. "Did you guys do it? Are you calling in secret from the bathroom? Was he good?"

Richard had inspired an intense lack of charitable feelings, but leave it to Angie to smooth Quinn's angry wrinkles mere seconds into the conversation. "No, nothing like that, but he did bring me to a Hollywood nightclub. Shows a little spark, doesn't it?"

"Hollywood? Does he know you?" The disdain in her best friend's voice was welcome commiseration. "Where are you?"

"A place called Sabini's." Quinn appraised the room once more. Large round bulbs suspended from the ceiling hung low and cast their warm glow over the bar, thus creating quite the snug little atmosphere. "I'm pained to admit it, but the private bar is sort of nice. It's the mosh pit of sweaty, spastic idiots in the dance room next door who frighten me. I can't believe that passes for dancing these days. I thought the first guy I saw was having a seizure. He's lucky I didn't shove my brooch in his mouth to stop him from swallowing his tongue."

Angie snorted. "A creative way to divest yourself of a fortune. I've been to Sabini's before. Your Richard's a classy one. Are you two having a good time?"

"Not exactly." Quinn explained in painful detail how her night had gone so topsy-turvy.

She waited in silence for Angie's reply. She imagined her friend working through the scenario in her mind.

Finally, a response. "Well, okay. I guess my question is why you're still there."

Quinn loved easy questions. She sucked the last drop of beer from the long-neck bottle and smacked her lips for emphasis. "To get drunk. Why does anyone sit at a bar and order booze?"

"Nice. Tomorrow you'll wake up not only divorced and homeless but with a hangover cherry on top. Way to take your power back, honey."

"I'm not homeless. I'm staying at a hotel."

"Homeless isn't synonymous with cardboard box. You don't have a home. You're homeless."

Quinn waved to the bartender. Time for another drink. "Shut up and tell me what I'm supposed to do. Am I overreacting?"

Angie clucked her tongue. "Had he taken you out for kung pao chicken, I'd say yes, but this is kind of a big deal. He dragged you to some shady Hollywood club wearing a thousand-dollar ball gown and million-dollar diamonds. Not just ignorant, mind you. Potentially dangerous. This is L.A., not Friendly, Texas. Letting him leave you there was even dumber, by the way."

"Probably." Quinn tried for a deep breath. It escaped as a depressed groan. "What do I do? Fire him?"

The mere suggestion made her stomach pitch. She mustered up a weak smile for Busty the Barkeep, who promptly deposited Quinn's second beer in front of her.

"There's only one thing you can do." Angie sounded apologetic but remained firm. "You have to kill him."

Quinn pressed the phone closer to her ear. The spectacle had ceased, and people were back to their regularly scheduled partying. "Like it's ever that easy."

Angie scoffed. "You have no problem scalping a sweet, vulnerable, and ruggedly handsome pediatrician with a chainsaw, but you can't kill Richard? You even murdered the poor doctor on the very same night he finally worked up the courage to ask that cute barista out on a date. It took a lot of courage for him to step out of his comfort zone. The guy had issues."

Quinn rested one elbow on the bar and said what she always said. "You're taking it too personally, Ang. You've got to quit falling in love with my subjects."

"What in the hell is a barista doing with a chainsaw in the first place, huh? Does she moonlight as a lumberjack?"

Quinn wanted to roll her eyes at Angie's protest but couldn't. She was too pleased with herself. Her life's work revolved around inspiring heartfelt emotion in others. More's the better if the emotions were dark ones like grief and loss.

They were sort of her calling card. "Look, if I wrote Richard into a story to give him a grisly death, I'm afraid he'd notice. He *is* my agent. And you'd understand why the barista had a chainsaw if you'd bother to finish the book."

"I can't, Quinn, I just can't." Her best friend sniffed. "You kill everyone I love."

"I'm sorry. I'll write you a happy ending one day. Promise."

Angie went from sniveling to haughty in the space of a single sentence. "The only happy endings these days are in massage parlors."

Quinn was still laughing when she ended the call and returned the slim black cell phone to the hidden confines of her ball gown.

Her silk strapless Carolina Herrera ball gown.

Every bit of good humor conjured disappeared. Quinn remembered where she sat and how she got there.

Richard, Richard, Richard. He'd really screwed up tonight. Angie's solution, while amusing, wasn't pragmatic and wouldn't solve anything. Quinn nervously rolled the beer bottle between her hands.

The idea of confronting Richard in his office made her queasy. He'd downplay the entire scene and make her out to be a dramatic prude. The smoothness she counted on for publishing negotiations would come back to bite her when she found herself looking down the barrel of it rather than grinning smugly from behind it, but what were her choices?

She had to make a stand. She needed to put him in his place, be the iron fist of the feminine movement.

Then again, there wasn't much determined avoidance couldn't patch up. Key West was fabulous this time of year. Cabanas, boat drinks, palm trees, and pool boys.

When had she last gone on vacation? Disneyland three years ago. With Blake. Quinn didn't want to think about that. She wanted to daydream about pool boys. For research, of course. She was far too old for a pool boy.

She'd need a pool *man*.

"You don't match."

For an instant, the deep voice coming from behind stunned her. Since she sat virtually alone on her side of the L-shaped bar, she had no choice but to accept the man—a pool man if her luck had improved any—intended the words for her. Some drunken fool trying to succeed where Richard failed. What had she been thinking staying here? She should've picked up a bottle of tequila and moved this pity party to the privacy of her hotel room.

He had an accent, although she couldn't place the dialect. Definitely European. Rather than turn around right away to face her new visitor, she took a long, hard look at the beer bottle in her hand. Too soon to order her third? She wanted fuzzy, not pickled.

She'd put it off long enough. Quinn swung around on the tail end of an eye roll to greet Bachelor Number Two. The smart reply she had ready died on her lips.

Meet the Author

A Florida native, Roxanne Smith has called everywhere from Houston to Cheyenne home. Currently residing in Asheville, North Carolina, she's an avid reader of every genre, a cat lover, pit bull advocate, and semi-geek. She loves video games, Doctor Who, and her dashing husband. Her two kids are the light of her life. Visit her website at roxannesmith.net, and her blog at smithrox.blogspot.com.